DRUID VENGEANCE

A NEW ADULT URBAN FANTASY NOVEL

M.D. MASSEY

D1417162

MODERN DIGITAL PUBLISHING

1

Living in an undead apocalypse is a real pain in the ass.

I know the more accepted nomenclature would be "zombie apocalypse," but that designation just didn't do the whole thing justice. This timeline, alternate future, or wherever the hell Click had left me was full of vampires, revenants, and ghouls. Not to mention a shit-ton of 'thropes as well—not all of them friendly.

Back in my own reality—because that's how I'd chosen to define it—most intelligent monsters were either kept under control or became civilized, even tame. As for the rest, human hunters and higher-order supernaturals killed lower-order supernatural predators on sight, which kept the feral undead population contained. Vampires, for the most part, tended to avoid preying on humans. The same could be said for most lycanthropes as well.

But here? Well, let's just say no prey was off limits to

the supernatural species who now dominated the landscape.

Yep, I'm gonna kick Click's lily-white ass the second I get back.

"Click," as he liked to call himself, was an incredibly powerful mage skilled in the forbidden art of chronomancy—the manipulation of time. He was also a sort of trickster god, a fact I'd worked out since he'd left me here. I'd known he was trouble, but hadn't realized just how cuckoo he was until he'd pulled this latest stunt. Since then, I'd obsessed over his true identity and how I might get back to my own timeline.

That is, when I wasn't preoccupied with staying alive.

Currently I was on a scavenging run, sneaking through the aisles of an IGA grocery store to gather supplies for the group I'd hooked up with. They were mostly kids, ages ranging from grade school to tween. Despite the best efforts of their guardian, they'd have been zombie snacks already if I hadn't intervened. Obviously, it took a lot of work to keep a few dozen school-age children alive in a zombie apocalypse, and much of that effort involved keeping them fed.

Maybe it's best Bells and I broke up, I thought as I drove a steel spike through a particularly corpulent zombie's skull from behind. The zombie was a thirty-ish Anglo woman in a gore-stained mumu, somehow still wearing a single battered flip-flop. *I mean, it's not like I'm going to want to have kids after this is all over. I'm pretty much burned out on the whole idea already.*

Using a bit of my Fomorian strength, I gently lowered

the now de-animated corpse to floor, opting for stealth over speed. Good thing I'd partially-shifted before I'd come in here. The object was to draw as little attention as possible—preferably none. High-population areas were crawling with deaders, and they would happily venture into the sunlight for the chance at a warm meal. Nothing was worse than drawing a swarm and then spending an afternoon fighting your way free. I knew, because I'd done it.

The shelves were barren of anything edible, so I moved toward the back of the store. Survivors, although they were few and far between, generally weren't in the habit of exploring dark and gloomy places. That's where the really dangerous undead lurked during the day, resting and waiting for some unsuspecting human to waltz into their lair looking for food and supplies.

More for me, then. In more ways than one.

I enjoyed going on these scavenger runs, partially because they provided a reprieve from scared, whiny kids. But going out alone also gave me the opportunity to let my other side loose, so I could vent my frustrations on the apex predators in this reality.

Vampires.

I'd never been a vampophobe, as most vamps I'd known had been civil toward humans, even friendly. Heck, one of my best friends back in Austin was the local coven leader, a guy I'd trust with my life. But not in this reality. Nope.

From what I'd surmised, when the zombie outbreak had gone down, the fae had left for Underhill, the 'thropes had become feral, and The Cold Iron Circle had either been killed off or voluntarily disappeared. That had left a power vacuum the vamps had been suspiciously ready to fill, a fact that hadn't gone unnoticed by yours truly.

There seemed to be no end to their number, which had puzzled me from the start. Where were they all coming from? It was hellaciously hard for a vamp to make others of its kind, because the vyrus didn't always take. Often, the young ones would end up making zombies or ghouls instead of vamps. It took an elder or master vamp to reliably turn humans into vampires, and always in limited numbers due to the time involved. How they'd multiplied so fast was a mystery to me.

I also wondered if the evil vampire covens had been behind the zombie outbreak, and took every opportunity to question said species whenever I ran across them. Which was often, considering I actively sought them out when I could.

Pushing the door to the stock room open, I triggered a cantrip to make my Fomorian-enhanced vision even better suited for the current low light conditions. I tossed an empty tin can into the room and waited, listening for a good thirty seconds for any sign that the undead were present. Then, I propped the doors open to let the weak, reflected light in, just like any normal human would.

I could see them, perched as they were like spiders clinging to the ceiling at the far corners of the warehouse, deep in the shadows and well away from any errant rays of sunlight. The would-be predators had likely been aware of my presence since I'd entered the store, and now their beady, bloodshot eyes followed me as I feigned feeling my way around in the dark. I suppressed a smile as I lit a candle with a match, playing it up for my audience until the very last. There were five of them, and they were all very much awake.

Jackpot.

Younger vamps would be forced to rest at this time, but this was an older coven. They'd been around before the shit hit the fan—decades, probably. That meant they were more likely to know what the hell had caused the dead to rise en masse, in concert with the low-intensity nuclear war that had decimated major population areas. Thus far, I'd only gotten bits and pieces, because I'd yet to come across a coven consisting of vamps more than a few months old.

But today—today I might just get the answers I'd been searching for over the last half-year or so. And I intended to have those answers, even if I had to drag it out of their cold, hard flesh. As I inwardly reveled in my good luck, the vamps began to creep toward me along the ceiling.

Come to papa, you bloodsucking pieces of shit.

BETTER PLAY *this one to the hilt—figure out who the leader of the bunch is before I let 'em have it.* I stumbled my way deeper into the room, knocking things over indiscriminately and blinking like I was trying to adjust my eyes to the gloom. All the while, the vamps skittered above noiselessly, positioning themselves for the inevitable pre-ambush build up that preceded the typical vampire feeding.

Up until a few months ago, I'd rarely seen vampires feed, and then only the less-advanced nosferatu variant of the species. While nos-types preferred to hunt their prey down and immediately feed with abandon, I'd discovered that higher vamps liked to toy with their prey. It had something to do with the flavor of the blood elicited by the release of certain stress hormones—or so I'd been told. For that reason, I jumped like a startled child when the doors to the warehouse swung shut behind me, even though I'd seen a vamp headed that way just moments before.

A heavy metal shelf then slid across the floor, blocking the exit. It was laden with cartons of clean drinking water and bags of water softener pellets, and way too heavy for any human to move. I dropped into a crouch, ostensibly searching the shadows for whatever dangers lurked there while silently cheering the find.

Thanks for pointing that shelf out for me, folks. Clean drinking water was a luxury in this world, and most in our group had suffered through weeks of diarrhea and vomiting before their stomachs had become accustomed to drinking less-than-potable fluids. I'd definitely be hauling a few cases of that water back to camp.

The chatter started right on cue, voices echoing from all directions. It was all part of the build-up, designed to have me pissing my pants before they pounced.

"What do we have here?"

"A little lost lamb."

"Lost, and far from home."

"Far from safety."

"Nothing is safe anymore, is it, little lamb?"

I pulled a pistol, swinging it around as if blind. "H-h-who's there? This gun is loaded—I swear I'll shoot!"

Their sibilant, hissing voices responded in kind.

"Thinks it can hurt us with that toy."

"It's not iron nor lead that can hurt us, little lamb."

"But we can hurt it, yes, we can."

"Hurt it..."

"Drain it..."

"Just a sip..."

"And then a gulp..."

"And then we drink it dry!"

Good grief, these clowns have been watching too many Peter Jackson films.

Finally, the leader revealed herself. She was a slight wisp of a thing with close-cropped purple hair, who hadn't been a day older than seventeen when she'd been turned. As the coven leader, she'd reserve the pleasure of taking me down for herself, drinking her fill before allowing her subordinates to feed. She scuttled across the exposed metal joists above, stopping directly overhead.

I quivered and let out a low moan, patiently keeping up my act until she dropped from the ceiling.

Gotcha.

I holstered the pistol and stood in one smooth motion, grabbing the coven leader by the neck in a left-handed death grip as she fell toward me. Over the last several months, I'd gained a deeper understanding of my Fomorian-derived talents, learning to alter my bone density and musculature while still retaining the bulk of my human features and form. It was a handy trick, especially when I needed access to my superhuman strength, speed, and durability without tipping my enemies off that I was more than human.

"*Solas*," I said, triggering the light spell I'd prepared before coming in here. In an instant, greatly-weakened but highly-effective sunlight I'd gathered outside before entering the store illuminated the room. I had no idea why the vyrus reacted so violently to sunlight, and I didn't care. All that really mattered was that the spell worked—spectacularly.

The coven leader went batshit crazy, screaming and squirming as her skin blistered and burned. The rest of her little coven cried out in kind. I held my captive off the floor, chuckling even as her hardened nails dug deep furrows into my arm. The noise of her struggle and the coven's screams would draw more zombies, but the vamps had done me the favor of securing the room. I had time to play.

Three of the others withered into shriveled husks as the vyrus in their blood reacted to the light. The fourth and sole surviving subordinate vamp had also been burned, but he was still on the move. The underling snuck around behind me, then sprang at me using his vampire speed.

Waiting until the last moment, I leaned forward and donkey-kicked him into a line of metal storage shelves. Before he could recover, I pulled a long, wickedly-sharp Bowie knife, one I'd painstakingly electroplated with silver shortly after arriving in this hellish timeline. I threw the knife in a fast looping motion and watched as the blade buried itself to the hilt in the vampire's forehead.

Turning my attention back to the coven leader, I stepped back with my right foot and spun, dropping to one knee as I slammed her hard on the concrete floor below. My light spell had already faded, but the damage was done; my captive had crippling second- and third-degree burns over most of her body. That and the concussion I'd just given her made her weak as a newborn kitten... and ripe for interrogation.

I pulled a sharpened length of rebar from my Crane-skin Bag and drove it through her shoulder, deep into the concrete below. The spikes were hooked on one end like a shepherd's crook—my own design. They served well for spiking deader skulls, and detaining vamps for questioning. I did a repeat to her other shoulder, then did the same to each arm at the wrist and each hip joint. Finally, I pinned her legs to the floor through her ankles. She cried out in agony every time, but the screams grew weaker the closer I got to finishing the task.

Satisfied she wasn't going anywhere, I took a casual stroll around the room. The place smelled of mold and death. A quick circuit of the warehouse revealed a stack of desiccated corpses and bones, past victims of this coven. I poked around in the pile, both out of curiosity and to look for ammo and other useful items.

My search turned up a handful of .22 caliber and nine-millimeter rounds, a serviceable machete, and a Buck 110 folding hunting knife, along with a more grisly and disheartening discovery. There were child-sized bones in the pile, and an infant's skull. I instantly regretted killing the others so quickly, but was comforted by the fact that I'd soon be taking my frustrations out on their leader.

This vamp isn't getting off easy. No fucking way.

Strolling over to a shelf, I grabbed a warm Mexican Coke from an open case. The cap popped off with a flick of my thumb, and I savored the soft hiss and slightly acrid smell before I took a nice long swig of the sugary, caffeinated concoction. I took my time walking back to the vampire, swirling the liquid in the thick glass bottle as I examined her like an entomologist eyeing a dead beetle pinned up for display.

"Baaaaaaah," I bleated, doing my best impression of a lamb.

"I thought we killed all the wizards," she spat. "How are you still alive?"

Her skin was slowly healing, so I grabbed a metal chair, unfolding it and placing the crossmember for the legs under her chin. I dropped my full weight on it, savoring the creak of metal as it pressed against her throat. Between the spikes and my extremely dense bulk holding her down, she'd be hard-pressed to free herself—vampire strength be damned.

"Brrrrzzzzzzzzzt!" I exclaimed, mimicking the sound of a buzzer. "Nope, not a wizard. Only two guesses left, darlin'."

"What are you?" she asked, with just the hint of a Texas twang in her voice. "You don't smell like an animal, but you've got the strength and speed of a 'thrope."

"Strike two," I muttered, downing the rest of the soda with a loud belch. "I'll give you a hint. I used to live in the capital."

Her brown eyes narrowed, then widened as realization dawned across her face. "Druid," she said in a hushed, fearful tone.

"Bingo! Give the bloodsucking fiend a prize."

"Impossible—they said you died in the blast. That was the whole reason we bombed Austin. You're supposed to be dead!"

I considered the implications of that revelation. *Guess I'll never meet my alter-ego from this timeline.* I didn't really know how I felt about that, to be honest, but I kept my face a mask.

"Well, they missed. I bet that really fucks up your week. Hope I didn't ruin your plans for world domination or anything." I looked her up and down, taking in her singed purple hairdo, worn leather biker jacket, razored t-shirt, sports bra, wide leather belt, black yoga pants, and high-heeled ankle boots. "Incidentally, Pat Benatar called, and she wants her wardrobe back."

Her eyes narrowed again. "We heard stories about you in the NOLA coven. They told us to stay away from Austin, to avoid any contact with you until it was too late."

Without taking my eyes off hers, I reached out to the wooden scales on my silver-plated dagger, calling them to me. The knife flew into my outstretched hand, like an iron filing drawn to a magnet. It was another trick I'd discovered, innovation under stress—a survival skill I'd picked up out of necessity in this sink-or-swim, kill-or-be-killed world. I couldn't do it with metal, but anything plant-based would obey my call, especially if I handled the item frequently.

My hand snaked out as I slapped the flat of the blade against the now barely-healed skin on her cheek. She hissed, wriggling and squirming in vain to get free as the silver burned and weakened her further. I trailed the blade up the side of her face, drawing a blistered line toward her eye. I stopped short of my intended goal, leaving the metal there to sizzle against the sharp curve of her cheekbone.

Time to seal the deal.

In one quick, violent motion, I drove the point into her eye at the corner, scooping out her eyeball so it hung against her cheek.

The vampire howled. She was trying to wrap her mind around what was happening to her and failing. When you've been an apex predator for decades, and suddenly something comes along that's even more dangerous and wicked than you, well—suffice it to say it's a shock to your system. In all likelihood, the last time she'd felt this sort of pain was back when she still had a heartbeat.

I examined my work thus far, then started poking and prodding at the exposed nerves and connective tissues from which her eyeball currently dangled. *Poke. Sizzle. Scream. Poke. Sizzle. Scream.* It didn't take much to cause pain when you were working with exposed nerves. She shrieked ever more desperately with each tiny stab and cut.

"What do you want? Tell me, and I'll give it to you," she panted. "Please!"

Pausing to wipe the blade on my pant leg, I pointed the tip at her other eye, leaning over the chair back as I let a bit of my Hyde-side show on my face. Her reaction waffled between revulsion and abject terror.

Nothing like showing the boogeyman who the real monster is.

"Let's start with your name." I really didn't care, since she'd be dead in an hour anyway. But I'd noticed that asking put the vamps I interrogated at ease.

"Clara," she said with a genuine sniffle. *Pathetic.*

"Alright, Clara. What I want is answers, namely about how this shit started. I want to know everything, including who was behind the whole fucked up mess. I want to know the key players, the planners, their triggermen, and who was pulling their strings."

"I can't! Every maker put their thralls under a compulsion to force us to keep our mouths shut. I couldn't tell you if I wanted to, druid—you gotta believe me!"

I chuckled. It was not a friendly sound.

"Compulsions can be broken, Clara. That's something I've learned through trial and error." I let the tip of the knife drift closer to her remaining eye, causing her to flinch and squirm.

"Please, don't," she said in a small voice. "I can't talk, mister. Honest."

I frowned. "Is that so?"

Ever so slowly, I ran the tip of the blade down one side of her face, around her jawline, and up the other side, watching her skin sizzle like bacon crisping in the pan. Clara let out a little mewling whine.

"Clara, after six months in this shithole I got nothing but rage and crazy inside. So, you and I, we're going to work through some of my anger issues together. Believe me, it's going to be one hell of a long day for you. But don't you worry your pretty little head, because I'm positive you'll give me what I need—soon enough."

2

I was on my way back to camp and deep in my thoughts when I nearly stumbled into a sizable group of zombies headed straight for our encampment. I'd have noticed them sooner, but the evil little coven leader had turned out to be a wealth of information—although it had taken considerable time to break the compulsion her maker had placed on her. In the end, she'd given me plenty to ponder. But now, I had more pressing matters to attend.

Our camp was located on a large isthmus that extended a half-mile or so into Lake Somerville, a man-made reservoir about nine miles northwest of Brenham, Texas. I'd chosen the location because it was remote and highly defensible, as deaders could only access it via a single narrow stretch of swampy land that was partially flooded at this time of year.

We'd been there for two weeks, and thus far I'd managed to hide us from the numerous wandering hordes of undead that now roamed the countryside. Almost every populated area had been overrun by the dead at this point, and vamps roamed at night in most sizable towns, along with the odd revenant or ghoul. The cities were no longer a safe place for children, so I'd led our group out here. It was far enough away from populated areas for safety, but close enough to allow for scavenging runs.

To this point, I'd only had to deal with encroachments by lone deaders. But this group consisted of at least two-dozen zombies and, from the looks of it, some of them were fairly fresh. *Probably that vamp coven driving them out this way. Damn—a herd this size might push their way through the swamp.*

I'd hidden a flat boat and canoe in the trees on the north side of the isthmus just in case, but I'd rather it didn't come to that. Finding locations where I could safely hide two dozen kids was never easy, and for that reason alone I didn't want to abandon camp. Like it or not, I'd have to take the herd out before they made their way to our camp.

Great.

In the six months since that bastard Click had stranded me in the middle of a zombie apocalypse, I'd learned a few things about killing the undead. For one, I'd almost imme-diately given up fighting them with firearms. Sure, you could take out a lot of deaders with an AR-15 and a decent optic, but even suppressed gunfire would attract more dead. I'd found stalking them from cover was best, and silent kills were the rule of the day.

Like I said, getting swarmed sucked.

After stowing the huge duffel bag of supplies I carried, I strung my longbow and nocked an arrow, holding it in place by wrapping my forefinger over the shaft. Then, I snuck through the swampy woods, keeping myself hidden behind thick brushy undergrowth and the oak, hickory, and sugarberry trees that dotted the area. The woods had gone quiet, except for the low moans and shuffling footsteps of the walking dead. Thus, I took great care to avoid snapping a twig or branch underfoot as I flanked the group of undead.

Peeking around a large post oak, I spotted the last few stragglers in the group. The herd was headed north, funneled toward our camp by the gradually narrowing stretch of land that jutted into the lake and blissfully undeterred by the dense vegetation and marshy soil. Deaders didn't much care about such things, mindless creatures that they were. Once they began walking in a particular direction, the only thing that would cause them to change course would be a high wall or a warm body moving in a different direction.

I leaned out from behind the tree and drew the bowstring to my cheek, sighting down the arrow's shaft at the back of a deader's head twenty yards away. The paracord silencers at either end of the bowstring, as well as my smooth and practiced release, muffled the twang. The brightly-fletched shaft hit the mark, burying itself in the zombie's skull with a *thunk*. My target collapsed, falling to the soft soil without alerting its companions.

One down, twenty-three to go.

I emptied my quiver by repeating the process,

following the herd at a distance and retrieving arrows along the way. Unfortunately, hunting the undead in this manner was causing me to lose arrows, as the aluminum shafts often bent as the zombs fell. Lamenting the loss of half my ammunition, I finally lost my patience and slung the bow over my shoulder so I could draw my sword.

Eight zombs left. Super easy, barely an inconvenience.

Another lesson I'd learned was that it paid to move with a purpose when taking on deaders in close combat. The last thing you wanted was to give a mob a chance to close ranks on you—better to keep them spread out and deal with them one at a time. The hand-and-a-half sword's blade was damned near three feet long, impossible to draw from the over-the-shoulder rig in which I carried it. So, I unslung it, discarding the scabbard and rushing the first zomb as I drew the sword.

At least, that's what I had intended. But as I started after the closest deader my foot landed in a hole, the entrance to some animal's warren or den. Since I'd been running at speed, I continued moving forward while my right foot and ankle remained solidly lodged a good six inches underground. Oddly, I heard my tibia and fibula snap before I felt it, then I was falling face first into the mud—all the while trying in vain to stifle my screams of pain so I might avoid alerting the deaders marching through the trees up ahead.

It shames me not in the least to say that I failed spectacularly on that count. Whether it was the loud, sickening crack my bones made as they splintered or the growling cry of agony that escaped my lips, or my sword clattering against a rock as I fell, I'll never know. What I did know was that I'd inadvertently alerted the remaining herd to my presence, and I now had eight starving zombies trudging my way.

I wondered, as I had many, many times since I'd been stranded in this hell on Earth, whether I might be transported back to my own timeline if I died here.

Fuck that—I am not going down like this.

With a thought, I began to shift into my full Fomorian form.

EVEN WITH THE benefit of rapid healing in my shifted state, I still had to pull my leg from the hole and line up the bones so they could heal quickly. If I left them alone, eventually my body would figure it out, but I didn't have time for that. With a fierce growl and much cursing, I set the bones by hand and held them in place until they knit back together.

And none too soon, since the first of the hungry horde was nearly upon me. Revenants and nosferatu steered clear of me in this form, and sometimes ghouls did as well. But zombs were too dumb to know when they were facing their end. They'd keep coming at me until I took them out.

Better me than the kids back at camp.

Early on, I'd learned that my thickened skin was nearly impossible for deaders to chew through, but they could still infect me in other ways. A stray speck of gore in the eye or a drop of bloody saliva in the mouth and I'd be fighting off the infection for weeks. It had already happened once, when I'd gotten swarmed scouting for supplies and survivors in Brenham. I'd played it off like I was suffering from the flu, but the nausea, fever, and chills had been far worse than any flu I'd ever had. Even with frequent trips away from camp to shift so my rapid healing factor could do its work, the illness had lasted for almost a full month.

Not caring to relive that experience, I hobbled over to a fallen tree and snapped off two branches as thick as my arm. Then, I began to lay into the deaders, using the huge lengths of wood like escrima sticks as I whaled on my enemies.

I struck an older man who sported salt and pepper hair, a golf shirt, and khakis upside his skull, pulping it and splattering the contents of his brain pan all over the zomb behind him.

Poor bastard, he was probably enjoying his twilight years out on the links before this shit happened. Most people plan for retirement, but nobody ever plans for a zombie apocalypse.

A young woman in an old-fashioned waitress skirt with half her face missing moaned and lunged at me from my left. With her bottle-blonde hair, pigtails, black and white oxfords, and vestigial make-up, she almost looked like an extra from *Grease*. She'd likely been looking forward to a long and happy life when the shit hit the fan. Maybe she'd had a hot date planned after work—who knew?

Fuck, I hate it when I do this. Why do I torture myself, wondering what these people were like when they were alive?

I teed up and took the woman's head off with a vicious

forehand swing, forcing myself to watch dispassionately as it sailed out into the lake.

I do it because eventually I'm going to get back to my own reality, that's why. And when I do, I'm going to rain hell down on the fuckers who are planning this. Who have planned it. Er, who are going to plan it—aw hell, I fucking hate time travel.

I dispatched five more zombs in like fashion, crushing skulls with an attention to detail that bordered on reverence. There was no telling how much these unfortunate souls remembered, or whether or not their minds were trapped inside their rapidly decaying brains. All I knew was that I'd hate to be one of them, so I took great care to release them completely, smashing their brains out rather than merely incapacitating them.

There's one missing.

I heard a twig snap behind me. A glance over my shoulder revealed a zomb had flanked me—a tall, husky teen with a crew cut and missing nose, in a red letterman jacket that said "Burton High School Band." This one had a little pep in his step, and it wasn't due to his age.

A ghoul—there's always one hiding in the pack.

That was the thing with deaders; some were trickier than others. You never knew when a ghoul might be laying low within a zombie herd, blending in so they could catch you by surprise. Ghouls were smarter, faster, and stronger than the average deader. Not smarter by much, mind you, but sharp enough to sneak around and attack you from behind.

I spun and punted the thing with a crisp *mae geri* that sent the creature sailing. His flight ended as he was impaled on a broken tree branch, some eight feet off the ground and fifteen feet away. Searching the area for additional threats, I came to the conclusion that the ghoul had been the last of the bunch.

Shifting back into my human form, I took in the tattered state of my wardrobe, lamenting my torn clothes and shredded combat boots. It happened whenever I shifted in a hurry—turning into a nine-foot-tall version of Quasimodo would do that. It was a hassle each and every time, because clothes were so damned hard to replace in the apocalypse. Not because you couldn't find about a zillion abandoned houses with drawers and closets full of stuff just there for the taking. No, it was because finding stuff that fit properly was up to the luck of the draw.

I dug around inside my Craneskin Bag, that bottomless pit that served as my own personal bag of holding. Early on in my time here, the Bag had saved my life more than once, proffering up food, water, items of clothing, and a variety of weapons I'd stored within its depths. Over time, my various stashes had dwindled to nearly nothing, and at the moment the Bag's clothes racks were bare.

"Shit. Looks like I'm headed back into town."

A MOAN DREW MY ATTENTION, causing me to turn a critical eye at the ghoul still squirming on the branch above.

His Chuck Taylors looked to be about the right size, and if the pants were a bit too large around the waist it was nothing a belt wouldn't fix. A quick search of the area revealed my hand-and-a-half sword sitting exactly where I'd dropped it. After retrieving it, I stood in front of the ghoul, leaning on the pommel as I looked him in the eye.

"Man, I bet you never even got laid before you died. That must suck." I paused, scratching the back of my neck. "Can't remember the last time I got laid. Oh, yes I can, it was right before that asshole of a magician stranded me here."

The ghoul moaned, gnashing its teeth at me.

"Yeah, I hear you. You never even got to ask that cute little waitress over there out on a date. Sorry about line-driving her head into the lake, by the way. Couldn't be helped. And sorry about this, too."

I drove the tip of my sword through the ghoul's left eye, ending its thrashing instantly. Then, I sidestepped and chopped the branch off cleanly at the trunk, thanking my lucky stars I had good steel in my hand. Reliable gear often made the difference between life and death in this world.

I'd grabbed the sword from a booth during the chaos at the Ren Fest, that very first day. Luckily it had been made by a smith who knew their way around a forge. Fucker was probably deader cheddar by now. Damned shame, because whoever "Angel Sword" was, they made one hell of a functional blade.

I relieved the kid of his duds, letterman jacket and all, and searched the pockets for useful items. *A lighter—keep. Ballpoint pen—toss. Wallet with cash—nope.*

As I went to discard the wallet, it flipped open to reveal a picture that featured a happy family of four. Dad stood on the left, his arm over his teenage son's shoulder. It looked liked Sis' was in the middle, hugging her brother while Mom stretched to squeeze the both of them in a hug. It was a happy picture, obviously snapped by someone on the fly—a brief moment in their lives when everything was good and right.

I looked up at the former band geek, comparing the face of the young man in the photo to the ghoul. *Yep, definitely him.* I discarded the wallet but held onto the picture, unwilling to throw the young man's cherished memento away. Curiosity caused me to flip the photo over, and sure enough someone had scribbled something on the back.

—*Remember, family always has your back. Love, Dad.*—

I snickered. *Well, you're all worm food now, so good luck with that.*

Yeah, six months in this hellhole had made me a little jaded.

After tucking the picture away, I washed the band geek's clothes as best I could in the nearby lake. Without soap, there was no way they'd ever smell spring fresh, but at least I could get most of the stench of death and decay out of them. Unfortunately, the letterman jacket was a lost cause. *Too much red, anyway—red just isn't a good color for gingers trying to survive this Hellpocalypse.*

After using a cantrip to dry the clothes, I got dressed. Then, I retrieved the supplies, bow, and pack, and headed home. Anna was on watch, so I gave her the signal—a bird call, of course—as I made the approach to camp.

The isthmus was about two football fields across, with a large clearing in the middle hidden by trees on all sides. It had once been a farmstead, complete with a couple of rundown shacks we were using for shelter. I hadn't bothered fortifying the place, because we would abandon it at the first sign of any real and imminent danger. Standing and fighting just wasn't a smart strategy for survival in the apocalypse.

"Looks like a good haul," Anna whispered as I passed.

"It was. Found some new clothes, too. What do you think?"

She frowned, her thick brown eyebrows coming together as she took in my shoes. "Why'd you get rid of the boots? Those things aren't going to last six weeks out here."

I shrugged. "Call it nostalgia. Anyway, I have fresh water and lots of canned food in the bag."

"Thank goodness. I was about to start boiling shoe leather. Mickey's getting some sleep. Can you check on the boys for me, make sure they're not getting into trouble?"

I nodded in reply and headed into camp.

Anna had long since stopped questioning me on how I managed to do the things I did. That included hauling two hundred pounds of supplies cross country, along with all my gear and weapons. Suspicion had long given way to a trust born from hunger and a desire to survive, and thus far I'd kept her, Mickey, and the boys alive. Apparently, that was enough.

They'd all been there at the Renaissance festival that first day. Anna ran a LARPing group for her little brother and his friends, and she'd taken them to the festival as a special treat. The boys had been looking forward to the trip for months, or so I'd been told, and the fact they were there had probably saved all their lives.

Mickey had been an employee at the Ren fest, an actor in period garb who was part of the entertainment. He was no fighter, but when I stumbled across their group he and Anna had been fighting off the deaders with reckless abandon. They'd herded the boys into one of the smaller buildings, but it was a losing battle keeping the zombs from overrunning the place. I'd gone decapitation happy, then got them back to their bus and drove us out of there. It'd been a snap decision, but one I'd never regret.

Matthew, Christopher, and the rest of the little rascals were playing a game of tag when I arrived. They played like any other kids, except for one difference—no matter how hard they played, the boys barely made a sound. They all knew that noise drew the dead, so instead of the raucous laughter and shouts you'd normally expect from a group their age, they spoke in whispers and expressed their excitement with gestures and high fives that always stopped short of contact.

It was a sobering sight, and one that always gave me pause. But I had no time to get maudlin, because once the boys saw me stroll into camp they swarmed me immediately.

"Colin's back, Colin's back!" they whispered, the enthusiasm in their voices nearly driving their chorus to conversational levels. "Whad'ja bring us?"

"Sssh!" I admonished. "Mickey's asleep. And besides, I killed a small herd that was headed this way earlier." The boys' dirt-stained faces grew somber, and several started looking nervously at the tree line to the south. "Not to worry—I took care of them, and Anna's keeping a sharp eye out for stragglers. You're all safe."

"Nobody's safe now, Mr. Colin," nine-year-old Matthew said.

I squatted down to their level. "That's true, and I'm not going to lie and tell you it isn't. The sad fact is, you're all responsible for your own safety now. So, you can't rely on anyone else to save you from any dangers that are out there. Which reminds me, shouldn't you boys be practicing your archery about now?"

"Aw, we already finished, and Mr. Mickey said we could play," Christopher said. Chris was Matthew's best friend, and one of the older kids in the bunch. A once-chubby eight-year-old, he'd leaned out over the last few months, his baby fat turning into rangy kid muscles. "'Sides, you never told us what you brought."

"I might have a bag of candy in this bag..." I said as I watched their eyes light up.

"But I'm only going to share it with you after you've each taken thirty more practice shots."

Despite a chorus of grumbles, the boys took off to grab the PVC bows and dowel rod arrows that Mickey, Anna, and I had made for each of them. None of the boys were strong enough yet to draw a bow that could pierce skulls, but they had hunted the isthmus clear of small game in short order. Rapidly adapting to their environment as kids often do, they had quickly gained proficiency at stalking and hiding. When they got older, their skills would serve them well for surviving in this harsh, unforgiving world.

I watched them scamper off, then put the supplies into storage and headed for the trees to relieve myself.

I sensed it before I saw it, the distinct bone-jarring hum that preceded a major magical working—a dimensional portal, for example. I spun toward the source, still zipping up my pants as the hole in time and space appeared.

"Why there y'are, lad!" I heard a familiar voice exclaim.

Quicker than I could react, Click stuck his head and arm through the doorway and yanked me into the portal.

3

I stumbled forward, landing atop Click on the hard asphalt of the junkyard parking lot. My hands found his throat of their own accord, and I began throttling the life out of him with considerable enthusiasm.

"You weaselly, sneaking, conniving little pile of excrement. Six fucking months! You left me in that hell hole for six—fucking—months!"

Click's face started turning purple, but instead of trying to free himself he kept pointing and looking over my shoulder. Realizing that my chances of choking him to death were zilch to nil—he could vanish at will, after all—I followed his gaze back to the portal we'd just exited.

Like a painting in still life, the scene framed in that seven-foot-tall oval chilled me to the bone. I saw Anna running into the camp from the south, her face twisted in a silent, desperate scream. The boys turned toward their ward, ever more slowly, and their eyes grew wide with fright as a shambling, shuffling mass of the walking dead emerged from the tree line.

The moment stretched out into eternity, likely due to Click's mastery over the forbidden, mystical, highly esoteric art of chronomancy. My hands went limp as I leapt to my feet. I spun and lunged for the portal, only to hear the sound of Click's fingers snapping as it closed in front of me.

Landing catlike in a three-point stance, I turned on the immortal chronomancer, grabbing him by the lapels of his leather biker jacket and slamming him against the junk-yard delivery truck. I hovered over him, my glaring counte-nance reflected in his strange, hazel eyes. Those orbs sparkled with madness and delight even as he watched me struggle to contain my bestial other half. I felt veins pop out all across my arms, neck, and face. My muscles started to swell, and my bones and joints began to creak and crack as the change started coming over me.

"Send me back—now!" I growled with low menace.

Click had the audacity to flash me a sheepish smile and shrug. "And what if I told ye that I'd only do so under certain—er, *conditions*?"

"Click—or should I say, *Gwydion*—this is not the time for your fucking games." I switched my grip, crossing my hands to reach deep into the collar of his jacket on either side. Twisting my hands, I pulled him into a cross choke as I slowly increased the pressure on both sides of his neck. "I might not be able to choke you out, but I can sure as hell pop your head off like a cheap fountain pen lid. Open the fucking portal, now!"

The little mage snapped his fingers again, and I found myself holding air instead of leather.

"Always scramming me clothes up, ye bastards are. Totally uncalled fer, I'd say." I turned in time to see him popping his collars and flicking imaginary dust from his jacket a good twenty feet across the parking lot. "So, ye found me out. I was wonderin' when ye'd solve that riddle. Well done, lad, well done. I believe my faith in ye is well-placed, indeed it 'tis."

I leapt at him, but he disappeared with yet another snap of his fingers. My eyes searched the immediate area, finally spotting him leaning against the junkyard fence. I jumped toward him and he vanished once more, this time reappearing atop a nearby light pole, legs crossed at the ankles and smiling for all the world like this was nothing more than a silly game.

"We could muck around all day, lad, and still accomplish nothin'. Are ye ready to settle down and listen?" I picked up a nearby chunk of concrete the size of my head and fastballed it at the little man. He leaned to the side at an impossible angle, deftly dodging the missile. "Alright then, 'av it yer way if ye like."

I grabbed an even larger piece, shifting further into my other form. Click cleared his throat and nodded toward the street. A group of kids on bikes were stopped on the sidewalk, gaping at the 'roided up freak handling fifty-pound rocks like tennis balls. I doubted they could even see Click, as good as the bastard was at making himself invisible.

The mage tapped his foot in the air above me. "I assure

ye, lad, I kin take ye back to that exact moment, anytime ye like. But not before ye hear me out, now that ye truly know what's at stake."

I hung my head with a sigh, dropping the chunk of rebar and dried mortar to the dirt. "Fine. But I'm almost tempted to say the hell with it and shift, if only to get you back for six long months of abject misery."

I marched through the junkyard gates, and Click appeared in front of me with a snap, walking backward to match my pace. He spread his arms in a magnanimous gesture, as if all could be forgiven that quickly. I growled at him, causing him to wince.

"Too soon fer a hug, then?" the little trickster asked with mock seriousness.

Before I could sock him in his smug little face, Jesse appeared over Click's shoulder in a swirl of leaves and faery dust, brow furrowed and eyes darting this way and that.

"Colin? There you are. O-M-G, I was *so* worried about you. One minute you were there, and the next you just vanished. I couldn't sense your presence at all."

I unclenched my fists and exhaled heavily. "It's okay, Jess. Click here was just showing me something. No harm done."

Jesse squinted for a moment, then twisted her mouth in a deep scowl. "He's responsible? Well, I'll just show him—"

The youthful mage snapped his fingers again. Instantly, Jesse froze in place, just as her hair began to billow out in a halo like Medusa's own locks—a sure sign she was about to have an ass attack of Hiroshimic proportions. I pursed my lips and tsked. Although I was still a bundle of raw nerves and pent-up rage, seeing Jesse put in her place calmed me down a bit.

"Huh. Now, that's a trick you're going to have to teach me sometime. You have no idea what it's like, living with her."

Click glanced over his shoulder at my ex-girlfriend-turned-power-crazed-dryad. "Eh, I've had the opportunity to court a few of the Greek fae in my time. Believe me, lad, I've an inkling. But we've more pressin' matters ta' discuss. C'mon then, let's chat before she finds a way to break outta me spell."

"So, I was right about your true identity, you sneaky Welsh bastard," I said as I toweled the water from my hair. It'd been a long time since I'd had a decent bath, and the cold water and new bar of soap in my outdoor shower had been nearly as welcome as a hot soak. I'd had to burn the clothes I'd been wearing. For now, I'd be dressing in the finest mechanic's fashions by Dickies, at least until I had a chance to go shopping.

Click sat on a nearby car hood, legs crossed at the knee as he leaned back against the windshield. As usual, he showed not a care in the world, despite the urgency of his words just a few minutes earlier.

"And *Cymru am byth*, at that," the little trickster god

replied. "Aye, 'tis me given name, such as it were. But I've not used it nor been called by it in quite a spell."

"Why all the secrecy?" I asked.

"Oh, I dunno. Perhaps it's because we tricksters tend ta' collect enemies like a Cardiff pub gathers drunken sailors. It goes wit' the territory, 'an sometimes 'tis nice to take a break."

Realization dawned across my face. "You're hiding from someone—and you tricked Maeve into helping you do it."

"From some*thing*, actually, if ye want to split hairs. But enough o' that. Let's talk about the task at hand, before the wee little nature goddess in yer backyard cuts herself loose o' me magic."

I did a double-take. "Whoa, hold up. Jesse's a nature goddess?"

The youthful-looking mage nodded. "A baby one, fer sure. But she'll grow in strength if ye don't find a way ta' rein her in."

"Any suggestions on how I might do that?"

Click squinted and arched an eyebrow as he looked up to the sky. "Nuclear warhead? Naw, I'm jest messin' with ya', lad. Ye should talk ta the Dagda, or that crotchety old druid ye call yer mentor. Either one'll have an insight or two ta share regarding how ta settle the lass down."

I cringed inwardly at the thought of explaining the whole thing to Finnegas, but I'd have to do it, and soon. Jesse grew ever more powerful—and ever more capricious —with each day. I simply couldn't put the dreaded task off much longer.

I waved his suggestion away with a flick of my hand.

"I'll take care of the situation before it gets out of hand, but right now I'm more concerned with preventing an undead apocalypse. Tell me the truth, Click. Everything I went through—is that really our future?"

He propped himself upright with his hands as his care-free smile vanished. "The most likely future, I'd say. I try ta avoid walking the Twisted Paths, as it's easy ta get lost, or ta go mad fussin' o'er all the possible futures and outcomes. But I look from time ta time—curse of the chronomancer, 'tis—and that one kept coming up, over and over again."

"So, if we don't do something to prevent it, we're facing a nuclear war, a mass invasion of the undead, and the near-extinction of the human race."

Click shrugged. "Ye saw it wit' yer own eyes. Do ye really want ta curse those poor little lads ta such a wretched and hopeless future?"

"Wait a minute, I was there. Are you saying it hasn't happened for them yet? That everything that I saw and experienced over the last six months went 'poof'—up in smoke when you pulled me back to this timeline?"

The immortal mage shook his head. "Not exactly, no. 'Twas real ta you though, aye? Well, that's the thing about the Twisted Paths, lad. Once ye experience a timeline, it becomes real ta ye, personally. Sure, in this timeline those lads are still wettin' their beds and dreamin' o' getting video game consoles fer Christmas. But in that other time-line, well—that really happened. Or, it is happening. And it will happen ta everyone ya' care about if we don't prevent it."

"You're making my heart ache and my head hurt, Gwydion."

"I know, lad. 'Twas kind of the whole point of the exercise." He looked around nervously, dropping his voice to a whisper. "And I'd be pleased if'n ya' didn't be callin' me that."

I nodded, promising myself that I'd find out who was after him and why. It never hurt to have leverage over a minor god. "*Click*, I can't help but think I have to get back to them. That Anna, Mickey, and the boys are going to be toast in that timeline without me there to help them survive."

A sly smile split Click's face. "Well now, that's the right lush thing about time magic, isn't it? O' course, I kin take ye back, anytime I please. But what if I told ye there was a way for us ta' jump the line with yer magic studies? Ya' know, ta help ye better deal with the enemies that're ta come?"

I sat down on a low pile of old tires. "I don't follow."

"Think, lad, think! Have ye noticed anything about the time ya' spend inside that great green pocket dimension ya' have over yonder?"

"You mean when I visit the druid grove? I hadn't thought about it."

Click scrunched his face up, giving me a look like I was the slowest kid in the class. "Have ye noticed that when ye enter said grove, ye come out at nearly the same time ye entered?"

"Honestly, I try to avoid spending much time in there

at all. I can't remember a single occasion when I spent more than thirty minutes inside the grove."

"Then listen close, lad. Time doesn't pass inside the grove like it does out here. The Dagda designed the groves in that manner when he created them, in order ta allow the druids ta delve deep into their studies, advancing decades in knowledge and wisdom whilst time virtually stood still here on Earth. Just think about how much yer skills advanced in the short time ye were away in that apocalyptic hell. Now, what if ye could do that multiple times?"

I clutched the sides of my head. "Shit! You mean all this time, I could've been using the grove to plan, study, heal—hell, to catch up on sleep—in a virtual chronological limbo, completely separate and detached from the flow of time on Earth?"

Click winked. "Give the lad a cookie."

"I am so going to give the Dagda a piece of my mind the next time I see him," I growled.

A LOUD RUMBLING erupted on the other side of the junkyard, and the oak tree's limbs began to shake and sway in the distance.

"An' that would be me cue ta leave," Click said.

"Wait a second—I have so many questions! Like, why can't we just bring Anna, Mickey, and the kids back here? And why can't we just send me back down our own timeline once the apocalypse starts, so I can tell myself how to fix it or who to kill to stop it?"

"She'll be free soon." Click gave a nervous backward glance toward the druid oak, then looked at me and sighed. "Look here, lad, and pay attention. Time travel is not ta be taken lightly, and there are consequences ta mucking around with timelines. Especially when yer meeting yer own self in another timeline. Things are sure ta go pear shaped if that happens. Which is why I can't bring those poor folks here, 'n why you can't go warnin' your future or former selves o' whatever trouble might be comin' down the pike."

"But you sent me to the future!"

"Yes, but 'twas a future without you in it." Click's eyes softened as continued in hushed tones. "Ah, I see it in yer eyes—someone told ya', they did. That's the only reason I could send ye there, 'tis."

"And why you chose me to help you fix this mess."

Click tapped the side of his nose. "Precisely, lad. I needed someone capable and invested, and yer it." A feral, high-pitched scream erupted from the general direction of the oak tree, causing Click to start slightly. "Aye, but she's a handful now, ain't she? Best be speaking to that druid friend o' yours, real soon. Now, I'm off, but be advised that we won't be able ta use yer grove for yer chronomancy lessons, fer obvious reasons. So, we'll need ta make other arrangements."

"What 'other arrangements,' Click?"

"All in good time, me lad, all in good time. Oh, and I almost fergot ta' mention—don't go tellin' a soul about yer little sojourn down the Twisted Paths. Fer one, certain powers that be frown on time travel, and second, ye might break the timeline if ye do."

"Wait—what?"

"Never ye mind, lad, it'll all work out fine. I'll be in touch."

And with that, Click disappeared. The ruckus in the junkyard continued, with Jesse ranting and raving about tearing "little gods" limb from limb. Roscoe and Rufus, our half-Pitbull, half-Doberman guard dogs, both hid behind my legs, nudging my hands and whining. The two were normally fearless, but they instinctively knew they were no match for Jesse's temper.

"Relax, fellas. I'm about to go deal with her." Rufus let out one last low whine, then lay down on his stomach, covering his eyes with his paws. Roscoe, on the other hand, hid underneath a broken-down van. "Sure, leave me to deal with her alone," I muttered as I headed for the druid oak.

Jesse couldn't stray very far from the oak, and until today I'd only seen her on this side when she was in contact with the tree. So, for her to appear even a few feet away from the source of her power was disconcerting, to say the least. I suspected it had to do with her worry over my absence from this reality. And, I sincerely hoped it wasn't a feat she could easily replicate. If she developed the ability to foray further from the oak, I'd never get any peace.

I turned the corner around a stack of junked cars and ducked back on instinct, barely dodging out of the way of a

Volkswagen engine that buried itself in the dirt a few yards past.

"Jesse, for fuck's sakes, calm down. It's me!"

"Sorry!" she replied. "I thought you were that weird wizard-god-thingy. He sort of defies convention—did you know that?"

"I did. Now, are you done pitching a fit?"

"So long as the little god is gone, I am. But I make no promises if he comes back."

I rubbed the back of my neck. I was exhausted, terrified about a future I might not be able to prevent, and my nerves were shot from spending six months on the run, fighting for my own life and the lives of my companions. I just wanted to crash and forget about everything for a few blessed hours of sleep. But first, I needed to make sure my mentally-unstable ex-girlfriend wasn't going to destroy my place of work.

I peeked around the corner of the stack I'd been hiding behind, only entering the clearing after I saw the dryad had calmed down. Since she'd taken this form, her moods had been as mercurial as any creature I'd seen, and while her range was limited, her powers were not. I worried that one day she'd expose her existence to the staff or, worse, do harm to an employee or customer.

"Jess, you can't just throw things around out here. For one, someone might see—or get hurt. And second, I have to sell that stuff to keep this place open. I know it's junk, but we have to keep it serviceable or else no one will want it."

She put on a long face and trailed a toe in the dirt. "Sorry."

Save for a few strategically-placed leaves, the girl was naked as the day she was born. While I was *gone* I'd had a lot of time to think about my feelings toward her, and how she'd been manipulating those feelings to her benefit. Dense as I could be about such things, eventually it had occurred to me that she had ulterior motives for her lascivious manner of undress.

Yup, this version of Jesse was as devious as the day was long. I needed to be on my toes around her, else I might end up in her thrall... or worse.

"Jess, it might help if you put some clothes on. And can you make yourself look more human? That way, if someone accidentally sees you, they won't freak out."

She struck a pose against the tree that reminded me of an old-time pin-up model. "What, you don't like what you see?"

"Look, it's not that—" I caught myself before I fell into one of her verbal traps. "Besides, that's not the issue at hand. What we were discussing was public safety, and not revealing to the staff that we have a dryad living in the junkyard."

"But you *do* like what you see?"

I grabbed a handful of hair with both hands. "Gah! You're impossible, you know that?"

"I can think of other ways to drive you crazy, Colin," she said, running her light-green tongue across her lips.

"Jesse, please—"

"It's been quite a while since I came back, you know."

She paused to cross her arms and place a finger on her lips. "How long has it been?"

"Long enough, believe me," I replied in all seriousness.

"Exactly," she exclaimed, cocking her hip. "And in all that time, you've barely given me a kiss on the cheek. Don't you think it's time to go back to the way we used to be? I know you want to—I can smell your testosterone levels rising from over here."

Her hips swayed seductively, and after six months without sex I was sorely tempted. But, there was no way I would do that to Bells, break-up or no.

"Sorry, Jess, but I'm just not there yet."

She winked playfully. "Give it time, Slugger. I'll wear you down eventually."

Without another word, Jesse disappeared from sight, presumably back to the alternate dimension that was the druid grove.

"That's what I'm afraid of," I whispered.

4

Some time later, I awoke to a strange yet familiar sound. I ignored it for a time until I realized it was my ringtone. I'd left the damned thing charging inside Crowley's death trap of a car when Click had taken me on the vacation from hell. Now, it sat on my nightstand, buzzing and playing the first few bars of "The Imperial March."

That could only mean one thing—Maeve was calling.

Rather, her people were calling, likely to send me on some errand or another in the name of fulfilling my duties as druid justiciar. Well, I'd had a lot of time to think about my role while I was gone, and fuck them. Fuck *all* of them. I let it go to voicemail and began drifting back to sleep.

Soon the phone rang again, this time playing "Born To Be Wild." Again, I ignored it, until the ring tone switched to "Vampires Will Never Hurt You" by My Chemical Romance.

Yeah, gonna have to change that one, for sure.

I rolled out of bed with a groan and grabbed the

phone, noting the date and time. More than twenty-four hours had passed. It was nearly 8:00 p.m. on the following day.

"Luther, what's up?"

"Is not Looter, you know he never uses modern technology," a woman replied in a thick Russian accent. "Is Sophia Doroshenko, *chudovishche.* There is, how you say, situation. I pick you up in ten minutes."

The line went dead. *So much for my coma.* My bed was calling, but this "situation" had to be serious if I was getting calls from the Coven, the Pack, and the Fae. Reluctantly, I got up and grabbed some clothes along with my Craneskin Bag. Then, I remembered that this thing called *coffee* existed, and my heart skipped a beat. I stumbled over to my espresso machine and grabbed my coffee canister, practically ripping the lid off so I could take a deep whiff of the contents.

"Oh, come to papa," I purred.

Twelve minutes and two sugary espressos later, I was nursing a third from a paper cup while sitting on the back of Crowley's car. *Going to have to return this heap, and soon.*

Tomorrow, I'd send one of the troops out to bring the Gremlin back on the flatbed and get someone to replace Crowley's windshield. Just before my little excursion to Hades, Bells had tossed me through it in a surprising outburst that involved her breaking up with me and the revelation that she was a serpenthrope.

Had I worked out how I felt about that? Depended on which part. The serpenthrope thing I could live with, but the break-up, not so much. We had a connection, maybe not as deep as what I felt for Jesse—the old Jesse—but a connection nonetheless. I'd never been the type to abandon people on a whim, and if she needed space or wanted to friend-zone me, so be it.

For a moment, I considered what it would be like if she busted out in scales while we were going at it. *Get your mind out of the gutter, McCool.* That was a tall order. After a long sleep and a megadose of caffeine, I was hornier than a rutting buck on Viagra. *Hell, even Sophia might look appealing to me, cold slab of meat that she is.*

When the vamp pulled up and I opened the door to her Corvette, I realized how far off base that stray thought had been. Her scent was a mixture of dried blood, expensive perfume, and the faint, almost imperceptible odor of decaying flesh. I paused before getting into the car, breaking out in a cold sweat that had nothing to do with my caffeine high or the chilly fall air.

Prior to being away, I'd never noticed the smell on higher vamps before, but life in the killing fields had sharpened my senses like no amount of practice or training ever could. They all had it to an extent—a musky pungency reminiscent of dry-aged beef. I doubted I'd ever be able to enjoy an air-ripened porterhouse again, and it took every bit of self-control I could muster to climb into that car instead of riddling it with bullets.

Sophia looked at me and clucked her tongue. "What is wrong, druid? You look as though you have seen ghost, no?"

"I—smelled something bad. It'll pass."

She gave me a sideways glance and put the car in gear.

The blonde vampire put her foot down, and we shot out of the parking lot like a rocket. "Druid does not seem like type to have weak stomach. I hope I did not leave a poor impression last time we worked together. My reaction to your... *unique* abilities... was unprofessional. It vill not happen again."

I looked at her, bug-eyed, then busted out laughing.

"Vat is so funny?"

Wiping my eyes, I took a few shuddering breaths as I calmed myself. "It's not you, Sophia, it's me. I forgot what it was like, being around vampires who—"

"Who what? Say it. I am no shrinking violet."

"Who have manners, is all."

She nodded as if what I said had made all the sense in the world. "Da, is true. Many vampires forget what it is like to be human and develop disdain for human ways. These kind fail to remember—civility is what holds society together, is what maintains peace. Manners matter, druid. And this is why I am ashamed for my behavior, last time we meet."

I rubbed the last bit of wetness from my eyes and took a couple deep breaths. *There it is again, the scent of death.* Suppressing the instincts screaming at me to plant a silver nine-millimeter slug in her skull, I wiped my sweaty palms on my jeans and smiled.

"There's nothing to be ashamed of at all. Believe me, your reaction was well-founded."

"Da? How so?"

I let just a hint of my Hyde-side creep into my voice as I

replied. "Because I'm the boogeyman to all boogeymen, Sophia Doroshenko. And don't you ever forget it."

Instead of waiting for a response, I leaned my head back and shut my eyes. And if my undead companion happened to grip the steering wheel a bit more tightly, I pretended not to notice.

SOPHIA DOROSHENKO DROVE us out near Buescher State Park, to The Virginia Harris Cockrell Cancer Research Center near Smithville. The campus itself consisted of a series of research buildings scattered over a couple of acres, nestled within the idyllic piney woods area of central Texas. I mostly stared out the window, admiring the view as we drew close to our destination. The surrounding area was both peaceful and breathtaking.

Much of the loblolly pines in the area had fallen victim to a massive forest fire several years back, but this area had remained relatively unscathed. It seemed an odd setting for a major supernatural emergency, so I asked Sophia to fill me in on what had happened there that might warrant a five-alarm response.

"Is best you see for self, druid," was her response. "That way, you may view scene with fresh eyes, da?"

The vamp briefed me a bit about the lab as we drove through the woods, saying the place was a primary research campus for M.D. Anderson Cancer Center. Scientists and physicians performed groundbreaking research on epigenetics and carcinogenesis there, seeking to find a cure for the deadly disease.

Or, at least, they *had*. Now, the place was a charnel house.

When we pulled off Park Road 1C and onto the campus' main drive, I felt a brief wave of panic envelop me.

Fuck me. It's started already.

Bodies were scattered all across the grounds, some in various states of dismemberment and evisceration. Others were decapitated or sporting large-caliber bullet wounds to the head. I'd witnessed scenes like this many, many times during my foray to the future, and I didn't need to be told what it was.

Zombie outbreak.

"Druid, please—is rental, and I would like to return this car in one piece."

I snapped to my senses, releasing my grip on the door handle as pieces of plastic and foam crumbled beneath my hand. "Sorry, Sophia. I—had a bad experience once, fighting the undead. Seeing this scene brought up some nasty memories."

"Da, you refer to battle at City Cemetery. We hear of this even in Moscow, no? News spreads fast among our kind." She parked the car and reached for her door latch. "Come, we see vat mess has been made, investigate—perhaps Druid will discover what happened."

Sophia stepped out of the car and I followed, but only after calming my nerves with a druid breathing technique. As I exited the vehicle I took in the macabre tableau in its entirety, turning in a slow circle as I watched the clean-up crews do their thing. An odd mix of fae, vampires, 'thropes, and humans were working the scene, chasing down stray zombies and putting those victims who showed signs of turning out of their misery.

Sophia Doroshenko grunted as she surveyed the scene, hands on her hips. "Fae living in nearby woods reported incident when started. Queen Maeve sent her people in, then called other factions when they realized was out of control. It took combined efforts of Fae, Pack, and Coven to keep outbreak from spreading to town."

I rubbed the stubble on my face with a rough, calloused hand. "Any survivors?"

"*Nyet.* All here were infected or killed."

We stood there a few more seconds, taking it all in. "I take it The Circle didn't get the memo?"

"We contacted them and they send, how you say, 'sub-contractors' to help with containment and clean up. Pfah! Cowards."

"Huh. I've tangled with them a few times, and I can tell you that The Cold Iron Circle doesn't hire cowards. No, if they're not here, it's because they didn't think it was worth their time and resources." *Or, someone called them off— someone high up in the chain of command.* "C'mon, Sophia— let's take a look around."

We walked the grounds, stopping occasionally to examine a corpse or gauge the state of the infected. There were two ways to cause a zombie outbreak. One was for a vampire to get sloppy with their feedings and leave a victim on the brink of death with a load of vyrus in their bloodstream. This could result in the victim becoming partially-turned, not fully becoming a vamp but instead transforming into one of the undead—either a revenant, ghoul, or zomb.

The other way an outbreak could happen was through necromancy. I'd seen such an event before, but typically necromancers preferred to work with the dead rather than zombifying live victims. It took time for an infection to spread, regardless of the cause of the initial outbreak. After being bitten, symptoms would appear within hours, but for the average human with no magical immunity to the vyrus, they'd turn some twelve to sixteen hours later.

However, it was clear that these deaders were very recently turned—dozens of them, scattered all across the campus. Most perplexing was that the zombies I examined were not just fresh; they were also *still warm*. Algor mortis, or the cooling of a body post mortem, generally resulted in a decrease in core temperature of one degree Celsius per hour. For these bodies to have not yet cooled, they must have been turned very, very recently.

I pulled off a pair of rubber gloves, turning them inside out and wadding one up inside the other. "Sophia, what time did the initial outbreak happen according to the fae?"

"Around four-thirty this afternoon."

I nodded, squatting over another deader corpse to gauge its temperature with the back of my hand. "Any family members call to find out where their loved ones are?"

"Da, some. But apparently is common for employees to work late. We have contained situation, thus far. But soon, authorities will be involved. We should wrap this up quick, so fae magicians can cover up what happened."

I held a hand up, signaling that I wasn't yet finished with my examination. To confirm my suspicions, I looked at the corpse in the magical spectrum, then reached out with my druid senses for a double confirmation. *There it is —necromancy.* I could both sense and see the dark magic, still hanging like a pall on the dead husk's cells and tissues.

The air exited my lungs in a heavy sigh as I stood. "This wasn't an attack. It was a test."

Sophia snorted. "Test? Of what?"

I shook my head. "Something we've not seen before, a combination of science and necromancy. From what I can tell, this is a new and highly virulent strain of the deader vyrus—one that can turn a victim within minutes instead of hours."

"*Blyad!* This is bad, Druid—very bad."

Triggering a cantrip, I created a small amount of fire that danced across the surfaces of my hands and fingers. I allowed it to burn until it singed the hair on my hands off, along with any trace of infection. Then, I turned to the tall blonde vampire, fixing her with hard, cold stare.

"Tell them to burn it, Sophia—tell them to burn it all. Scorched earth response. Not a trace must be left, you understand?"

"Will be hard to come up with cover story, but I vill pass request along."

"If anyone gives you any grief, tell them they'll have to answer to The God-Killer. Now, I'm off to decon the hunter teams before one of them takes this shit home to their family."

ON THE WAY back from the hunters' staging area, I saw Sophia arguing with a tall, thin, male fae. The mage looked as though he'd just stepped off the runway in Milan, decked as he was in Ralph Lauren from head to toe and lush, shoulder-length blonde hair. I decided to watch from a distance.

"I know is causing panic!" the vampire groused. "Druid would not ask if were not of utmost importance. If infection spreads, vat vill happen then, *feya*? Hmm? Think queen gets panties in bunch now, wait until haf entire city of undead."

Huh, her accent gets thicker when she's upset. Or nervous.

Maeve's mage crossed his arms and looked down his nose at Sophia, which was quite a challenge due to her similar height. "Still, I simply cannot level an entire human research facility. For one, the amount of magic it would require would drain our reserves for months. And second, the Queen would never allow it. Besides, I do not answer to the *druid justiciar*."

He said that last bit like he was referring to something he'd wiped off his shoe. *We don't have time for this shit.* I shifted underneath my skin and closed the distance in a single breath, lifting the mage in the air with one hand clamped around his throat.

"Maybe you didn't get the memo, Legolas," I growled as

he clawed at my fingers in vain. "As far as you're concerned, I am judge, jury, and motherfucking executioner to any supernatural, hunter, or magic-user who threatens to out the World Beneath to the mundanes. All you motherfuckers answer to me, because every last one of you are in *my* jurisdiction."

A female fae cleared her throat nearby, one who bore an uncanny resemblance to Sandra Bullock. "Ahem. That's exactly what Andariel was trying to avoid. Surely you don't think such an extreme act would serve to draw attention away from us, do you?"

Still choking Andariel with one hand, I turned on Sandra Bullock's twin. "And just what do you think will happen when that mutated strain of vyrus I found causes a mass outbreak? If you think the government will swoop in for an act of terror, just wait until they see World War Z going down in Dubya's backyard. You haven't seen heat like you'll see if that happens, cupcake."

She tilted her head, then touched her fingertips to her temples.

A fucking telepath. So, Maeve is using technomancers now. Hmph.

After a few seconds, she nodded to the other fae who were standing close by. "The Queen agrees. Burn it to the ground." Sandy turned to me with a polite smile. "And she asks that the God-Killer not break her mage's neck."

I looked up. Legolas had passed out. I tossed him to a fae medical team. "Here." Then, I walked off to help decontaminate more human hunters.

"Damn, Colin. I figured you'd take our break-up hard, but that was uncalled for."

Bells was standing nearby, leaning against a blood-spattered Ford Taurus. Her arms were crossed and she was looking at me like I was the most pathetic son of a bitch in Texas.

I tried to keep a straight face, but I couldn't help but toss a little eye roll her way. "Seriously? You think I did that because I'm pissed that you broke up with me? I care about you, Bells, but I have bigger things to worry about right now than patching things up between us. So, why don't you take your inflated ego and your pissy attitude somewhere else? Because right now, I honestly don't have the time or the patience to deal with you."

Bells' face turned cherry red, and her eyes flashed a golden hue, but her voice was low and cold. "Oh, sure. Now that your ex is back, you can just kick me straight to the curb. That's fine, *pendejo*. I don't need someone as wishy-washy as you in my life, anyway."

It was hard to see in the dim light, but with my enhanced eyes I could see the scales popping up on her chest and neck.

"Careful now," I whispered. "You expose yourself in front of all these hunters, you're going to give the Circle carte blanche to declare you a dangerous supe so they can make your life hell. Don't throw away your career just because you're a little upset."

"I already threw my career away—for you, *tonto*!" she replied. "Obviously, I made the wrong choice."

"You're being childish, Bells. Just stop, alright? People are starting to stare."

"Me? Childish? Listen here, man-child. I—"

"I don't have time for this." I flashed her the hand, spun on my heel, and walked off to find Sophia so she could give me a ride home.

Bells was in full-on hissing and spitting mode behind me, her mouth going a mile a minute. "Don't you walk away from me, *pinche cabron*! *Te haré lamentar el día que me conociste, hijo de puta...*"

My second ex was still ranting and raving by the time I located Sophia Doroshenko. "Druid, your people skills never cease to impress," she quipped.

"Are you talking about the fae, or my ex-girlfriend?"

She nodded. "Yes."

"I—have a lot on my mind. Let's get out of here before I cause an interspecies incident, alright? Besides, I don't want to be anywhere near this place when the fae trigger that bomb spell."

5

The explosion was all over the news the following morning. "Bombing in Bastrop" seemed to be the headline du jour, as "Terrorist Attack at a Medical Research Lab in Smithville" didn't have quite the same ring to it. The fae had made it look like a terror bombing, using magic and the liberal application of fertilizer and diesel fuel to mimic a large-scale AMFO bomb. The authorities swallowed it, hook, line, and sinker, and now every alphabet-soup agency from the BATF to the DHS were investigating the incident.

Of course, the story had already gone viral, and all the primetime and cable news networks had descended on our fair city to cover it. *If it bleeds, it leads,* I thought as I clicked off my news feed and shut my laptop.

Despite being wired on caffeine, I'd crashed again soon after Sophia Doroshenko had dropped me off. Physically, I was almost back to my old self—Fomorian healing powers will do that for you. But mentally? I was still a wreck.

No rest for the weary. With one crisis narrowly averted and more certainly to come, it was time to get to work finding the ringleaders behind the coming apocalypse.

Unfortunately, when I woke up I discovered I didn't have any decent clothes to wear—a minor concern when the fate of the world was at stake, but a concern nonetheless. Out of habit, I'd long ago taken to keeping all my spare clothing in my Craneskin Bag. It was fortunate I did, since it had saved my bacon a time or two during my jaunt through the apocalypse.

However, that also meant I didn't have a stitch of clothes to my name besides the Dickies pants and mechanic's shirt I'd donned two days ago. I picked the shirt off the floor and sniffed it, recoiling at the overwhelming stench of stale body odor, gasoline, and brake fluid.

This simply will not do.

One thing was universal when it came to vamps and the Circle: they were well-connected. Those assholes had money, and they were prone to spend it. In tracking down the bastards who were about to fuck up this timeline, there were places I might have to go that would require me to *not* look like a homeless person. I needed to go shopping, stat —and that meant I needed to check in with Maureen.

My beautiful half-fae friend and occasional trainer in the warrior arts was in the front office as usual, keeping the business humming along for me. Seeing her through the window working her ass off, I felt bad that she now had to do all the managerial stuff that Ed had used to do around here. But despite my own guilt, I was pretty sure she enjoyed it.

Maybe it had something to do with fae and their penchant for counting money—I had no idea. That wasn't a topic I cared to broach with Maureen, for obvious reasons. Another little detail complicating matters was that I couldn't thank her directly, because that was a no-no when dealing with the fae. Lacking any polite alternative, I simply resolved to make frequent comments about what a great help she was and call it a day.

I walked in the office and found my usual steaming-hot mocha waiting for me. How she did it, I'd never know, but it was damned skippy of her.

"Mmm... good coffee," I said as I took a sip.

"Ye've been burnin' the candle at both ends again, I see. And what happened ta yer hair? Did ye shift inta' that great lout of an alter-ego and forget ta shift yer mop back agin?"

While I was in the "Hellpocalypse," as I often referred to it, Mickey had been cutting my hair. He did the same for all the boys, so I was familiar with his work and well aware that my hair looked a wreck. The man's calling had definitely *not* been to be a barber.

"That's what I'm about to fix, Maureen, along with my wardrobe. I just need some cash to do it. How are we looking? Any of the cars sell yet that we brought back from auction?"

She chuckled. "Cash is not yer concern at this point. Yer first month's stipends came in and added a few zeroes to yer bank accounts."

"Um, how many zeroes?"

"Enough ta keep this place afloat, and fer ya' ta move

outta that dump you call your living quarters." She paused and looked at me askance. "You *are* goin' ta move out, right?"

"Not on your life. This junkyard is the only place I feel safe now."

"Aye, the wards and metal and such do well enough at keeping things out that don't be needin' entry. It's enough to even make me a bit jumpy at times, even though I'm only half-fae." She pointed the eraser end of a pencil at me. "But you'd do well ta remember that no young woman's goin' ta want to settle with a guy who won't place a decent roof o'er her head."

I held my hands up. "Least of my worries right now, Maureen." I looked around the office, scanning the counters and shelves. "Do you know where the checkbook is?"

"'Course I know where it is. But ye don't need it. I already paid you a salary and deposited it in yer account."

"I have a bank account?" I asked in all seriousness.

"Yes, that's somethin' else I took care of for ye, ya' big dumb lout. And yer also the sole owner and manager of yer very own consulting company, MacCumhaill, LLC. Thought it might draw a wee bit of attention, a junkyard getting large electronic deposits fer 'consulting fees' when the only thing ya' seem to consult around here is those mutts."

She handed me a stack of business cards and a debit card with a PIN number written on a piece of masking tape on the back. I took a moment to examine the business cards. They were simple linen card stock with my name in a fancy font. Underneath my name she'd added the ambiguous title of "consultant," the company name, and a phone number—Maureen's line in the junkyard office.

"These are nice. Well done on the name."

"I thought it fitting—and besides, there was no MacCumhaill in the books when I searched the state records online."

I tucked the cards in my pocket. "So, what do I consult about?"

"Smart alecky responses and backhanded compliments, I'd assume. Cernunnos' sakes, I've no idea. Make somethin' up, why don't ye? That was the whole point of making you a consultant in the first place. The druids have been doing it fer ages, mind you—'twas the original bullshit job."

"How about, oh, I dunno—security consulting?"

Maureen rubbed her chin. "Hmm... it might work, at that. There's probably some paperwork ta file with the state, but I'll hire one of Maeve's fixers to take care of it. Now, off with ye then. Go get that pile o' brambles on yer head trimmed, and buy yerself some decent clothes fer a change."

I mock-saluted her. "Aye-aye, cap'n!"

Maureen balled her slender, delicate fingers into a fist and shook it at me. "I'll do somethin' ta yer eye if ye don't quit yammerin' and let me finish this work."

Despite her threats, I walked around the counter and gave her a half-hug and kiss on the forehead. "I really missed you, you know that?"

Maureen's eyes were misty as I stood up. I pretended I

didn't notice. "What're ye on about? Go on, get out of here so a woman can get her work done."

I waved the debit card at her as I exited the office. "Thanks for my allowance, Mom—don't wait up!"

I was pretty sure the door slamming behind me wasn't the wind. Still, it was good to know that I was loved, to be reminded that I had friends looking out for me here in my own reality.

Alright, Colin. Time to get this piddly-ass shopping trip out of the way so you can see to keeping those people safe, sound, and zombie-free.

I WAS HEADED out the door of a custom boot shop in SoCo when I heard a familiar voice call my name.

"McCool..."

It was almost a whisper, but not quite. My senses were pretty damned sharp, both from my druid training and six months of living and dying by my instincts in the Hellpocalypse. After a moment's vacillation, I zeroed in on the source and walked around the corner of the shop, into a narrow drainage alley that separated the store from its neighbor.

The skinwalker stood in the shadows of the alleyway—the same one who'd tried to capture then kill me outside of Keane's little hideout. His look was a hard one to forget, with his dark skin, Eurasian eyes, stringy black hair, hooked nose, and lean, rangy build, reminiscent of a coyote. He had a hippie-looking teenage boy in a rear-naked choke—not tight enough to put him out, but enough to make him hold still.

There was a ball of sickly green and black fire in the skinwalker's hand, which he'd placed behind the kid's head. Little wisps of death magic kept licking at the kid's hair and dancing around his skull like a diseased halo, withering hairs and slowly destroying his man-bun. Thankfully the kid couldn't see it, or this rescue would require a mind-wipe from one of Maeve's fixers. Still, if I didn't do something soon, the poor little bohemian was going to go bald before he exited puberty.

Let's see if I remember how to bullshit properly.

"Oh, I remember you," I said with a smile. "You're the freelancer who tried to catch me for Keane and his buddies. You know, you're looking a little gaunt there. How've you been? Skinwalker life treating you good?"

"Keep talking, and the boy doesn't live to see his first set of tits," the skinwalker replied. "Just do exactly as I say, and no one will get hurt."

The boy actually had the balls to speak up. "I-I've had some tit before. I-I'm n-not a v-virgin."

The skinwalker and I both shouted at the teen in unison. "Shut up, kid!"

Catching the kid's eye, I added, "Let the adults in the room talk, and you might just live to see third base."

The kid clamped his lips together and stared at the ground.

Forcing myself to remain calm, I made a show of looking around the alley. "Where are your little fur-babies?"

The skinwalker grimaced. "Scattered."

I nodded. "Ah, I see. So, what do you want, then?" I snapped my fingers. "Hey, are you still sore about that *stole* I stole from you? I mean, that matted old coyote skin?" The look he gave me said I'd hit the nail on the head, so I started fumbling around in my Bag. "Pretty sure I left it in here somewhere."

"Stop! I'll kill the kid, I swear I will!" the skinwalker screeched.

"I think he means it, mister," the kid whimpered. "And I don't feel so good."

The boy was starting to look a little green around the gills, so I froze and locked eyes with the skinwalker. "Geez, chill out, dude. I'm not reaching for a weapon—just looking for something."

"What are you looking for?"

I arched an eyebrow at him like he was stupid, because he was. "Duh, your stole—er, I mean your coyote *skin*—so I can return it."

The guy looked genuinely perplexed. "Why would you do that?"

"Well, it's not mine, is it? Besides, I just took it from you because I needed to get away, and I didn't want you chasing after me in your other form. But that was all just business, right—part of the job?"

"I guess..." he replied, still confused.

I dug around in my Bag some more. "Ah, there it is!" I exclaimed, pulling the coyote pelt out of the Bag. "Here, catch."

I lobbed the pelt at him using a bit more speed than

necessary. Obviously, the skinwalker couldn't "catch," because he had his hands full of death magic and teenage boy. My throw was meant to hit him in the face, and it did. The coyote skin landed exactly where I'd aimed.

As soon as his vision was obscured, I leapt forward and clocked him as hard as I could through the pelt. Luckily, my punch caught the skinwalker right across the jaw, and he dropped like a ton of bricks, straight to the asphalt beneath our feet.

The kid still stood there, unharmed but looking more confused than the skinwalker had been. "Um, why'd that guy grab me, and what did he use on me that made me so nauseous?"

Digging around in my Bag, I grabbed a plastic "junior police academy" badge that I'd snagged off my friend Sgt. Klein over at the Austin PD. It wouldn't fool a pro, but it'd do just fine for a woozy, confused teen.

"Chloroform—he used chloroform on you," I replied.

"B-but, who are you, and why did he want that mangy skin back so bad?"

"Stolen property." I flashed the plastic badge at him. "Look, kid, I'm bail enforcement, and this is one of my skips. He didn't want to go back to jail, so he thought he'd use you for leverage."

"Like that guy on that show with the beard and the mullet?"

I nodded. "Just with better hair, and no camera crew."

"Y-yeah, but he was waiting for you when you came walking by. Why didn't he just run?"

I waved his protests off with a smile as I knelt over the

skinwalker. "Don't try to understand the criminal mind, kid. It'll drive you nuts. Now, go on about your business, and pretend this never happened. Smoke a blunt or something—it'll make you feel better."

The kid shrugged and stumbled down the alley, shaking his head and mumbling about deranged kidnappers. *Hmm, maybe I should've called in a fixer. Now, let's see who this guy is.* I dug around in the skinwalker's jeans until I found a wallet. *Stanley Bylilly—better make a note of that, for future reference.*

The address was somewhere on 183 North, way past Cedar Park out in the sticks. I took a picture of his I.D., stuffed his wallet back in his pocket, and draped the coyote pelt over his chest.

"Sweet dreams, Stanley. Better hope you don't try this shit a third time. I won't be as patient then."

MAUREEN HADN'T BEEN KIDDING about the size of the stipend payments I'd received. Except for the Cold Iron Circle, the members of each faction had been around for quite some time. In the case of the fae, they were near-immortal, and both 'thropes and vamps lived much longer than humans—centuries, in fact. Thus, they all were able to amass incredible amounts of wealth over the course of their very long lives.

I supposed it made sense that they should compensate me accordingly. No supernatural creature liked owing favors to humans, especially not the fae. Paying me handsomely ensured they wouldn't feel any obligation beyond the delivery of my stipend each month.

And wow, what a stipend. Maureen said she'd deposited a portion of it into the account she'd set up for me, leaving the rest to keep the junkyard afloat. Quite frankly, what she'd deposited in my personal account amounted to lawyer money. I had no idea what I'd do with all that cash, but what I did know was that I wasn't shopping at the Army surplus store.

After leaving the boot shop on SoCo, I drove to an outdoor shopping center on the north side of town that had row after row of upscale stores and shops. The very first thing I did was find a men's clothing store. Of course, walking into a high-end clothing store in a grease-stained mechanic's uniform and slush boots earned me quite a few stares.

Walking out in a new pair of jeans, a cable-knit sweater, and a classic men's overcoat made me less of a spectacle—but not by much. It might have been the haircut, or perhaps the haunted and shellshocked look in my eyes, but I was betting on the slush boots. A trip to the barber's and some shiny new shoes took care of the rest. Soon, I was looking like my old self—if not a more gaunt, hollow-eyed version.

A few hours later, I had several shopping bags full of fashionable yet serviceable clothing sitting on the truck seat beside me. Along with that were six pairs of tactical boots, several pairs of Chuck Taylor high tops, the pair of custom dress boots I'd purchased earlier, and another bag of clothes that were suitable for special occasions.

Got that little chore out of the way—what's my next step?

The answer to that question lay in tracking down the vamps who would soon be responsible for starting the apocalypse. But I couldn't tell a soul about *why* I was meddling in vampire and Circle affairs. At least, not if Click was to be believed. I knew squat about chronomancy, so I'd need to keep my investigation on the sly and my motivations to myself, at least until I could affirm or disprove the trickster's dire warning.

Of course, being the druid justiciar meant I had some leeway regarding where I went and who I spoke with in the supernatural world. I only hoped my authority would be enough to explain away the actions I'd have to take in the coming days. And I hoped those actions wouldn't put me at odds with Luther.

Luther—what's he going to do if I have to kill one of his coven? Maybe I'll be able to cross that bridge without burning it down.

Based on what the Eye wanted, and my experiences living in that hell on Earth for six months, I'd long had a sneaking suspicion it had manipulated both the Cold Iron Circle and the vamps to fulfill its ultimate goal. The Eye had once said that by allying itself with the Cold Iron Circle, it had a very good chance of fulfilling its prime directive—namely, to destroy all the earthbound fae. Once that happened, the Eye would be free from the geas Balor had placed on it all those millennia ago.

There were no fae in the other timeline, at least none that I'd ever come across—and no Cold Iron Circle, either. The distinct absence of fae in that reality told me either the Eye had used the vamps to destroy them all, or they'd split back to Underhill when the vamps and other undead took over.

That had been my theory, anyway—then my little chat with Clara had cinched it. During her interrogation, the diminutive coven leader had indicated that the vampires were at least partially responsible for triggering the undead Armageddon. She also told me they'd killed all the Circle's wizards... all except the one who helped start the apocalypse. Clara said they feared that one, because the wizard possessed an object so powerful, it could burn the strongest vamps to ash with a thought.

I only knew of one magical artifact that could give a human wizard that kind of power, and that was Balor's Eye. The way I figured it, the Eye had offered to lend its power to whoever stole it, so long as that person helped it get rid of the fae. Then the wizard helped the vamps take over, in exchange for their help killing the fae off or chasing them back to Underhill. In fact, the only way the gates to Underhill could be opened again was with the Eye's power, because that's what I'd used to seal them.

The more I thought about it, the more it all made sense. And if I was right, I simply needed to discover which vamps were responsible for throwing the proverbial shit into the fan, then I could track them back to whoever currently had possession of the Eye.

As for how I intended to deal with the vamps, I planned to take them out one by one, following them like a trail of breadcrumbs back to the Eye. Without a doubt, someone at the Circle had the artifact, someone connected who knew how to cover their tracks. Vamps... Cold Iron Circle... Balor's Eye. Unless Clara had lied, that's where the trail would lead.

Thankfully, I doubt whoever took the Eye will be able to use it. Fomorian genes don't exactly grow on trees these days.

Or, at least, that's what I hoped. Not that it couldn't choose to cooperate with whoever stole it. It was an independent intelligence possessed of free will, after all. But for whatever reason, the Eye had to channel its powers through a willing agent in order to utilize them fully. And only a person with Fomorian genes could wield it. But eventually, the thief *would* find a way, else they wouldn't have stolen it. So, I needed to get it back before then.

Could I march into the Cold Iron Circle's headquarters and start busting heads, demanding they give me the Eye back? Sure, but I'd probably only last a few minutes against the combined might of the Circle. Once the Council showed up, I'd be facing dozens of hunter-mage teams plus eight master magicians.

No bueno.

In my last brush with the Circle, I'd had a rough enough time taking out Commander Gunnarson and his much smaller tactical unit. I didn't care for the odds I'd be facing if I went into their HQ guns blazing, so I'd have to go another route. What I needed was proof, something I could take to the Council that would force the turncoat— or turncoats—from hiding. And once I flushed the thief out, I would get the Eye back and make sure that it never saw the light of day again.

Find the Eye, save the world... or something like that. And thanks to Clara, I knew just where to start.

TEN HOURS later I was in New Orleans, headed into this anonymous dive bar in a seedy part of Bywater near the metal factories and docks. The place didn't have a sign, nor did its boarded-up façade offer an entrance that a tourist or passerby might easily notice. You had to go around the rear of the building and down an alley to get to the entrance. Around back, you'd find an unmarked and windowless metal door, scratched and covered in a half-dozen layers of peeling, multi-colored paint.

Here be monsters, eh?

There was no doorman or bouncer there to keep the riffraff from coming in, because if you were at this place you either knew what you were about or you were about to meet your end. It was a vamp hangout, plain and simple, and no human would turn up there without good reason. My sources—vampire chat rooms buried in the deep, dark web—indicated this place belonged to Remy DeCoudreaux, leader of the New Orleans coven.

Just the vamp I wanted to see.

Unlike the Austin coven, NOLA vamps weren't exactly human-friendly. They still kept to the old ways, hunting humans at their whim and leisure, ruling NOLA's world beneath with an iron fist. So, how did they get away with it?

After Katrina, lots of people just up and vanished, and

even to this day the population in poorer areas tended toward transience versus permanency. New Orleans was a city where people came to disappear, and local law enforcement was notoriously lax about following up on missing persons cases.

Case in point... In 2012, a journalist won a judgement in a Freedom of Information Act lawsuit, and his attorney was allowed to search NOPD's record storage room. And guess what? They found not a single missing persons record in storage—not one. Thus, New Orleans was just about the perfect place for an evil vampire coven to operate.

In the short time we'd spent together, Clara had given me lots of info but little *actionable* intel—save one critical detail. She'd said her maker was a member of Remy's coven, which was why I'd decided to start my search for the Eye here in New Orleans. Somebody in this coven knew something, and I intended to find out who.

But first, I'd need to gain Remy's trust. I still owed him a favor, which gave me an excuse to show up on his doorstep. Remy's coven consisted of dozens of higher vamps, and a great number of them were more than a century old. Older vamps were tougher to kill, because they got stronger as the years went by, and they typically started developing special skills around the century mark.

That could mean teleportation, the ability to take another form, hypnotism—the list went on and on. Older vamps were also more resistant to sunlight. Sure, they could be damaged by it, but UV light wouldn't always boil their blood and kill them outright like it would a younger vamp.

Meaning, if I were to take on Remy's coven, I'd be facing a few dozen incredibly fast and strong vamps. Many would possess special skills and abilities, and a good number of them would be at least partially resistant to my sunlight spell. *Shit.*

I'd fought an ancient vamp years before, a nos-type, and his powers were so far beyond mine I wondered if I'd be able to take him even in my full Fomorian form. And while Remy's crew was nowhere near as powerful as that vamp had been, I didn't like those odds any more than I liked my chances of attacking the Cold Iron Circle in their own headquarters.

Which was why I was walking into a known vamp bar, at night, alone, to find the one individual who might possibly lead me back to the Eye.

I slammed the front door of the bar open and stood in the doorway. Almost instantly, every set of eyes in the place was drawn to the scent of human blood... and the sound of a warm, beating heart.

"Alright—which one of you leeches do I have to fight, fuck, or feed to get an audience with Remy tonight?"

6

As it turned out, walking into a vamp bar and calling them all leeches was a great way to start a fight. *Who knew?*

A tall, stocky, bald vamp with pale skin, numerous jailhouse tats, and a bare chest under a black leather biker vest stood up... and up... and up. The guy was big, taller than my friend Hemi and just as wide.

Well, the bigger they are, right?

"You're going to regret saying that, human," the giant vamp said as he smacked his fist into his palm.

I looked across the room, taking in the many hateful and hungry glares I was receiving. Then, I turned my gaze back to Goliath. "Ah, so we're going to fight then. That's great, because there was no way I was going to feed or fuck one of you walking cold cuts. You know what it's like, being human and trying to snuggle up to something that cold and clammy? Me neither, and I don't intend to find out."

Someone shouted from the back of the bar. "Get him, Polly—make him pay for dat smart mouth of his!"

My index finger shot into the air, and as it did I slipped my other hand in my coat pocket. "Whoa, hold up. Is that 'Paulie,' like Rocky's brother-in-law, or 'Polly,' as in 'Polly wanna cracker?'"

The big vamp looked around, as if daring another patron to laugh. "The second. It's short for Polycarpe. I was named after a saint."

"Huh. If it were me, I think I'd start going with the first option," I said, shaking my head as I fiddled with the device in my pocket. "It's just not right for a dude to be called Polly. Kind of like that 'boy named Sue' thing. It's a life-long invitation to an ass-kicking. At least with the other spelling, you have an out."

Polycarpe's chest swelled. "Ain't nobody gonna be calling me a girl, no. An' in a minute, you gonna regret all you say 'n more."

"Alright, Polly, I got time to tussle. Before we do that, there's something I want to show you," I said as I pulled an object from my pocket.

I held it overhead for all to see. It was an M-26 frag grenade, one of several I'd purchased at an Army surplus store. I'd wrapped this one in a necklace made of sterling silver beads, and the beads shone in the neon light as I displayed it to everyone in the room, along with the pin that dangled from my pinkie finger.

Of course, the grenade was inert, but the vamps didn't know that. I fully intended to pack them with explosives and rig new fuses later, but for now, this one would have to serve as a bluff to prevent an all-out fight with a bar full of vamps.

A hiss went up from the bar's patrons as they caught the scent of silver. I'd learned from Luther that the distinct metallic tang could be detected by his kind from dozens of feet away. To them, it was like the smell of death, and they tended to react poorly to its presence.

You could cut the tension in the room with a knife. All the bar's patrons were up and on the move now. Some gauged whether they could take me out and keep me from triggering the grenade, while others looked for an escape route. Truth was, most of these bloodsuckers could clear the bar before the grenade went off—that is, if they made an orderly exit. The only problem was that I was blocking the only public entrance, so they'd have to file past me to leave. And if they rushed the door, not all of them could make it out in time.

Suddenly, someone began clapping, ever so slowly, in the very back of the bar.

"Why, I do declare—if it isn't Colin McCool in the flesh," a deep, sultry male voice with a mild French-Caribbean accent said. The crowd parted, though none of them took their eyes off me. As they did, Remy DeCoudreaux strutted his way through their midst.

Remy was of mixed African and European descent, with dusky skin, dark brown eyes, and dark, close-cropped hair that hugged his scalp in tight curls. His facial features reminded me of a young Lenny Kravitz, and he had the swagger to match. As at our last meeting, he was dressed to the nines in a white silk dress shirt, an Egyptian blue double-breasted suit, matching Berluti crocodile loafers, diamond stud earrings, and enough gold jewelry to make a statement without being gaudy.

"You're looking well, Remy," I said, meaning it. Every ginger wishes they had more melanin in their skin, after all.

He laughed—a full, rich guffaw that echoed to every corner of the now eerily silent room. "I should say the same of you, but I'd be lyin' now, wouldn't I? You been missing sleep lately, cher? Looks like t'em folks down in Austin are runnin' you ragged, no?"

"Something like that," I replied with a crooked smile. "Now that I have your attention, you mind if I put the pin back in this thing? Normally I wouldn't make such a scene, but I figured my chances of walking into this place without someone trying to snack on me were slim to none."

Remy tilted his head slightly. "You come to square up wit' ol' Remy, den?"

"Let's just say I needed a break from my duties back in Austin, and figured I'd take a long weekend in your town to kill two birds with one stone."

"Hmpf. Maybe you won't get much relaxin' done this weekend, no? But I do have work for you, and that's a fact." He beckoned to me. "Come, no one will harm you. Now they know we have business to attend."

Just like that, every vamp in the bar went back to doing, well, vampire stuff. One second I was on the menu, and the next I was invisible. I slipped the pin back in my dummy grenade and followed Remy to the back of the bar.

———

REMY LED me through a small maze of halls and corridors, quickly covering enough distance so that the music and chatter of the bar faded behind us. As we walked through the building, my enhanced senses picked up the scent of fresh blood and sounds of vampires feeding. This was obviously where they kept their Renfields and Lucys.

It took a supreme act of self-control to restrain myself from killing the vamps who were feeding on humans just feet away from me. But the truth was, I had no right to interfere. For all I knew, the people behind those doors were volunteers, humans who had willingly offered themselves up as blood donors. It wasn't unheard of for my kind to do so, and some crazies even thought it was an honor to be bled out by a leech.

Keep your eyes on the prize, McCool, and just keep walking.

We stopped at a metal door that opened seemingly of its own accord to reveal a lean, dangerous-looking vampire standing guard behind it. Apparently, it was invitation-only beyond this point, even for the bar's patrons. The sentry's mouth tightened at the sight of me, and he shared an inquisitive look with his boss.

"He's not here to cause trouble." Remy glanced over his shoulder at me. "Are you, druid?"

I shrugged in response to the question, noting that

Remy's accent had faded now that we were alone. "As long as no one causes trouble for me."

"See?" Remy purred. "Tame as a newborn kitten."

The doorman stepped aside, but he never took his eyes off me despite his coven leader's admonishment. I winked at him as I passed his guard post, earning a silent snarl behind Remy's back. Not that he didn't catch it, of course.

"Manners, Silvère, manners."

Silvère, huh? Well, ain't I just a lucky fucker.

The wiry, dark-skinned vamp pointed two fingers at his eyes, then at me. Message delivered, he went back to guarding the entrance to Remy DeCoudreaux's lair. With an amused chuckle, I followed the coven leader further down the arched, stone-lined corridor, which seemed to stretch on into infinity.

"I take it we're not in the bar anymore?"

Remy gestured broadly at the expanse of stone and mortar around us. "I own the entire block, and much more of the city beyond. For our convenience—my own, and those chosen few of the coven I trust, that is—nearly every building I own in New Orleans proper is connected by private corridors and tunnels. Some of them date back to prohibition days, some are even older, and still others I had built in my time as coven leader."

As we walked, I noticed that arrow slits lined the corridors at ten-yard intervals. There were also holes perforating the ceiling above, where I assumed vats of acid or other surprises might be hidden and ready to trigger at a moment's notice. It felt more like I was walking inside the walls and ramparts of a fortress than through an underground access tunnel. I took it as an indication that Remy was both paranoid and a much more careful leader than I'd originally thought.

I gave a grudging nod. "Impressive, considering the engineering required to build anything underground in this city."

"And necessary. I tend to work at all hours and can't have the sunlight get in the way of running New Orleans." He made a casual gesture over his shoulder. "My apologies for Silvère, by the way. He's rather protective, to the point of inconvenience at times. I saved him from a slave owner's posse back before your Civil War. He'd been shot and infection had set in, but the Dark Gift took care of that. He's looked out for me ever since."

"Doesn't talk much," I proffered.

"His former owners cut out his tongue long before I met him."

Well, shit. There goes my plan to interrogate the sumbitch. "How awful," I said, meaning it.

"Indeed. After he was turned, I allowed Silvère to go back to their plantation so he might return the favor. The plantation's ownership reverted to the bank shortly after, so I purchased it and gifted it to him, as a memento of sorts."

I didn't need the details to understand what Remy was getting at, because I'd seen the ruthlessness and wanton violence of predatory vamps firsthand. My mind flashed back to the bone pile at the supermarket where I'd questioned Clara, and my heart began to beat faster in my chest.

Silvère must've passed his habits down.

"Are you alright, cher? You seem a bit... distracted." Remy eyed me with interest, obviously noting that something he'd said had upset me.

Damn it, get your shit together already.

Although the slip in self-control had been a rookie mistake, shaking it off was easy; all it took was a little druid breath control to calm my nerves. After I'd settled down, I realized I'd been unconsciously reaching for the silver-plated knife at my back. I allowed my hand to drift back to my side under Remy's watchful gaze.

"I'm fine. Just not a fan of slavery, in any time period."

The vamp shrugged. "We do it all the time to humans who volunteer for such treatment. I suppose it is the way of things, for the predator to subjugate its prey. But to do it to one's own kind, or perhaps even to an entire species, well—that would be an unconscionable act, no?"

I kept my dark thoughts to myself. I was here for intel, not to start a war—although I *was* here to prevent one. If I had to kill Remy's entire coven to achieve my goal, I would. Yet I had no idea who the key players were. Even if I killed every vamp in New Orleans, it wouldn't necessarily bring me closer to my goal.

I'll play it cool, for now. But once I get what I came for, all bets are off.

The coven leader was still looking at me, waiting for an answer. "I'm a druid, Remy. We tend to look at events in terms of centuries instead of years, secure in the knowledge that the tide always turns, eventually." It was bullshit of course, at least as far as I was concerned, but I needed to maintain an air of neutrality to quash any suspicions Remy might have about me.

He nodded. "The implication being you wouldn't care to involve yourself in such matters. Interesting. But as I understand it, there aren't that many of you left—druids, I mean. Seems like that approach is not working out so well, no?"

"One druid, one riot," I said, bastardizing the unofficial motto of the famed Texas Rangers—the law enforcement agency, not the baseball team—to make a point. "You know as well as I that if we started multiplying it'd make the faction leaders in Austin nervous."

"I doubt very much that Luther is concerned with druid affairs."

"It's not Luther I'm referring to."

The vampire gave a tilt of his head. "You make a fair point. I forget that in Austin you have a truce between the factions, and that the vampires don't rule the city."

I thought it unlikely that Remy ever forgot anything, but I was curious as to how the vamp felt about the contrasts between his city and mine.

"Do you think Luther should seize power, Remy?"

The vampire's voice grew deadly serious. "I think he's weak, to abdicate power for the sake of peace. He should have chased the fae, the wolves, and those wizards from his city long ago. Vampires should not share power—with anyone."

"I'll be sure to pass that along," I replied disinterestedly, despite the intensity and nature of his response. *Congrats, leech—you just moved up on my shit list.*

Remy chuckled humorlessly, then remained silent for the rest of our short journey. Perhaps a minute later, we stopped in front of another metal door.

"Ah, here we are," he said. "My own personal retreat, right in the heart of the city."

"No guards?" I asked.

"None needed—at least, not at this time of night." The coven leader opened the door, gesturing for me to enter. "Come, let me show you around."

WE EXITED THE DARK, gloomy, stifling confines of the private corridor into a large garden courtyard lit by candles and old-fashioned gas street lamps. Rather than a single barren expanse of stone or concrete, the space was instead broken up by koi ponds and vegetation, with meandering walkways connecting individual patio areas paved with intricate patterns of bricks and tiles. Marble and bronze statues adorned Remy's garden, and even my untrained eye deduced that many of them could easily have been museum pieces.

Flowering plants and vines grew all around, covering the walls, overhead lattices, and archways, but all were carefully trimmed and manicured so as not to obscure a view or present an obstacle to passage. In the pale moonlight and fire-lit glow of the candles and lanterns, the place was stunning and almost magical in its charm and elegance. But more than the sheer beauty and opulence of the place, I was struck by the activities that engaged its current inhabitants.

The place looked like a scene from a Roman bacchanalia, complete with naked bodies, scantily-clad servants of both sexes, and the occasional ménage à trois or orgy happening on over-sized beds, couches, and the odd divan all around the garden. Yonder laid a naked man, easily handsome enough to have strutted the catwalks in Paris or Milan, and at each wrist and one inner thigh, a vampire eagerly lapped the lifeblood from his veins while he writhed in ecstasy.

I suppressed a shiver and forced my eyes to wander on.

Over there was a model-thin woman performing an oral act on a vamp, all while a female vampire with a strap-on drilled her from behind at warp speed. And there, a naked older man was restrained in velvet-padded stocks, his head and arms trapped while a female vampire in a black Naugahyde getup tore strips of flesh from his back with a cat o' nine tails, pausing to lick the blood off between each swing. Everywhere I turned, the most violent and ribald scenes played out like *Caligula* adapted and reenacted for modern times.

I stood stunned for a moment, as I'd never before seen the like outside of watching *Spartacus* or *Game of Thrones* on cable television. Of course, I knew such things happened, and I also knew that certain members of the supernatural community engaged in X-rated acts on a regular basis. But I'd never realized just how visceral and revolting an experience it might be to witness such depravities firsthand. Combined with the psychological aftereffects of my recent apocalyptic jaunt, the scene before me was almost too much to take.

Remy turned to me with a tsk. "Oh, cher, you are upset, no? I thought maybe a young strapping man like you might want to sample the wares, eh? But perhaps I misjudged the situation. My mistake."

His expression told me there had been no mistake; Remy had brought me here on purpose to see how I'd react. He wanted to know for certain whether I could be trusted to handle coven matters without interference on my part. I quickly considered what I was willing to put up with and how far I'd go in compromising my values and morals to prevent the hell I'd seen from coming to pass.

"I don't care what you and your people do behind closed doors, Remy. Just as long as there aren't any kids involved, I'll choose to look the other way." *For now.*

"What, you want a child? That can be arranged," he teased with a sly grin on his face.

I clenched my fists. "Remy—"

The old vamp laughed. "Oh, lighten up, you! We're vampires, not savages. Do you see any children round here? No? O' course not, because even old Remy has rules he lives by." The vampire's expression became subdued. "But enough with these distractions. Come, I take you away from this place, and we discuss what Remy needs from you to settle your debt."

"Fine, but no more games, Remy. My ability to deal with silly bullshit only extends so far."

"Then let us retire to—less *lascivious* environs. There, I'll explain the task at hand."

Without another word, Remy headed back through the door from which we'd exited. I forced myself to take one last long look at the courtyard, committing the scene to memory. Once finished, I swallowed the rising bile in my throat and followed the coven leader back inside.

7

A short walk down the passageway led us to a cleverly-hidden door in the wall. Remy pulled out his phone and dialed in a passcode, and an electronic whirring noise came from just on the other side of the concrete. When the sound stopped, he pushed on a section of wall, causing it to pivot as smoothly as the lazy Susan on my mother's kitchen table.

Beyond was a well-lit lounge complete with large, comfortable-looking couches, a wide-screen television, and a wet bar stocked with an assortment of expensive liquors. Soft jazz played in the background at low volume from wireless speakers, and a second large-screen television displayed peaceful, sunny outdoor scenes like some larger-than-life screen saver made into nouveau art.

"What's with the pictures?" I asked.

The vamp gestured at the screen. "For those who were gifted with the second life, we often wish to see scenes such as these again. Does that surprise you, that a predator could enjoy such beauty—even long for it?"

I shrugged. "I hear sunscreen and UV-blocking window tint goes a long way."

"True, but the colors are always muted, and it never looks quite the same." He paused before nodding toward the bar. "Would you care for a drink?"

I shook my head with a grunt. "Enough pleasantries, Remy. Tell me what you need so I can square this debt and be done with it."

"Of course. Sit, please."

He sat on one of the couches and tilted his head at the adjoining love seat. I stood for a moment, then took a seat. As I did, I wondered if I was going to lose my cool and kill him before he explained the job.

"This matter I would have you take care of, it is a delicate thing," he stated without preamble. "Not delicate work—no. But a matter that must be handled discreetly and with the utmost haste."

I pinched the skin on my forehead with my fingers. "I find it difficult to believe that this 'delicate matter' just so happened to pop up right before I did. Seems a bit convenient, and damned obvious."

"I prefer to view this as propitious timing. In fact, I had considered contacting you to call in that favor. But here you are, offering to pay me back just when I have an issue that requires someone of your unique talents." He paused to rub his chin. "Perhaps it is I who should be suspicious, no? But I believe in the hand of fate, and when you've lived as long as I, you learn to see through people."

I kept my face blank, but it took some effort. "Just tell me who you need killed, and I'll tell you if I'm willing to do it."

"Oh, you'll be willing to kill this one, for certain. Have you ever heard the legend of Jacques Saint Germain?"

I lifted a hand off the arm of the couch, wavering it back and forth. "It vaguely rings a bell. Enlighten me."

"More than a hundred years ago, Jacques Saint Germain was the coven leader here in New Orleans—my predecessor, in fact. But Saint Germain was much too bloodthirsty, and he flagrantly broke the laws of vampire society."

"Such as?"

Remy propped an ankle over his knee and draped his arms across the back of the couch. "Such as the dictate that we must keep our way of life, and our existence, a secret. Instead of preying on those who would not be missed, he took familiars from the highest levels of society as his cattle. He threw lavish parties and flaunted his talents and appetites among the social elite and city leaders. But perhaps his most egregious crime was getting caught in the act—and with a common prostitute, no less."

"The act, meaning feeding on a human."

"Indeed. He drank so much blood and wine one night that he forgot to mesmerize the whore he'd been feeding on. She leapt from a second-story window of his home in broad daylight, drawing the attention of local citizens and the police. This would ultimately result in his downfall."

"How so?" I asked.

Remy gave a lazy wave at my question. "A tribunal was

called, and the coven determined him to be unfit for leadership. We chased him from the city and left just enough evidence at his mansion to make him look like a madman instead of the supernatural threat he was."

"And now, he's back."

"Just so, and he wants the city—and the coven—back."

I ran a hand through my hair. "Why should I care? I mean, besides the fact that I owe you a favor, and I don't want it hanging over my head any longer."

"Because, cher, he's a monster. What you saw tonight, I know it offended you. But, although we are predators, we have rules. We only take volunteers for familiars, and we only hunt violent criminals, those who would be incarcerated or on death row—if only the human authorities were more competent at solving crimes."

The truth was, I was starting to get very, very interested in this Saint Germain. The way DeCoudreaux described him, he might well be the vamp I was looking for, the one who would help trigger the damned apocalypse. However, I couldn't allow myself to appear too eager and tip my hand to this putz. For all I knew, *he* was the one I wanted, and not this Saint Germain.

"Remy, you almost make your outfit sound like the Salvation Army."

He scoffed at my remark. "Oh, hardly. We are perhaps the most aggressive and feral vampire coven of any in the United States. But compared to Saint Germain, we are—"

"Tame as newborn kittens?"

"Hah, yes. As I said, we live by rules that were designed to ensure our survival as a species."

"How heart-warming." I rubbed my temples, because Remy's stench was giving me a headache. "Of course, I have to ask—why not handle this yourself?"

The vampire tsked. "I will tell you why, druid. The last time, it took the combined might of the coven to chase Saint Germain off. Believe me when I say he is not a vampire to be trifled with, mon cher. Unfortunately, he's managed to draw many of the city's bloodkin to his side—those who desire a return to the more savage days of old." He waved off nothing. "I simply lack the power to chase him off."

I chose to keep what I was thinking to myself. *The truth is, you need a monster to kill a monster.*

Remy examined the back of his hand, perhaps to admire his rings or assess the state of his most recent manicure. It was a gesture meant to convey nonchalance, but I could tell by the tension in his voice that this was no small matter for him.

"So, druid, will you do it?"

I nodded ever so slightly. "Yes, I'll track him down. And if he's as bad as you say, I'll kill him. But I'll make that determination for myself. If I decide otherwise, I'll chase him out of your territory, and you'll have to make do with that. Deal?"

The old vamp nodded. "Deal. But if you kill him, I want proof."

"Fair enough. Just point me in the right direction, and I'll handle the rest."

Remy raised his chin at me. "That should be easy. He's taken up residence in his old chateau, at the corner of

Ursulines and Royal. It's as if he thinks it's some grand joke, to return to the home that he soaked in blood. You will find him there tomorrow evening. He's having a party, so you shouldn't find it very hard to gain entry. Oh, and just so you know, any vampires who attend are to be considered traitors, and therefore fair game."

"Understood. Is there anything else I should know?"

The coven leader's voice went cold. "He's old, dangerous, and he uses hospitality to draw in his prey. In the old days, he housed his abattoir upstairs. Chances are good you'll find the proof you need there."

THE PHONE RANG twice before she answered.

"If it isn't Colin McCool. Tell me, stranger, to what do I owe the pleasure?"

"Fallyn, how would you like to enjoy a free weekend in New Orleans?"

Her raspy Southern party girl voice dripped with sarcasm as she replied. "Is this a trick, golden boy? Or did you finally get tired of that little Spanish tramp you were shacking up with?"

"It's not a trick, and we weren't shacking up." She scoffed at my denial. As much as I stayed over at Belladonna's, and her at my place, we may as well have been living together. "Anyway, I'm headed to a party with a bunch of vamps, and I need a plus one."

"You need back up is what you mean. So, you and the hunter are on the outs? Because when she hears I spent the weekend with you in N'awlins, she'll be out for blood."

"Normally I'd ask her, but she broke up with me."

The female 'thrope laughed, short and quick. "Ah, so I'm your back-up plan." For several seconds all I heard on the other end of the line was silence, followed by a sharp intake of breath. "Wait a minute, druid—what the hell are you into this time? And does Samson know?"

Samson was the alpha of the Austin Pack, of which I was an official but somewhat estranged member. I'd gained honorary pack member status based on certain duties I'd performed, in addition to passing their induction trials. I'd qualified for membership by way of the fact that I was a shifter, albeit of the "caused by fae magic" variety.

Samson had recently had a fit when I'd stirred up a bunch of trouble with the fae without realizing my actions would create some blow back for the Pack. Since Samson was Fallyn's dad, she certainly didn't want to be caught up in anything that would raise her dad's hackles. Besides, she'd been way more pissed about the trouble I'd caused the Pack than her dad had been. So, I had to convince her that what I was about to do would *not* reflect poorly on the Pack.

"I promise, this'll have nothing to do with the Pack, because it's all going down in another demesne. I'm doing a job for the leader of the New Orleans coven, to pay back a debt I owe him." *And I'm trying to prevent the apocalypse.*

"Hmm—Remy DeCoudreaux is quite a shady character. How'd you end up owing a debt to that creep?"

"Long story, but it happened when I was chasing down Claw. Remy agreed that he wouldn't interfere in exchange for some future favor." Claw was one of a secret cabal of fae who'd infiltrated the Pack to attempt a coup against Samson. I'd uncovered their plan, and Fallyn and I had prevented them from pulling it off by killing their leader. But Claw had escaped.

"Huh. Since it was a debt you incurred while taking care of Pack business, I suppose I could lend you a hand. What's the gig?"

"I need to infiltrate a vampire masquerade ball to get intel on an elder vamp who is vying for Remy's spot as coven leader."

Fallyn whistled softly. "So, basically, we're going to be in enemy territory, hunting an old and dangerous vamp, surrounded by potentially hostile bloodsuckers, and I'm going to be the only shifter there? Wow, druid, you don't ask for much."

"The only *other* shifter. I'll be by your side the whole time."

"When you put it that way, sugar, I'm all in," she said in hungry voice. "But fair warning, if this is going to involve wearing a dress, you're going to owe me after. Big time."

"It's a high-society event, Fallyn. You know how vampires are. They love dressing up and showing off. But since it's a masquerade party, we can use that to our advantage. I'll get us some suitable masks, and I'll cast a spell to cover your scent so no one knows you're a 'thrope."

"Sounds like a plan. And if you find what you're looking for at this party? What then?"

I took a moment, wondering just how much info I should share with the female werewolf. "If he's as bad as they say, I'll do what it takes to end him."

Fallyn snickered. "You just don't do things halfway, do you, Colin? I haven't had a good scrap since we took out Sonny and his cronies, so count me in. How soon?"

"Tomorrow night. Your flight leaves in a few hours. You'll get the ticket in your inbox shortly, and I'll pick you up at the airport tomorrow afternoon."

"Ooh," she cooed softly, laying the Texas accent on thick. "A weekend away in the Big Easy, with the world's sexiest druid all to myself. My, my—whatever shall I wear?"

"This is going to be purely a working weekend, Fallyn. Believe me, I have girlfriend problems out the wazoo right now, and I don't need to complicate that situation any further."

"And that's exactly what I'm counting on, my cute little ginger wizard."

Fallyn hung up on me before I could respond.

"Ah, fucking great. What did I just get myself into?"

AFTER I PICKED up the alpha's daughter from the airport, we headed back to my hotel, along with the half-dozen or so items of luggage she'd brought with her. For a tough, no-nonsense werewolf who was raised in a biker gang, she sure didn't know the meaning of "traveling light." Once we arrived at the Monteleone, I paid the bellhop a rather large tip then showed her to her room.

"Nice room," she observed. "Being the justiciar for the demesne ain't too shabby, is it?"

"Financially? No. Otherwise? The jury is still out on that."

"Yeah, I sign the checks for the Pack, so I know what you're getting paid." She quickly surveyed the room again, and her eyes lingered on the bedroom doors. "Again, my compliments on the digs, but did you really have to get a two-bedroom suite? I'm Pack, Colin. We aren't exactly known for our modesty."

"As I'm well aware. Like I said, my life is complicated enough as it is, and your dad isn't exactly keen on us becoming an item. So, let's keep it professional, alright?"

Fallyn frowned, but her almost yellow-hazel eyes danced with mischief. "Spoil sport. Now, if you'll excuse me, I have to get ready for a ball."

The pretty werewolf spun away with a toss of her chestnut ponytail. Then, she snatched three suitcase handles in each hand, lifting them with nary a sign of effort as she headed to her room. She stopped just inside, glancing over her shoulder to give me a wink. Without setting her luggage down, Fallyn raised her right leg to deliver slow, head-high hook kick that gently nudged the door closed.

Werewolf strength. Figures.

"You could've saved me a twenty if you'd carried your bags upstairs earlier!" I yelled.

Fallyn's dusky laughter was her only reply. I turned the

television on and watched survivalist shows for the next hour, checking the time every fifteen minutes while I waited. The sound of a shower running, and later, the high whir of a hair dryer were the only indications of life I heard from the next room.

Another hour later, I knocked on Fallyn's door. "Hey, you alive in there? The party started at nine."

"Nobody shows up on time for those things. Hold your horses and let a girl get ready," was her muffled reply.

Suitably rebuffed, I took a shower in my room and changed into dark jeans, black dress boots, a white dress shirt, and a classic black blazer. Then, I paced the floor for several more minutes, noting the fact that the hair dryer had stopped at least a half-hour earlier. I checked my phone for the time, then I knocked on the girl's door again.

"Seriously, Fallyn, you've been in there for over two hours. C'mon already—I'm going to be an old man by the time you're ready."

"Just a minute!" she called.

With a loud harrumph, I sat on the bed and scrolled the social media feeds of a few prominent New Orleans vamps, those Remy had indicated might support the usurper. As I suspected, one of them had already posted pics of their arrival at the ball.

"So, what do you think?" Fallyn asked. I hadn't heard the door open, a testament to the she-wolf's ability to silently stalk her prey. And my, what a dangerous predator she was.

The girl wore a strapless, shoulder-baring satin gown in

fuchsia, with a ruffled high-low hem that showed plenty of leg in the front, from mid-thigh all the way down to her four-inch flesh-colored pumps. The top half of the gown was a folded, ribbon-style halter with a straight-across neckline and exposed back that accentuated her athletic build, showing off her round shoulders and lean, well-defined arms.

She had obviously applied her make-up in painstaking fashion, but somehow it looked natural and not at all over-done. The subtle war paint deftly accentuated her high cheekbones and full, lush lips, along with a dash of eyeliner that added a smokiness to her eyes I'd never noticed before. For the coup de grâce, the she-wolf had pulled her hair up in a sort of puffy high ponytail that draped just past her shoulders, with long wisps of hair trailing down to frame her face on either side.

"Well, don't just sit there with your jaw in your lap." Fallyn did a little pirouette, just fast enough to fan the hem of her dress. "Do you like it or not?"

I closed my mouth and took a few moments to gather my senses. To date, I'd only seen the girl in tight jeans, t-shirts, and leather jackets. And also in the buff during my training with her father. Being a gentleman, I had done my best to avoid staring on those occasions.

But this? The visual impact she made could not be done justice by words alone.

"You look amazing, Fallyn. Honestly, you do."

"Why, thank you, druid," she said, giving me a small curtsy.

"It's the truth. I mean, wow."

"Just some old thing I pulled out of my closet," she demurred.

Suddenly, the 'thrope glided across the room toward me. I stood in a display of manners so my eyes wouldn't be at the level of her breasts. She fussed with my collar a bit, straightening it needlessly—I'd checked it twice. Then, she licked her thumb and smoothed down my eyebrows.

It was a little gross, but sexy too, and it made me recall something that Fallyn's packmate Trina had told me. *If you ever see a 'thrope grooming another 'thrope, you can bet they're staking a claim.*

Gulp.

Fallyn's sultry voice drew me back to the present. "You don't clean up half-bad yourself, golden boy. Most of the time I see you in ratty old jeans and Army surplus trench coats. This is a look I could grow to like."

She smiled at me, and I almost forgot my earlier admonitions. *Purely business, Colin—keep it purely business.*

"Um, thanks," I said as I backed away, nearly tripping over the corner of the bed.

Fallyn giggled at me. "You're such a schoolboy, Colin."

"Here's your, uh, mask," I said as I held it out to her, for all the world looking as if she might bite.

Hers was a colorful, feathered thing, with a bouquet of plumage that swept up to cover the right side of her face. Mine was a full-faced *bauta* done in faux silver filigree, which I hoped would keep anyone from recognizing me. As I handed hers over, I noticed that by chance alone, I'd managed to color-coordinate Fallyn's disguise with her dress.

As my "plus one" took the mask, her strong, delicate fingers brushed over my own. Rather than meet her gaze, I glanced down, noticing that her manicured nails matched her dress almost exactly.

Some old thing, my ass. Full court press, anyone?

She placed the mask on her face. Rather than obscuring her beauty, it only added to her allure.

I cleared my throat and held out the crook of my arm. "Shall we, then?"

"And the boy wonder recovers," she chided. "Alright, druid, let's get going. The night awaits!"

8

I had a cab drop us off a few blocks from the mansion, and we walked the rest of the way there. The idea was to blend in, acting like just another well-heeled member of New Orleans' supernatural underbelly, here to appraise the man who would be king. Once inside, we'd sneak upstairs and look for evidence to justify Saint Germain's demise. The masks would prevent us from being recognized, and hopefully the rest of my plan wouldn't blow up in my face.

Just don't kill any giant serpents, and you'll be fine.

The last vampire party I'd attended, I'd ended up killing a god. Or, at least, its avatar. I kept wondering when that Mayan deity would come looking for me. Texas wasn't all that far from the Yucatan, after all—you only needed to scroll any Austin soccer mom's vacation pics for proof of that.

One more enemy to add to the collection.

I hoped there wouldn't be a repeat of that last performance this evening, but my gut told me this was going to end in a brawl. Not wanting to catch Fallyn flat-footed—as if that were possible—I leaned over and whispered in her ear as we neared Saint Germain's home.

"Stay on your toes and stick close to me. The spell will cover your scent, but everyone will think you're human. Smelling like a mundane, you might get singled out for some vamp's meal. I'd rather you didn't reveal your true nature unless things get ugly."

My "date" turned her head toward me, her lips brushing my ear as she replied. "And I take it things *will* get ugly at some point, being as this is your gig and all. But don't worry about me—I didn't wear this dress simply for the sake of showing some leg." She playfully poked my chest with a manicured finger. "If we have to fight or make a tactical retreat, just make sure *you* keep up."

Two big vamps were standing guard at the door, looking like matching extras in an Elmore Leonard movie adaptation. They sported black, skin-tight V-neck t-shirts, color-coordinated sport coats and slacks, dark sunglasses, slicked back hair, and muscles that probably came from a needle long before they were turned. The smaller of the two halted us with a raised hand as we approached.

"'Dis here is a private pawty," he said in a thick Yat accent. It sounded like he was from Brooklyn, but with just a touch of a Southern drawl. "You an' your dawlin' awda move along now. Dis ain't no place for y'all to be."

I held my hand out, palm up, and triggered a fire spell. A ball of yellow-orange flame appeared an inch above my skin, hovering for a few seconds before winking out of existence.

"I'm sure we'll be just fine in there," I assured him. "Now, if you two don't mind, Charlotte and I are just dying to meet the host. As we hear it, his parties are to die for," I said, finishing with a knowing wink.

I winced inwardly for overplaying it, but it seemed to do the trick. Thing One looked at Thing Two, and the larger bouncer shrugged. Thing One looked back at me with a frown.

"I s'pose y'all can enter. But don'cha go gettin' stupit, else I'll be shooing y'all out da doah."

"I'll certainly take that under consideration," I replied. Thing Two held the door for us, and we marched right into the dragon's lair.

Inside, well-dressed, model-thin vampires mingled and chatted quietly in small groups and trios while classical music played softly in the background. I recognized a couple of vamps I'd killed in my previous, future life. Fallyn must've felt me tense up at the sight of them, because she squeezed my arm a bit harder than necessary.

"Smile, champ," she whispered. "Remember, we're supposed to be blending in—not glaring at the guests."

"Uh, right," I said, taking a few breaths to calm myself before I continued to scan the room.

Servers stood at strategic positions all around the house, some holding trays of hors d'oeuvres while others served champagne. Contrary to portrayals in popular fiction, vampires didn't serve plain blood in glasses unless it was fresh from the vein due to coagulation. Luther's coven seemed to prefer mixing it with alcohol to keep it from clotting, but at a fancy party like this, I doubted they'd serve bloody Bloody Mary's.

"By the way—Charlotte?" Fallyn grumbled, drawing my attention back to her and away from my scan of the party guests. "Seriously? Do I look like a Charlotte dressed like this?"

"Hey, it was the best I could think of on short notice."

She narrowed her eyes at me, then smiled like the cat who ate the canary. At that moment, a tall, pale couple approached us. The man wore an almost Victorian-style get-up—a regency tailcoat over a blood red paisley double-breasted vest, with a matching satin puff tie over a high-collared dress shirt. His face was partially obscured by a silver and gold half-mask with an obscenely large nose. The man's companion wore a maroon and silver vintage dress in a baroque, Rococo style, with a bustle, ruffled sleeves, and a velvet choker.

"Oh, you must be the service!" the man said in a nasally, somewhat effeminate voice. "How wonderful. Mitzy and I are fit to be famished."

His—wife? lover?—Mitzy nodded in agreement while fanning herself with a lace collapsible fan, which she snapped open and closed every few seconds. "George, be so kind as to drain me a few ounces in a champagne glass, would you? I don't want to ruin my lipstick on the young man's neck, and he utterly reeks of grease and gasoline."

I was just about to straighten them out when Fallyn jumped into the conversation ahead of me. "I hate to disappoint you, but *Beauregard* and I are here at the request of the host."

Mitzy looked down her nose at us. "And what, pray tell, do you do?" she asked, aiming the question at me more than Fallyn.

"Oh, he runs a wizardry practice out of Houston. Does exorcisms and luck charms for NASA, mostly. Rather droll, but it pays handsomely." She pinched my cheek so hard it hurt. "Quite the little earner, my Beauregard is. Aren't you, dear?"

A booming man's voice with just a trace of an Eastern European accent echoed from the upper landing of the grand staircase above. "How interesting. I don't recall inviting any wizards from Houston. Vampyr, yes—but wizards?"

———

STROLLING down the stairs toward us was a robust-looking middle-aged man of average height, muscular with a slight paunch and a full shock of wavy brown hair. The vampire —because he was a vamp, that much was evident from the way he moved—had a prominent, aquiline nose and dark eyes that peeked out from behind a black leather domino. He wore a light-grey, double-breasted, V-neck vest and matching trousers. His white dress shirt was rolled up at the sleeves to bare his thick, pale forearms, while a black, grey, and pink striped tie adorned his neck. A pink satin pocket square, gold Rolex Oyster, and expensive Italian dress shoes finished off his understated ensemble.

Better recover quickly, Colin—else this is going to become a shit show a lot faster than you anticipated.

"I'm afraid you have my wife and I at a loss, Monsieur Saint Germain. In all honesty, I've been trying to get a magician's contract with Remy DeCoudreaux for years, but to no avail. When I heard someone might be challenging him for the position of coven leader, well—I just couldn't pass up the opportunity to introduce myself."

"Oh, how gauche," Mitzy said under her breath from behind her fan.

The host's brow furrowed slightly, and for a moment his eyes seemed to look right through me. I felt a quick touch of something—*other*—brushing against my skin and wards, and then it was gone.

Magic. The fucker is using magic on us.

Vampires and magic were bad news, because they could amass a great deal of knowledge and power over their very long lives. Most vampires frowned on its use, however, deeming it an unnecessary crutch in light of their innate supernatural abilities. When you ran into a vamp who deigned to use magic, you had to be careful.

The vampire relaxed and flashed us a news anchor's smile. "I go by Germain now, Jack Germain. You know how it is with the authorities who govern the mundane. When a citizen lives past one hundred and twenty years, they start to get suspicious."

"Just so, my good man," George said. "Why, just the other day—"

Germain ignored him, cutting him off with that booming, game show host voice. "Ah, that explains why you're carrying that hideous bag," the vamp said as he eyed my Craneskin Bag with contempt. His eyes met mine, and he flashed his smile again. "What's your magic specialization, Beauregard? Once I'm in charge of the coven, I'm sure we'll be looking for decent help."

"Exorcisms, wards, and charms," I replied. "I, uh, mostly do contract work for the government."

Germain's eyes tightened, revealing just the slightest hint of crow's feet at the corners of his eyes. *Must've been turned late in life—or he's even older than Remy suggested. Shit.* The older the vamp, the more dangerous they could be. This job was turning out to be a lot more complicated than I expected.

"Hmm. Be sure to leave your card with my second, Cornelius. I'm certain he's around here somewhere—but if not, you can speak with one of his sons, Gaius or Lucius. Now, I must be off. Enjoy the party."

"We most certainly will," Fallyn called after his retreating figure.

After a pregnant pause, Mitzy huffed in indignation at the rebuff they'd received. The female vamp shot us a look that could curdle blood, then grabbed George by the arm and pulled him away. "If you'll excuse us, my husband and I are going to go find someone to eat."

After they walked off, Fallyn smirked. "I guess that means we're not getting invited to Mitzy and George's next backyard barbecue. Oh, darn."

The girl spun like a flamenco dancer, deftly snatching three champagne glasses from a server who'd been passing behind her. She downed two and tossed the empty flutes in a nearby potted plant while holding the third in reserve. "This party blows. Let's go find your evidence so we can kill this dude, then we can go get hammered on Bourbon Street."

"I'm up for everything except the last part, but we need to move now. Those three vamps he mentioned—Cornelius, Gaius, and Lucius? I kind of cut Lucius' hand off, then helped Luther kick his dad's ass."

"When did *that* happen?"

"A while back at Mateo's garden party. It was when I killed that Mayan god's avatar."

"You *what*? Damn it, Colin, you really need to let me know when you're going to do stupid crap."

"Hey, it had nothing to do with the Pack—"

"I'm not upset because of that, dumbass. It's because I hate missing all the fun."

"Well, now's your chance to participate," I said as I grabbed her hand. "Let's pretend like we're looking for a place to make out and sneak upstairs."

"Did you just say, 'make out'? Fuck's sakes, but you are a boy scout."

I held two fingers up while leading her up the stairs. "Guilty as charged."

Fallyn giggled. Normally, I'd blame it on the alcohol, but it took a lot to get a 'thrope drunk. I didn't know whether to hope I was right about her having a crush on me, or hope I was wrong. My luck with women hadn't been the best of late. And I sure as hell didn't want to screw up our friendship—and have her dad on my ass to boot.

When we reached the top of the grand stairway, I looked right and left. In both directions, the blood-red carpet trailed off toward identical, bifurcating halls.

"Eeny, meeny, miny—oh fuck!" I exclaimed as Lucius and Gaius appeared around a corner and headed toward us from the left hall. They were deep in discussion with a buxom, dark-skinned female vampire who seemed to be enjoying their combined attentions.

"Fuck what?" Fallyn asked.

"That's Lucius and Gaius," I whispered.

Hearing their names, the brothers looked up at us. Gaius took a quick glance and went straight back to working game on the female vamp, but Lucius' eyes lingered. *Damn it, he's going to recognize me*, I thought as I began to prepare a spell.

Before I knew it, Fallyn had me pressed up against the wall, her lips locked on mine, one leg hitched up as she ground her pelvis against mine. The female wolf smelled of "Fucking Fabulous" Tom Ford perfume, champagne, and musk. She kissed me hungrily as her hands clutched my ass and lower back.

After an enforced six-month dry spell, my body responded as expected, and I felt a growing, throbbing ache in my nether regions. Certain I was blushing furiously, I maintained the deception until Gaius and Lucius had gone downstairs. Fallyn held the ruse for a moment longer than necessary, then she backed away, allowing her hand to trail across my chest.

"I knew you were hung in your other form, but damn, son—I do believe you've been holding out on me. No wonder that little Spanish girl has it so bad for you," she said with a lascivious smile.

"Fallyn, I'm fully aware that Pack members are fairly casual about sex, nudity, and such, but—"

"I know, I know—this is where you tell me you're a one-woman man and all that crap." Fallyn winked, clutching my hand as she dragged me down the hall with her werewolf strength. "I *do* believe you—but every man has his limits."

ONCE WE'D SNUCK around a corner and were safely out of sight of the guests below, Fallyn released my hand. Instantly, she transformed from a giggly, drunk party girl to a deadly 'thrope on the hunt. She raised her nose in the air, sniffing like a wolf on the scent.

"I smell blood," she said.

"It's a vampire's home, Fallyn. There's bound to be blood scent everywhere."

"True, but this is both fresh and old, and from the same person." She tapped the side of her nose with one slender finger. "You might be able to cast a spell to help those weak human senses out, but I was born with a sense of smell that's one thousand times more sensitive than yours. Trust me, we need to check this out."

"Lead the way, then," I replied as I swept my arm toward the other end of the hall. I was trying to play it casual, but my eyes darted everywhere. Being around so many vampires was making me jumpy.

"You sure you're alright?" Fallyn asked as she sniffed her way down the hall. "You seem awful, I don't know—skittish lately. Plus, you look like you've lost weight, and those dark circles under your eyes say you're not sleeping right. Besides that, I could hear your heart start beating faster as soon as we saw those bouncers earlier."

I shrugged, still scanning up and down the hallway as I followed her. "So?"

"So, the Colin I know has ice water running through his veins. Or at least he did the last time I worked with him. Nothing ever seems to get you rattled. It used to be that you almost had a death wish or something. Now, you're about as jumpy as spit on a hot skillet. What's the deal?"

I scratched my nose with a knuckle and kept watching out for stray party guests. So far, we were the only ones up here, but that could change at any moment. I sensed Fallyn looking at me in anticipation of an answer.

"Fallyn, you wouldn't believe me if I told you. Suffice it to say that helping me with this job is probably the most important thing you could be doing right now. So, let's stay focused on the task, because there's a lot riding on us tonight."

Fallyn's shoulders stiffened as she replied. "Have it your way then, druid. You're not the only one who can keep secrets."

"Hey, look—it's not like I don't want to tell you—"

Fallyn stopped and held a hand up, causing me to stop as well. She wrinkled her nose like she'd smelled something sour, then waved a hand in front of her nose before pointing at a nearby door.

"Whoever it is, they're in there. Smells like they got put in timeout for about a week with suspended bathroom privileges. Nasty." She tried the door. "Locked. We going in?"

"Yup. Move back and give me a minute," I said as I took a knee in front of the doorknob.

I looked at the door in the magical spectrum, and it was warded as I'd expected. The ward was a simple alarm spell, but it told me that either Germain already had a mage on staff or was an adept himself. Earlier I couldn't be sure, since some vamps had innate talents that mimicked magical spells. But now, I was almost certain of it.

I picked apart the weaves with my own magic, which was child's play since wards and traps really *were* my specialty—exorcisms, not so much. I cast another cantrip to unlock the door and caught Fallyn's attention with my eyes as I stood.

"Hear anyone coming?"

She cocked her head, listening to the sounds around us. "Nope, everyone else is downstairs."

"Then we'd better hurry. I have a feeling Germain is going to wonder where we snuck off to. He doesn't strike me as the trusting type." I glanced at my companion. "You ready?"

She flicked her fingers open in front of my face, and her nails extended into long, razor-sharp claws. "Always. Damned shame I have to mess up this manicure, though."

I chuckled despite myself as I readied a spell, realizing

that I *had* missed working with Samson's only daughter. Her scent still lingered on me, and notwithstanding my current case of the nerves, I found it to be a pleasant distraction.

Focus, Colin—focus!

Shaking off those stray thoughts, I drew the silver-plated Bowie knife from my Bag and burst into the room with Fallyn close on my heels.

9

As soon as I entered the room, the odor hit me like a tidal wave. The stench was a powerful combination of curdled blood, piss, shit, and the distinct miasma of human fear. I'd smelled a lot of nasty stuff during the time I'd spent in that future hell on Earth, so it didn't even faze me, but Fallyn gagged softly behind me.

The room, however, was clean. It was a bedroom, well-appointed with a large four-poster bed, side table, mirrored dresser, and tasteful paintings on three of the four walls. A door to our left caught my attention, and I heard a small shuffling noise from the other side.

Fallyn and I shared a glance and a nod, and I headed for that door. This one wasn't warded, only locked. I opened it with a quick spell and swung it wide with my knife, another spell at the ready. Behind the door was a bathroom, complete with a pedestal sink, a toilet with a bidet—I mean, how often did you see those in America?—and a clawfoot tub.

Inside the tub sat a thin, older black man tied to a kitchen chair, bound and gagged and bleeding from at least a dozen cuts. He was semi-conscious, possibly from blood loss, and it was apparent from the wounds on his neck and inner arms that he'd been fed on repeatedly. He'd also been badly beaten, because his face looked like fresh-ground hamburger. In short, the guy was a wreck—on the verge of death, even. And he was most definitely human.

"Shee-it, golden boy. They worked this fucker over but good," Fallyn exclaimed in a low voice. "What's our move?"

Rather than ice in my veins, I felt fire flowing through them—a slow, hot burn that spread from my gut out to my extremities, flushing my face and causing me to clench my fists in anger. I'd felt that same feeling many times over the past few months, on each occasion when I'd come across some vampire-caused atrocity. I wanted to shift and tear the place down to its foundations. But first, I needed to get this man to safety, if I could.

I grunted. "Help me cut him free."

A few swipes of my knife and Fallyn's claws, and the man collapsed in my arms. He mumbled incoherently, something about no more, he didn't know anything, and so on. My rage built inside me as he bled all over my clean white shirt. I laid him gently on the bed and began cutting pieces of the bedspread and sheets to dress his wounds.

"Colin..." Fallyn laid a hand on my arm, just a light touch. I ignored her and continued to apply first aid. "Colin!"

Her voice was more insistent now, so I looked up at her.

"He's dead, Colin. We got here too late."

"But it appears we arrived just in time—didn't we, Lucius?" a cultured, almost female voice said from the doorway.

"Indeed we did, Gaius. Indeed we did," a similarly epicene voice answered.

I spun with a growl, knife held low and pointed at the threat with my other hand held high in a tight fist. The brothers were almost twins, tallish in height and lean in the soft way the leisurely rich were versus that of the active and athletic. Each had removed their masks, revealing their pale skin, flowing blonde locks, and elongated, Hapsburgian features. The siblings were dressed stylishly in matching Italian three-piece suits, but neither one would win any Brad Pitt lookalike contests.

I was certain they wouldn't like what I held in my hand —no, not at all. All that kept them from suffering that fate was I was saving it for their master.

"Well, hello, boys. Lucius, I see you grew your hand back," I said with venom in my voice.

Lucius's eyes lit up with recognition. "Druid!"

"One and the same," I replied with a slight nod of my head. "If you'd be so kind as to step aside, I'm about to go kill your boss. Or I could kill you first. It's no skin off my nose either way."

Lucius giggled in a high, girlish manner. He responded to my threat in a detached, almost pleasant tone. "Good luck with that, druid. Even if you could get past us—which you won't—you have no idea what you're dealing with when it comes to Saint Germain. He's old, crafty, and has skills that are of a very... *unique* nature."

Gaius calmly nodded in agreement with his sibling's assessment, a single curl of blonde hair in the middle of his forehead bobbing with him. "I'd almost be tempted to let him pass, brother, to watch the master teach him a lesson. But he did cut off your hand, and his meddling also cost Father his chance at revenge. I don't believe we can let those insults pass, do you?"

"Not at all, brother, not at all," was Lucius' reply. "Shall we?"

"We sh—" Gaius' reply was cut off as Fallyn pounced across the room to drop kick him in the chest. She landed with both feet, likely in an effort to stake him with one of those four-inch heels she wore.

"You boneheads talk too much," Fallyn asserted as they both flew out the door.

That left Lucius and I inside the room, and I wasted no time closing the gap. While the two dandies had been chit-chatting, I'd already stealth-shifted to increase my muscle and bone mass. Right now, I was as strong as any young vamp, and nearly as quick. My blade was already headed straight for the dandy's throat a split second after I initiated combat.

LUCIUS'S EYES GREW WIDE, but he recovered quickly. He might have been a fop, but he was a relatively mature vamp, and apparently he'd had some training. The bloodsucker leaned back, just enough to avoid my blade with time to spare.

Good reflexes, even for a leech.

After months spent fighting for my life against Lucius' kind, I'd anticipated that he might respond with just such a move. While I didn't want to release the spell I was holding, I thought I could let a tiny amount of that power escape without releasing the entire thing. And that's exactly what I did.

Since I'd put the vamp on his heels, I simply stepped in with a looping, overhand left that caught him square on the cheek. The punch snapped his head back and crushed his cheekbone with a loud crunch. It was a satisfying enough result, but the real payoff was the sizzling, crackling sound that filled the air as a trickle of light from my sunlight spell fried the skin from his face.

The scream the vampire released was unearthly loud and unreasonably effeminate. I'd seen Fallyn and Bells both take way worse hits than that and not howl like Lucius. Of course, half his face had melted off, and I knew from past experience that vamps didn't heal from sun burns without a shit-ton of fresh blood and rest.

Unfortunately for Lucius, I was determined he'd never get the chance. I followed the attack by thrusting my blade into the soft flesh between his throat and his chin, driving it through the soft palate into his brain. My heart warmed with the satisfaction of watching the light go out in his eyes.

Better make sure he's dead.

I grabbed a handful of those curly golden locks and

lopped his head off with a backhand, then a forehand stroke of my blade. Thick black blood splattered across the wall behind his corpse, and I kicked the body away to keep any of his filth from getting on me. Human blood was one thing, but vamp blood was rife with the vyrus. It was best to avoid it whenever possible.

Fallyn sprinted back into the room at that moment, barefoot and grinning from ear to ear. She stopped and her mouth formed an "O" as she took in the carnage I'd visited on Lucius.

"Damn, druid. You do not fuck around."

"Did you kill him?" I asked.

Her grin faltered. "Naw, my heel must've missed his heart by a fraction of an inch. But I managed to get this as a souvenir." She held up what looked like a bloody blonde wig, but there were bits of skin and tissue around the edges.

"You scalped him?"

"Meh. I tried grabbing him by the hair so I could twist his head off, but the little fucker took off at vampire speed in retreat. I had a good fistful of this mop when he decided to split, so he tore his own scalp clean off when he ran." She tossed it over her shoulder. "With the Dumbo ears he was sporting, the prissy little bitch is going to look damned funny without all that hair to cover them."

It took but a moment's consideration to decide that I didn't want Gaius to have his scalp back. I stuck my knife in Lucius' chest. "Hold this," I deadpanned. Then, I spoke a single word in Gaelic. "*Spréach.*" A spark flew from my now outstretched hand, landing on Gaius' scalp and lighting it aflame.

"Now, he'll have to grow it back the hard way."

"Wow. That's petty, but I like your style." Fallyn nodded at my other hand. "What do you have there, his nose?"

I chuffed. "You'll see. Just be sure you close your eyes when I raise my fist over my head."

"Whatever you say, golden boy." She pointed a thumb at Lucius' head. "No growing that back. Think his dad is going to be pissed?"

"I'm counting on it." I grabbed Lucius' head by the hair, like Perseus claiming his Gorgon prize. "Now, let's go find Germain."

When we exited into the hall, I could already hear a commotion coming from downstairs. Gaius was babbling incoherently, and a chorus of angry voices echoed from the foyer below. I calmly walked to the top of the stairs and tossed Lucius' head down the steps, watching every bounce with gratification as it left a dark and bloody trail all the way to the bottom landing.

"That's what I do to vampires who prey on humans," I stated in my Hyde-side voice. "Now, bring me Saint Germain."

My left fist was still clenched in anticipation of the vampires' inevitable response. I just wanted to get my target in full, clear view before I cut loose with my spell.

Speak of the devil.

Jack Germain walked out of the parlor, nudging his way through the crowd of vamps below. "I knew you were more than you appeared, Beauregard—if that even *is* your name. That's why I sent Lucius and Gaius looking for you when you vanished. Although it appears I may have underestimated the threat you pose."

I pulled my mask off, tossing it away. My cover had already been blown, so there was no sense maintaining the masquerade. "Colin McCool, actually. But most folks call me the Junkyard Druid."

Fallyn leaned in and whispered in my ear. "We're revealing our identities? You didn't tell me we were revealing our identities!"

"Relax and keep your mask on." I whispered back. "Bad enough they know who I am now."

Germain squeezed Gaius' shoulder to comfort him while the rest of the vamps below hissed up at us. The younger vamp cowered in his father's arms, bleeding all over him, but Cornelius only had eyes for me.

The chubby old vamp's voice simmered with low menace as he spoke to his master. "He's Luther's pet, but let me kill him and I'll swear allegiance to you for all eternity." Germain said nothing, so the chubby popinjay looked up at me with hatred in his eyes. "Before, I owed you a quick demise—but now, I'll surely make your death linger."

Cornelius released his son, handing him off to a nearby vamp before taking a step toward me. Germain, on the other hand, stood his ground as he eyed my clenched fist. The would-be coven leader spoke almost inaudibly in French.

"C'est un piège. Fuir."

Two things happened in the next instant. First, every

vamp in the place scattered, just as their master had commanded. Second, I thrust my fist high in the air and released my sunlight spell.

As anyone who has ever dealt with vamps knows, they're faster than hell. Even the young ones can move like Usain Bolt on speed, and the older ones often appear as a blur to human eyes when they pour it on. However, in my shifted form I was also hellaciously fast—if not vampire fast, then at least werewolf quick.

Of course, no vamp is faster than the speed of light.

I'd spent all afternoon meditating and gathering solar energy out on the Audubon Park Trail, so this spell was a doozy. White-hot light suffused everything around, with the exception of Fallyn and me. Most of the older vamps were already out the door or in the adjacent rooms when my sunlight spell went off, but several others weren't so lucky.

The younger vampires burst into flames immediately. Some collapsed on the spot, continuing to burn like tallow candles on a sconce, while others managed to escape, leaving trails of smoke that smelled like putrid bacon burning on a skillet.

Within seconds, the spell was spent. Although I'd killed at least a dozen vamps and wounded easily two dozen more, Saint Germain had escaped.

Damn it.

PURSUIT WOULD'VE BEEN FUTILE, as Germain could probably move faster than both Fallyn and I put together.

Well, that didn't quite go as planned.

Apparently, the sight of several burning figures running down Royal Street was cause for commotion. By the time I'd checked all the bodies to make sure we weren't leaving any stragglers behind, we could already hear sirens in the distance. Rather than stick around to explain all the charred corpses, I unlatched a window in the rear of the house, just in case I wanted to come back in the morning. Then, we left by jumping the garden wall out back.

Back at the hotel, I showered and changed, then plopped down on the couch to watch some late-night television. Fallyn was not nearly so relaxed, however. She paced the floor, alternating between being excited about the brief scuffle and worried she might catch hell from her dad.

"Do you think you killed anyone from our demesne?" she asked.

"Fallyn, for the hundredth time, I made sure I didn't recognize anyone there before I triggered my spell. I know just about everyone in Luther's coven, and I'm positive those were all local vamps. Trust me, there won't be any blowback on you or your dad."

"Yeah, but they know it was you now. And that means Dad is going to hear about this. If he finds out I was with you, he's going to have a shit attack of major proportions."

"Maybe, but I'm a neutral entity now, remember? I don't answer to Samson anymore, or Maeve, or Luther, because the druid justiciar works to protect every faction in the demesne. That makes it even less likely anyone will associate the Pack with what we did tonight. Besides, you didn't even shift. If anyone asks, I'll say I hired a human hunter for backup. Problem solved."

Fallyn arched an eyebrow. "A human hunter with superhuman strength and reflexes?"

"I dunno. Maybe they'll think you're on steroids."

"Colin..." she said in a low growl.

I sat up, running my hands through my hair and then throwing them up in the air. "I thought you wanted some excitement. I mean, you knew what the job was before you stepped on that plane. Why are you getting cold feet all the sudden?"

She winced, tight-lipped, so I stood up and walked to the mini-fridge to give her time to decide what she wanted to say. Anyway, I had a feeling this was going to be a "serious discussion," and if so, I was going to need a drink.

I plopped back down on the couch with two beers. Fallyn sat down on the love seat catercorner from me, knees together and feet askew with her hands in her lap. "Colin, you don't know what it's like being Pack. Not only am I Samson's daughter, but I'm also his second now."

I popped the cap off a bottle with my thumb and toasted her with it. "Oh yeah? Cheers then, Fallyn. That's great news." The she-wolf frowned until I held the other bottle up. She nodded, so I tossed it over and took my seat again.

Samson's only daughter took a long swig from her beer, then held it to her head. "Yeah, it kind of *is* good news, but it's also a lot of pressure, you know? I mean, being the alpha's kid, the whole nepotism thing comes up—"

"Sure, but I've hung out with the 'thropes in your Pack. Heck, Fallyn, you're three times the wolf any of the other candidates are—Sledge and Trina included."

She gave me a wry smile. "Thanks, but you know as well as I do it doesn't matter. Whatever I do reflects back on Dad."

"Making it harder for you to step out from behind his shadow," I said before taking a swig of my beer.

"Exactly. Dad has always kept close tabs on me, even though he likes to think he lets me do as I choose."

"I know that. Last time I spoke with him, he pretty much warned me off you. Didn't help that you practically propositioned me in front of him, though."

Fallyn squinted. "Um, sorry?"

I chuckled. "Hey, don't sweat it. I've, uh, done *a lot* of thinking lately, and I decided I'm not going to worry what people think about me anymore. I have a lot of responsibility and a lot of people counting on me, and I can't be second-guessing my decisions based on the opinions of others. So, I guess what I'm saying is—"

"Fuck 'em?"

I raised my beer and winked. "Fuck 'em."

Fallyn clinked the neck of her bottle against mine, then downed it. As she stood, my eyes lingered on her lithe, athletic form.

I looked away quickly, setting my beer down on the side table. "I should really be going to—oof!"

I suddenly had a lap full of female 'thrope. Fallyn sat

astride me on the couch, her yellow eyes reflecting the hunger we both felt for each other.

"Fallyn, if you keep coming at me like this, I may not be able to resist."

"That's what I'm hoping for, golden boy."

The girl leaned in and ran the tip of her tongue up the side of my neck. When I felt her hot breath on my ear, she nibbled on my earlobe and ground her hips against me, causing me to respond in kind.

"I'm not sure this is a good idea," I whispered.

Fallyn leaned away from me, looking me in the eyes with her hands clasped behind my neck.

"Poor conflicted Colin," she said without a hint of condescension in her voice. "You're just too good for your own good, champ. But eventually, you'll come to your senses. And when you do, I'll damned sure make it worth your while."

Fallyn gave me a lingering kiss, then hopped up and walked to her bedroom, closing the door behind her. Of course, I watched her go.

Door's still open just a crack. Belladonna did break up with me, right? And Jesse is batshit crazy. Maybe a little harmless sex with a sane, reasonable woman is just the thing I need.

I sighed, realizing that I needed to settle things with both Bells and Jesse before I started playing the field. Besides, I didn't want Fallyn to get the wrong idea. She seemed to take a pretty casual attitude toward sex, but as far as I knew, she'd never hooked up with anyone in the Pack. Female wolves might act all brazen and brassy, but they tended to mate for life. If Fallyn had actual feelings for me, things with her could get complicated real quick.

Besides, you have bigger fish to fry right now, Colin old boy.

I growled in frustration, covering the throbbing in my lap with a pillow. Fallyn's door beckoned. Instead of doing the obvious thing, I chugged the rest of my beer and headed to bed.

Man, I am such a fucking martyr.

10

The next day, Fallyn flew back to Austin. We both agreed that if she was seen around NOLA with me, people would put two and two together and realize she'd been involved in the attack at Saint Germain's place. So, back home she went.

When I dropped her off at the airport I gave her a hug, she snuck a kiss, and we parted with a lot left unsaid between us. I watched her walk *all the way* away, this time with just a single bag, since she'd checked all the rest of her luggage at the curb. And damn it if I didn't almost chase her and ask her to stay another day.

There I go, thinking with the wrong head again. Man, I really do need to get laid.

But, more importantly, I needed to take out Saint Germain. Not just because what he'd done to that poor man was an intolerable offense; it was also because I needed Remy's complete trust so I could move around in his coven at will. Then, I could find the key players who were going to trigger the apocalypse and take them off the board.

Would that stop it? I honestly had no idea, but Click seemed to think it would. I hated to rely on the opinion of a slightly-wacko trickster god, but it was the best I could do at the moment. Once I got back to Austin, I'd ask Finnegas what he knew about chronomancy and chronourgy and see if Click was yanking my chain.

But until then, I had to focus on Saint Germain and the NOLA coven.

I headed back to Saint Germain's, but the place was empty. It wasn't just that there were no occupants—the damned place looked like no one had lived in it in ages. Much of the furniture had been removed, and what was left had been draped in sheets of linen and plastic. Even more surprising, there was a layer of dust all over everything, and cobwebs hung from the light fixtures and high corners of every room.

Moreover, not even the scent of blood remained. It was one hell of a clean-up job, so good I almost suspected he'd hired one of the fae to do it for him. But the magic smelled human, not fae—and that worried me.

Either Germain has a freaky-talented mage working for him, or he is one himself. And if that's the case, he's going to be hella hard to kill.

I was starting to wish I was getting paid for this job, because it was damned sure turning out to be a pain in the ass. A call to Remy had revealed that the coven leader was as clueless as I regarding his rival's whereabouts. DeCoudreaux admitted with some chagrin that Germain had ways and means of staying hidden that foiled even his extensive intelligence network.

In fact, it appeared to be yet another reason why he'd asked for my help in the matter; Remy had assumed I could use magic to track Germain down. Due to that assumption, he accused me of trying to get him to do my work for me instead of doing it myself. I assured him I was only trying to save time, and hung up before he could ask how I intended to track Germain down.

Best to keep the fucker guessing. With any luck, I'll get to kill that prick too.

Lacking any local contacts beyond the coven leader, I had no way of figuring out where Germain had gone. Still, I'd expected I might need outside help to get things done in New Orleans, and thus I'd come to town with an ace up my sleeve. After hanging up on Remy, I quickly pulled up my list of contacts on my phone, finding the one I wanted. I clicked the call button and waited to hear it ring.

"Madame Rousseau's, where your future is our business. This is the Madame speaking. How can I be of service?"

"Hello, Janice."

"Colin McCool, what a surprise! It's good to know you're not so busy saving the world that you can't take time to call a friend and chat." I let the silence hang between us for a bit. "Hmm—so you didn't call to chat, then. What's up?"

Janice—also known as Madame Rousseau—was Austin's resident expert on all things voodoo, a fact that I found rather humorous considering she was as pale and ginger as I was. How a little white girl like her had become a high-level *mambo*, or voodoo priestess, was beyond me. I just assumed that voodoo society was way more egalitarian than the mundane world, and had never questioned her about it.

"I happen to be in your old stomping grounds, and I need an assist."

"You're in N'awlins? I wish I had known you were visiting. I'd have offered to come along and show you my city."

"The company would have been welcome, but unfortunately, this was a business trip."

Janice laughed. "It's *always* business with you, Colin. Such a shame." Her voice trailed off, and she cleared her throat. "So, what can I help you with?"

"I'm tracking down a rogue vamp, and I need a local who can help me find him." Silence. "Tall order?"

"No, it's not that. Any number of local mambos or *houngans* could track this creature down. However, I can't think of any who would help you do so. Long ago, the N'awlins voodoo society decided to stay out of vampire affairs, under agreement that the vampires would do likewise. Outside of a few *bokor* I know of, I doubt anyone would take the work."

Bokor were spellcasters for hire who often used black mojo to achieve their ends. I didn't want to mess with a bokor, that was for sure. Dealing with all these evil vamps was bad enough.

"Eh, that's out of the question. Any other options?"

I heard Janice exhale, short and quick. Not quite a sigh, but close. "Well, I do have someone I can send you to. But,

I can't promise you'll walk out of her home without paying a steep price."

"This is important, Janice, and I'm willing to do what it takes to get the job done. Besides, I can take care of myself. Who is this person, anyway?"

"It's my maw maw, actually. But Gran Brigitte doesn't normally take kindly to visitors, so you're going to have to butter her up if you want her help."

JANICE SENT me to an address in the Garden District, with the admonishment to bring her "maw maw" a special rum infused with ghost peppers and a black rooster.

"And don't harm the rooster," she advised. "Not on your life."

Great.

So, there I was, walking through an upscale neighborhood in the Garden District, past multi-million-dollar homes with a mason jar of homemade hooch in one hand and a black rooster under my other arm. As we got closer to the address Janice had given me, the rooster started clucking and screeching. I didn't think it was out of fear, because it didn't try to get away—obviously, the rooster knew something I didn't. Regardless, all the noise it was making was getting me some strange looks.

"Shut up, you," I whispered.

"Baw-ka-bak-bak-bak," the rooster clucked in reply.

I soon reached the address, a beautiful pale-yellow two-story home on Prytania with a white picket fence, black shutters, a huge covered front porch with white Roman columns, and second-story dormer windows peeking out over the street. I decided a little magical recon was in order, so I walked past while scanning it in the magical spectrum.

That's... odd? How about not possible?

The place was spelled up, just as I'd expected from a skilled voodoo priestess. However, the magic used to create the protective wards and charms wasn't human at all. Instead, it had a peculiar signature, one I would recognize anywhere.

Tuatha Dé Danann. What the actual fuck?

I walked all the way around the block, taking time to work out just why in the hell a voodoo priestess would be using Tuatha magic. When I came back for a second pass, an older, regal-looking black woman sat on the front porch, slowly rocking back and forth on a bench swing that hadn't been there moments before.

She was tall and slender, but in a healthy way, with a skin color that a slave owner might have once called redbone—not quite Melungeon, but close. Her dark, reddish-brown hair was straightened and pulled back into a bun. Her nose was prominent and wide, but not unpleasant, her lips full and sensual, and her grey eyes sparkled with mischief. Her outfit spoke of money and a casual disregard for convention, as she wore denim skinny jeans, sensible pumps, and a lovely pussybow peplum blouse in an African print.

"Might as well come up here an' greet me, boy," she said in a full, rich voice that virtually rang with command.

Her accent that was both familiar and peculiar—Southern, but with traces of Ireland as well. "Everyone an' their sister done seen you strutting past me house with gifts for the goddess. 'Sides, only a fool could think you're on a casual afternoon stroll with that fat black rooster under your arm. Get your pretty pale ass on up here and tell me what brings you."

Busted.

I opened the gate only after the wards had been dropped, and stepped onto the porch while eyeing the woman with polite suspicion. By the time I stood before her, I had it figured out.

"Gran Brigitte, I presume? Or should I say, Brigid?"

Her lips curled into a smug grin, dimpling her cheeks as well. "Da' said you were sharper than you looked. I s'pose he was right. You can set that fucking bird down— he's not going anywhere. And leave the rum on the coffee table, if you don't mind."

One second we were on her porch, and the next I was standing in the middle of a cozy, well-lit sitting room. Sunlight poured in from nearby windows, bouncing off the pastel yellow wallpaper and white, raised-panel wainscoting. Colorful paintings in gold-leaf frames adorned the walls, including one that looked to be a castle in the Irish countryside. Victorian-style couches and chairs were arranged neatly around the space, and a stack of books sat on a side table near a particularly comfy-looking chair set close to the windows to take advantage of the ample natural light.

Maman Brigitte, sometimes known as Gran Brigitte

and also Brigid in the Celtic pantheon, was nowhere to be seen. However, I heard the whistle of escaping steam and the clinking of china and silverware coming from an adjacent room, so I assumed she was preparing tea. I set the rum on the coffee table and stood by the window, admiring the garden view.

"You have a lovely home," I called out.

"An' you have a lovely ass," Maman Brigitte said directly behind me as she pinched my posterior. She balanced a small silver tea service set in her other hand, complete with china tea cups and saucers, which she gracefully set down on the coffee table. "Now, tell me what brings such a fine-looking young man to my home. I assume it's not to deliver a strip-o-gram."

MAMAN BRIGITTE SAT in a high-backed easy chair and gestured to a nearby couch. I sat. The goddess crossed her legs and rested her elbows on the arms of her chair, steepling her fingers as she watched me like a bobcat eyeing a fat, juicy rabbit.

"Mmm, what I could do to you," she purred as she unscrewed the lid from the jar of rum I brought her. "You ever fuck a goddess, druid? It'd be an experience you wouldn't soon forget."

"Um, no, ma'am, I can't say that I have."

She rolled her eyes and took a long drink from the jar, wiping her mouth with the back of her hand after. "You can drop the 'ma'am' thing. I'm anything but a polite

Southern matron. Fuck sakes, but it's been forever since I had some dick." Maman Brigitte set the jar down and grabbed her breasts from underneath, giving the tips of each a pinch as she pushed them up. "Makes my nipples hard just looking at you."

Well, this isn't uncomfortable at all.

"Um, thanks?"

She tossed her head back and laughed, a rich, deep belly laugh that lasted for several seconds. "Janice said you were uptight, but I had no idea." She wiped her eyes with a knuckle. "I'm just giving you shit, druid. Although I could use some dick, and that's a fact, but I think my granddaughter has a thing for you."

I pondered that statement for several seconds before responding. "Don't take this the wrong way, Maman Brigitte, but you're definitely not like any of the other Celtic gods I've met."

"Met a few, have you?" She began counting off on her fingers. "Let's see—my da', of course, Lugh, Niamh, and Fuamnach, plus the others who haven't revealed themselves." She chuckled. "Oh, don't look so shocked. The whole lot of them have been meddling in your life for some time now. Fuckers don't know when to leave well enough alone. S'why I left, in fact, and took up with the Ghede. Not only are we a hell of a lot more fun, but we don't mess with humans unless they call on us first—unlike those bastards back in Underhill."

In the voodoo tradition, the Ghede were the loas of death and fertility. They were known to be boisterous, foul-mouthed, and fond of a good party. In the short time I'd been with Brigitte, I could see why she took to them.

"How did you end up here, anyway? If you don't mind my asking."

She gave an almost imperceptible shake of her head as she snatched the jar up again. "Not at all. I got here the same way Niamh arrived in Austin—the Irish brought me. They called, I came. Then I met the Baron, and the rest is history."

I nodded, feigning contemplation as I considered how to frame my next question. "And... this?" I said, moving my hand in circles in front of my face. "Don't get me wrong, you're a lovely, um, death goddess. I'm just curious as to why you changed your look."

"Oh, that?" Maman Brigitte said. "That wasn't my doing. Most don't know this, but the gods and their aspects are shaped by those who worship them. After I was taken up by those who practice voodoo, my appearance began to reflect that of the people who worshipped me, African and European both. Honestly, after being a ginger for so long, I think having some color is an improvement." She waggled her eyebrows at me. "Care to see if the thatch on the roof matches the carpet in the foyer?"

I waved my hands back and forth in front of me. "Um, no! I mean, I'll take your word for it. No offense—on either count."

"None taken. Political correctness is just a cruel joke that Anansi, Kokopelli, Coyote, Iktomi, and Heyoka played on the white man for fucking over their children. The other tricksters thought it was such a great gag, they spread it all over Europe and Australia too. You should hear Loki, Reynard, Veles, and Crow go on about it. Now, enough dicking around—why don't you tell me what you came here for?"

"Have you ever heard of a vampire by the name of Saint Germain?"

The goddess tipped the rim of the mason jar at me. "Ah, 'The Man Who Wouldn't Die.' Yes, I've heard of him. Louis XV was rather fond of the vampire, you know. Germain finally grew tired of the king ignoring his advice, so he disappeared and eventually ended up in N'awlins. Was on the losing end of a power struggle within the local coven, oh, a hundred years ago or so. But that's vampire business, and we stay out of it. What of him?"

"I have to kill him."

"If he's back in town, he shouldn't be hard to find. As I recall, he threw the most elaborate parties. Shouldn't be hard to sneak into the next one he puts on." Maman Brigitte must've read something on my face, because she clucked her tongue with a chuckle. "Tripped over your dick and let him escape your clutches, hmm? And now you need Maman Brigitte to tell you where he is."

"That pretty much sums it up, yes."

"Did my granddaughter tell you my price is steep?"

I bobbed my head. "She did."

"And you're prepared to pay?"

"In all honesty, that depends," I replied.

"Good answer." Maman Brigitte laughed. She took another slug of rum, wiping her mouth on her sleeve this time. "Easy to see you've dealt with the Tuatha before."

She rubbed her chin with the tip of her thumb. "Hmm, I should make you pay in sexual favors, but then you'd keep owing me ad infinitum."

"Wouldn't the Baron get mad?" I asked, not wanting to cause offense by turning her down a third time. I was fairly positive she was merely joking, but no sense tempting fate.

"Pfah! That old prick is always chasing mortal tail. It'd serve him right, but you might not survive the curse he'd put on you if he found out. Now, let me think a moment."

I waited, eyeing the tea service and cookies she'd laid out but resisting the urge to partake. She knew I wouldn't touch it, but it wouldn't do to not offer me anything, either. Gods were weird like that.

Suddenly, Maman Brigitte thrust a finger in the air with a shout of, "That's it!"

"What's it?" I asked.

"I got it—I know how you can pay me back."

"Go on—"

She winked at me with a wolfish grin. "You can take my granddaughter out on a date."

"Seriously?" I asked, with perhaps a bit more disgust in my voice than I'd intended. Janice was attractive enough, but I had enough women problems as it was, and I certainly didn't need to compound the issue.

Maman Brigitte's voice lowered an octave, and I swear the temperature in the room dropped a few degrees. "What's wrong with my granddaughter?"

"Nothing, nothing! It's just that one girlfriend just broke up with me, my ex is living in my backyard, and the alpha's daughter is working me, hard."

The goddess frowned. "Oh, poor you. Still, it sounds like you're free and clear to play the field." She crossed her arms beneath her breasts, pushing them up, and sat back in her chair. "Nope, there's no way around it, because I won't accept any other form of payment. You *will* take Janice out on a date, sometime before the next full moon."

The moon had nearly been full the night before, so I wanted to make sure I was clear on the timeframe. "So, basically, I have to take her out before—say, midnight, four weeks from today?"

"Correct."

"And what if she declines?"

Maman Brigitte batted her eyes. "Then, I suppose you'll have to take me out on a date instead," she said in a husky voice. "But my granddaughter won't say no."

I scratched the side of my head and sighed. "Fine, I'll do it. Now, how do I find Saint Germain?"

11

————

That's where I fucked up. I should have said, "Where do I find Saint Germain?" But instead, I'd asked "how." Rule of thumb when dealing with the fae and Tuatha—always say exactly what you mean, leaving no ambiguity in negotiations and requests.

I'd failed to do that, which was why I was sitting in the front of an airboat, speeding through the swamp in search of a supposedly insane and incredibly dangerous werewolf.

The boat's engine cut off, and we glided up on the shore of a marshy island, way out in the middle of the swampland south of Houma. My guide was a stoic, aged black man named Odilon who was one of Maman Brigitte's houngan. Odilon was tall and stoutly built, with thick ropy forearms and shoulders as broad as a cypress trunk. I watched as he secured the boat, waiting for him to let me know our next move.

Instead of talking to me, Odilon marched off into the

swamp. The old man moved fast, and before I knew it, his tan fishing vest and matching boonie hat had disappeared into the trees. I followed the sound of his waders squishing and sucking in the mud as I hurried to catch up.

"I take it we're walking the rest of the way?" I asked as I caught up to him.

Odilon grunted. "That or we let ol' Jean-Michel know we're coming."

The old man spoke with just a touch of backwater Louisiana accent, but he was an educated man and an expert on bayou myths and legends. Maman Brigitte had told me he was a retired professor of anthropology who'd taught at Tulane, which was how he'd become one of her priests. His specialty was folklore and religion, and his research had led him straight to her doorstep.

"Fair enough. Just point me to him, and I'll take care of the rest. I've dealt with plenty of werewolves in my day."

"Pfft. Not like Jean-Michel. For one, he's old— hundreds of years, maybe. Second, he wasn't turned by another lycanthrope. He became what he is today because he was cursed by a bokor."

I squashed a mosquito that had been feeding on my arm. "But he's still a 'thrope, right? I'll just shoot him up with silver rounds, then when he's weakened, I'll force him to tell me where to find Saint Germain. Piece of cake."

Odilon looked at me like I was bent. "You always go barreling into situations not knowing what the hell you're getting into? I'm trying to tell you, silver doesn't work on the Rougarou. He's all magicked up, and his power doesn't come from the wolf vyrus. All silver bullets are going to do is piss him off."

"Damn. I suppose I could decapitate him or burn him —going to be kind of hard to question him when he's dead, though."

The old man snorted. "Have fun, you." He stopped and scanned the area for a moment, then he continued. "Look, when the time comes, I'll help as much as I can. Frankly, I'd have put him out of his misery a long time ago if I had the strength." He gave me a backward glance. "But if you're as tough as Maman Brigitte says, maybe Jean-Michel can finally have some peace."

"Maybe." I watched the old man for a while as I trailed him. "You sure seem to know your way around out here."

"I was raised in these swamps. Now, hush. We're getting close to Jean-Michel's stomping grounds, and I don't want to scare him off."

"Scare him off? I thought he was a big bad werewolf?"

"Haven't you listened to a word I said? He was cursed. When he turns, he gets the moon sickness and can't control himself. That's why he lives way out here in the swamp. If he sees us coming before nightfall, he'll just run away."

"And after nightfall?"

Odilon harumphed. "You better be ready for a fight."

We walked the rest of the way in silence, me preparing spells and Odilon picking a careful path through the swamp. As we walked, I considered what Maman Brigitte had told me.

The Rougarou was once friends with Saint Germain. If the

vampire is back, he'll surely check in on his old friend. If you're lucky, you'll catch him there. But if not, Jean-Michel should know where to find him.'

To be honest, I was pissed about getting such a sketchy plan from Maman Brigitte. For a goddess, I'd really expected more from her—like a map with a big "X" on it, or a magical homing device that would lead me right to Germain's hideout. I sure as hell hadn't thought I'd have to beat the vamp's location out of some super-thrope, that was for certain. As far as I was concerned, she could find some other putz to take her granddaughter to the voodoo cotillion ball if this didn't work.

Odilon stopped, raising a fist in the air as he crouched low to the ground. I came up alongside him, crouching down as well. He pointed toward a wisp of smoke drifting up through the trees ahead. I cast a cantrip to enhance my senses, and the smell of woodsmoke, tobacco, and gumbo plucked at my olfactory receptors—along with the stench of old blood and rotten flesh.

It wasn't quite dark yet, so I tapped Odilon on the shoulder and turned my palms up in the universal gesture for, *What now?*

He tapped at his wrist, then pulled a rain poncho out of a fanny pack, spreading it out on the ground next to the trunk of a black tupelo. My guide sat and leaned his head back against the tree, pulling his hat down over his eyes. Within less than a minute, his breathing became slow and rhythmic.

Well, great. I guess I'll keep watch then.

I'D BEEN NODDING off when we heard the first terrifying howl.

Besides coming up with a cantrip to keep the mosquitos away, I had nothing better to do but watch the swamp decompose while we waited for night to fall. I briefly tried meditating so I could tune into the local fauna and use them to monitor the region, but something was blocking me near the cabin, like there was a dead spot around the Rougarou's home. I could detect no sentient life within a hundred yards of the place—not even the supposed inhabitant.

I reached out to shake Odilon awake.

He whispered before my hand reached him. "What do you want?"

"I've been using druid magic to try to monitor the cabin, and I can't detect a thing there, especially not a human."

"That's the bokor's black magic at work. Trust me, he's there. Now, let me sleep."

After that, I sat and watched and waited until the monotonous whine of the cicadas and mosquitoes lulled me to sleep. When that first howl veritably shook the swampy forest around us, it startled me into instant alertness.

"Looks like he's awake—and on the hunt," Odilon said in a soft voice. "Won't be hard to find, so you do what you got to do, and I'll be out there backing you up."

"No plan, just attack?" I asked.

The old man scowled. "You're the expert on hunting these creatures, aren't you? I just study them, mostly." He let that hang in the air for a couple of beats. "Just don't shoot any gators. They're not here to do you any harm."

"I—huh?" Odilon was already gone, having slipped off into the trees like a swamp ninja.

Fuck. Alright, time to confront the Rougarou.

I had some spells prepped, but earlier I'd decided I'd like to see how plain-old firepower would work on the beast. If that didn't work, I'd resort to spell craft. If that failed, I'd shift and go hand to claw with him.

Now, to find our furry friend.

Another roar came from the direction of the cabin.

Alrighty then. Here I come.

While I'd been fighting for my life hunting vampires in the Hellpocalypse, I'd managed to amass quite the gun collection inside my Craneskin Bag. It's amazing what people will leave behind after they've been overrun and eaten by a zombie horde, military units included. One of the beauties I'd picked up was an AR-15 modified and chambered in .458 SOCOM, a round with nearly identical ballistics and stopping power to the much larger and scarier-sounding .50 Beowulf round.

Honestly, I wasn't enough of a gun nerd to know that—some military dude who later got eaten had shared that little tidbit with me. All I knew was the rifle spat out big-ass bullets that punched holes in bodies like a freaking disintegration ray. I'd seen it rip softball-sized chunks of flesh from a vamp's torso, so I figured it'd probably slow down our super-thrope, too.

I pulled the black gun from my Bag, slapped a thirty-round drum on it, and chambered a round. The drum made it heavy, but the weight was nothing to me in my stealth-shifted mode. I clicked the fire selector to full-auto and headed toward the cabin.

Since I was shooting at night, I'd chosen to rely on a vision-enhancing cantrip and open sights instead of using a night-vision optic. I could acquire a sight picture quicker with open sights anyway, and as fast as a 'thrope could move, I'd rather have the slight edge in speed than target visibility. I snuck through the marshy forest with the rifle shouldered, sighting down the barrel and scanning the trees as I went.

Bingo.

Rustling and snuffling from up ahead alerted me to the presence of my prey. While I couldn't see the Rougarou yet, it sounded more like a grizzly moving around than a 'thrope. Creeping closer to the cabin clearing, I rounded a tree and sighted in on the biggest fucking werewolf I'd ever seen.

Hole-lee shit.

The Rougarou was down on all fours, sniffing the ground like a wolf on the scent. Then, he stood up on his hind legs, revealing himself to be well over eight feet tall. Either Jean-Michel was a giant of a man, or the bokor had shot him up with steroids when he'd cursed him.

Now I know why everyone is so scared of this thing.

The creature's fur was shaggier than a normal lycanthrope, black and matted with what looked like dried blood and swamp detritus. He was in the classic half-man, half-wolf form, bipedal but with huge claws and long teeth set into an elongated, lupine jaw and snout. The Rougarou was muscular, but lean and built for speed. As he balanced on his reverse-jointed legs, I couldn't help but admire what a magnificent and terrible beast he was.

Then, he turned and looked at me. Maybe he'd caught my scent, or I'd shifted my weight and snapped a twig. I couldn't honestly recall, because one moment I was observing the damned creature, and the next he was bounding on all fours at me like a freight train.

Understandably, I opened up on the fucker.

In the lighter AR-15 platform, the .458 SOCOM round kicks like a motherfucking mule. However, I was able to keep the muzzle down with my enhanced strength and mass in my stealth-shifted form. By my estimation, at least twenty out of my thirty rounds hit the wolf as he bore down on me.

Chunks of flesh and splinters of bone flew from the creature, spattering thick black blood on nearby vegetation as each shot hit its mark. And yet, the beast barely faltered as the heavy, hard-hitting rounds did their work, chewing away at him like a school of piranhas on a drowning cow.

By the time the beast was on top of me, he looked like a wet, fur-covered tatterdemalion. He'd lost maybe a third of his mass as the bullets carved jagged, cavernous paths through his body. One of the rounds had even taken a chunk from his skull, revealing ruined gray matter bordered by white bone that glistened in the pale moonlight.

How is he even still moving?

BEFORE I COULD ANSWER my own question, the Rougarou tore the rifle from my grasp and sent it sailing into the swamp. *Damn it, I liked that gun.* I had no time for remorse, because I was flying through the air a split-second later, the result of a backhanded blow from the beast that felt like a cannonball striking me in the chest.

I bounced off a giant cypress, discovering that the folds and creases in the trunk of said species made for a shitty landing pad. I heard ribs crack, then gravity took over and I fell some fifteen feet to the ground. "Oof," was about all I managed to say as I hit the dirt below with the wind knocked clean out of me.

In this state, my Fomorian lungs and physiology could go without oxygen for several minutes with little ill effect, but the amount of time I could stay in this partially-shifted form was limited. Back in the Hellpocalypse, I'd managed to hold my stealth-shifted form for up to an hour, but it had taken a toll on me to do so. And if I had to fully shift, being in this state beforehand reduced the length of time I could hold my larger, fully-Fomorian form.

I was beginning to suspect I'd need to completely Hulk out to take Jean-Michel down, and I needed to do it fast if that was the case. The last thing I wanted was to be in a prolonged fight with the Rougarou, then collapse due to magical and physical exhaustion while the fight was still on. I only allowed myself a moment's respite, willing my diaphragm to stop spasming so I could take a decent breath and get on with the fight.

The clock is ticking, Colin. Move!

It'd take me several seconds to finish the shift, so I needed a distraction to give my Hyde-side time to come out and play. I wobbled to my feet just as the giant 'thrope came at me in a rush to finish me off. His wounds were already nearly healed and he looked fresh, which kind of put a damper on my plans to use magic to defeat him. Yet all I needed was a momentary diversion, something to keep him busy while I made the shift—and magic might just do the trick.

I reached into my Bag for the first surprise of many I'd prepared while in the Hellpocalypse.

At the last moment, I spun out of the way, tossing a small semi-spherical object at the Rougarou's head. Six months of surviving against overwhelming odds with limited resources had taught me a lot, and one thing I'd learned quickly was how to take down a 'thrope, fast. Since I hadn't always had silver rounds on hand—I'd run out of what I'd had the first week, and good silver hadn't always been easy to come by in an apocalypse—I went for the next best thing.

Fire.

The glass bulb burst on impact, and a sticky, viscous liquid soaked the beast's fur. Light bulbs were the most fragile container I could easily find in that hellhole, and one that would shatter and release a payload nearly every single time. It would never have worked if I'd had to carry them on my person, but my Craneskin Bag kept them intact until I needed them. The hardest part about turning them into Molotovs was cutting the foot contact off without breaking the glass. After that, it was just a matter of filling them and plugging the hole with melted wax and duct tape.

The combination of gasoline, kerosene, dish soap, and dissolved styrofoam splashed all over the Rougarou's head. A spark flew from my hand, igniting the solution so the 'thrope's head burst into flames. The beast roared in fury at being momentarily blinded. I hoped like hell his senses of smell and hearing would be greatly diminished as well.

I backpedaled away from the creature, getting enough space so he couldn't easily locate me while I shifted. I tore off my clothes along the way, shoving them inside my Bag. *No way I'm messing these clothes up—not after what I paid for them.* Once I'd stripped down to my skivvies, I triggered the shift.

Like every time I'd done this, I knew that shifting as fast as I could would be a living hell. First, my skeleton would thicken and lengthen, splitting my skin and tearing muscle and tendon from bone as I gained two feet in height in seconds. Then, my muscles and sinews would catch up, healing and reattaching themselves while they doubled in mass and density. My skin would follow suit next, repairing the bleeding rents left earlier in the transformation while transmuting into something akin to rhinoceros skin—thick, rough, and nearly bullet-proof.

And while this was happening, my body would become twisted and misshapen, grotesque and malformed. Every time I shifted, I developed a huge kyphotic hump in my shoulders, the result of a knot in my spine that caused me to hunch like a larger, uglier version of Quasimodo, with one shoulder always higher than the other. My right hand would become almost club-like, with my forearm, fingers, and palm swelling until the whole limb became a Morningstar made of flesh and bone. My left hand, however, always warped into a claw-like appendage, with long, sinewy fingers that ended in sharp nails I knew could tear through skin and muscle like a hot knife through butter.

Finally, my face and skull would change to ensure my visage was as terrifying as the rest of me. My jaw would widen and lengthen, giving me a mug reminiscent of Lockjaw from those eighties *He-Man* cartoons. In much the same manner, my teeth would grow into long, jagged rows of yellowed ivory, reminiscent of the Dolomites and pretty much an orthodontist's nightmare. And finally, my brow would jut out from my forehead as my beady, dark eyes recessed, obviously serving function over form to protect the most vulnerable and exposed organs this mangled form possessed.

When the change triggered on its own, it happened almost instantaneously. That near-instant change was presumably the product of genetically-encoded survival mechanisms, and it was a phenomenon that had saved my bacon on multiple occasions. Partial shifts were easy as well—especially "stealth-shifting," since it didn't require an increase in mass or size. Plus, I'd gotten better at it with practice during my time in the Hellpocalypse.

But the fastest I could completely shift into my full Fomorian form was just a hair under twenty seconds. And while I made that change, I was understandably preoccupied and fairly vulnerable, as least until the process was complete.

Thus, I lost track of the giant 'thrope as soon as I started to shift.

I was only halfway through the process when the Rougarou rose from the waters of the swamp not ten feet in front of me, the flames from the napalm extinguished and his eyes and fur almost fully healed. The creature sighted in on me immediately, bursting out of the water in a massive leap that would bring him right on top of me, well before I completed my transformation.

Well, this is going to suck.

12

Time seemed to slow, and I watched helplessly as the Rougarou descended upon me, arms outstretched and slavering jaws spread wide. Clearly, the beast intended to rip me limb from limb as soon as he landed, and I had full confidence that was exactly what was about to happen.

Just as I'd resigned myself to a very unpleasant and bloody demise, a huge crocodilian head snatched the creature from the air, clamping its jaws down before flinging the 'thrope away across the clearing. My eyes followed the trajectory of the Rougarou's flight, then I looked back to take in this new potential threat.

Standing in front of me was a creature that was not wholly reptilian and not wholly man. The monster was covered in skin that was thick, scaled, and marked just like a gator from the bayou. It had the head of an alligator on top of a humanoid body and a thick, ridged tail that was nearly as long as the rest of it. Although it stood seven feet tall balanced on its hind legs and tail, it had to be twenty feet long from nose to tail.

The crocothrope opened its massive jaws, and a harsher, deeper version of Odilon's voice came out.

"You might want to hurry up, druid. I don't think I can hold him off for long."

The wolfman came loping out of the swamp at speed, colliding with Odilon in an apparent attempt to tackle this new threat. The crocothrope managed to stay upright by bracing himself with his tail, but that didn't keep the werewolf from ripping and tearing at the alligator man with tooth and claw. Soon, the two of them were locked in mortal combat, each grappling for dominance as claws struck and jaws snapped in an effort to disembowel or exsanguinate the other.

In the few short seconds it took to complete my transformation, it was clear that Odilon was engaged in a losing battle. While he had the advantage in size and the sheer massiveness of his jaws, the Rougarou had the edge in speed and reach. The crocothrope put up a good fight, but he could never seem to lock his teeth on Jean-Michel's body. Every single time Odilon snapped at the were, the beast would slip out of the way, leaving the crocothrope to snap at empty air while taking a vicious claw swipe across the snout.

By the time I stood, Odilon's face had been shredded and he'd been blinded in one eye as well.

"Feel free to jump in any time now, Druid," he croaked in his deep, crocodilian voice.

"Don't mind if I do," I growled.

I ran at Odilon's back, attempting to stay in his shadow and the wolf man's blind spot as I entered the fray. Of course, the Rougarou spotted me coming anyway, and he kicked the crocothrope in the chest, causing him to stumble into my path. I had anticipated the move. Instead of tripping over my companion, I stepped on his thigh, then on his shoulder, running over him Jackie Chan-style in order to leap on our opponent.

I landed on the surprised 'thrope, our bodies crashing into each other as I bowled him over. We rolled and tussled like two badgers fighting over a comb of honey, biting and ripping and clawing at each other faster than the human eye could see. I was fresh and he was not, but that didn't matter since the werewolf healed from each wound I caused almost as soon I injured him.

Equally frustrating was that the beast gave as good as he got, and I didn't heal near as quickly. I'd fought giants, fae, vamps, 'thropes, and more in this form, and to my recollection nothing had given me this much trouble—not even close. The werewolf was cutting me to pieces, and even with Odilon circling us and snapping at him here and there, I feared the battle would rage on until my magic ran out and I transformed back into my human state.

Then, I'll be well and truly fucked. Time to find this thing's weakness, and fast.

I fended off a particularly nasty swipe at my eyes, ducking under the 'thrope's arms as I went for a double-leg takedown. It wasn't the smartest of moves to attempt against a humanoid creature with claws that could rip even my hardened flesh. But I needed to be close enough to protect my eyes from the thing's razor-tipped fingers while I looked at it in the magical spectrum.

I grappled with the Rougarou as he shredded my torso and back, my arms in a death grip around his waist and my head tucked up under his right armpit so he couldn't reach my eyes. I shifted the focus of my sight, switching my vision so I saw only magic and not natural light. At first, all I picked up was his life force, a swirl of color dominated by the silver-grey glow that all 'thropes possessed.

But on closer inspection, I realized his aura was streaked with small black lines, almost like a spider's web. It was clear that each of those lines were connected to a central hub, a small sphere that looked like an inky black ball of twigs. It beat like a heart at the center of the wolf man's aura.

That's the spell—the source of the bokor's magic.

The question was, was it only made of magic? Or did it have a physical component that existed in our world, a focus that contained the magic of the spell?

One way to find out.

I released my left hand from my right, loosening my grip significantly so I could attack with that hand. Driving my fingertips like a spear, I stabbed my hand into the Rougarou's side, splitting his hide and slicing through organs and muscle. The beast howled, renewing his attacks on my body with a vengeance, but I kept on, burrowing my hand deep into its body while I used my magic sight to guide it home.

And while I tried to find the source of the spell, the Rougarou ripped me to pieces, weakening me as I kept digging around in his body—all in a desperate gamble to end the fight against this seemingly invincible creature.

THERE.

I felt my hand brush up against something—an object that felt like it was made of thorns and bramble, but pulsed like a heart beating in someone's chest. I spread my fingers wide and grabbed at it, clutching it like a monkey grabbing a ball of rice inside a coconut trap. And just like the monkey, my hand felt stuck as the magic inside the Rougarou resisted my attempts to dislodge it from the 'thrope's body.

Hot, slick blood ran down my waist and legs, leaking my life out on the ground with every second I grappled with the creature. Odilon had one of the Rougarou's arms trapped in his jaws, pulling it away so the 'thrope could only tear at me with one clawed hand. But his efforts had come too late. I was weakened by blood loss and was losing my grip on the 'thrope.

Once I bled out, it'd be over. The Rougarou would trample me underfoot, then he'd rip me to bloody shreds, probably while I transformed back into my human self.

No way I'm going down like this. I refuse to be killed by a fucking werewolf.

With one last Herculean effort, I pulled with all my might at the source of the spell. I felt a tearing sensation as something gave inside my opponent. Filled with rage and pain, the lycan let out a terrifying howl, and suddenly, the thing I held tore free. My hand slipped out of the 'thrope's innards, and I shoved him away as he fell limp to the ground.

Stepping back on shaky legs, I slipped in my own blood and fell to my knees. My gaze dropped to the thing in my hand—an effigy of a heart, not a human one, but similar. *A wolf's heart, maybe?* It had been made from tatters of cloth and string wrapped around a heart-shaped mass of black, thorny vines.

I crushed it in my hand, then spoke a single word in Gaelic.

"*Losgadh.*"

The focus for the bokor's curse burst into flames. I heard someone cry out, a human's voice. When I looked up, the Rougarou had turned back into a man—small of stature and thin, with short, close-cropped black hair, a scholar's soft hands, and a poet's soulful brown eyes. The gaping hole I'd left in his side was still there, leaking blood like a sieve and pouring his life out into the swamp.

"*Merci, Monsieur*," he gasped, "for breaking my curse. Who could have guessed it would take a monster to stop a monster, eh?" He spoke English in the way only the French can, making my rather ugly language sound prosaic.

I was already shifting back to my semi-human form as I leapt to his side, my own wounds healing as I attempted to staunch the bleeding from his wound with my hands. For the first time, I fully realized I hadn't fought a monster, but a man cursed. The weight of it only hit me now that I could see him for what he truly was—just another poor schmuck fucked by magic.

"Ah," Jean-Michel said sagely, "I see I am not the only one who is cursed."

"Shit, it wasn't supposed to go down this way. We'll get you to a doctor—just hang on." I looked around the clearing, frantic. "Odilon. Odilon!"

Jean-Michel gripped my hand. "Even if you could save me, I have no desire to live. I remember every innocent life I've taken. The things I've done—*merde*, but it is too much too bear."

"I—I guess I can relate." His eyes closed, and they began to flutter behind his eyelids. I shook him gently until they popped back open. "Jean-Michel! Hey, don't die on me yet, man. I need to know where Germain went. Please, tell me where he's hiding."

"Germain...." he whispered. "He tried to cure me—didn't know how."

"Where is he, Jean-Michel? Where has he gone?"

"Back—to Texas, to the town named for that *bâtard*, Austin. War—war is coming."

Don't I know it.

Jean-Michel's grip on my hand grew weak, then he gave a death rattle and was no more. Although he'd thanked me for killing him, it wasn't exactly the kind of mercy I cared to give. I said a silent prayer for the man before standing on still-shaky legs.

"You gave him peace, druid," Odilon said as he clapped his hand on my shoulder. The man damned sure could move quietly when he wanted. I simply nodded in response, deciding it wasn't worth debating.

"Can you help me bury him?"

"But of course."

I found a shovel in a small shed behind Jean-Michel's cabin. I probably could have coaxed the earth to swallow him whole, but doing it the hard way seemed somehow —*right*, for lack of a better word. When it was done, I said another prayer while Odilon stood silent. Then, I nodded again, signaling it was time to go.

"I have to get back to the city, and quickly, Odilon."

"We'll go as fast as the boat can carry us. I assume Jean-Michel revealed where Germain ran off to?"

I frowned. "Jean-Michel said he went to Austin. There's only one thing he could be going there to do, and believe me, it's not good. I have to stop him."

"Come, then, let's get back to the boat. I can get you to your car before the sun rises." He took off into the trees, back the way we came, and I followed close behind. As we walked, he spoke without looking at me. "And, druid?"

"Yes?" I had a feeling I knew what was coming, but I didn't want to make assumptions.

"I'd prefer it if you told no one about what you saw tonight. Maman Brigitte's magic protects me from discovery, but if word got out—"

"—Remy and his coven would chase you out of town." I paused. "Odilon, when someone saves my life, I'm not the type to forget it. Don't worry, your secret is safe with me."

The old man said nothing, because he was a man of few words and there was nothing else to say.

On the long hike back to the boat, I thought about how he hadn't had to help me fight Jean-Michel. The more I considered it, the more I doubted he'd done it at Maman Brigitte's behest. Despite his silence on the matter, I vowed that if Odilon ever needed my help, I'd repay the debt in kind—and then some.

ONCE I GOT BACK to my rental car, I used dry erase markers to place a look-away spell on it, praying I wouldn't hit rain on the way back. After I was certain I wouldn't get pulled over for speeding, I put my foot down and made record time back to Austin. My first stop was the junkyard, if only to get a quick shower and check in with Maureen.

When I popped my head in the office, Maureen didn't even look up. "The Seer is out back, waiting for you—and he doesn't look happy."

"He's old and cranky. What else is new?"

Maureen continued to type as she glanced over the counter at me. "While that may be true, he seems a bit more peeved than usual."

"You think he found out?"

"'Twas only a matter o' time, was it not? Best you go appease him, afore he blows a gasket."

I hung my head, cursing under my breath. This was not a conversation I was looking forward to having. "Th—I mean, I'm glad you gave me a heads up."

"There ya' go, slippin' up again. Don't forget yer coffee."

There was a steaming cup sitting on the counter that

hadn't been there moments before. I snagged it and headed for the yard, remembering that Finn still liked to sit in front of the van where he used to sleep back before he kicked his drug habit. I found him there, way in the back of the yard, sipping a can of Pearl beer. As usual, a roll-your-own cancer stick smoldered between his fingers, a long length of ash drooping from the end.

"Have a seat," he said. It wasn't exactly a growl, but it was close.

Didn't even look my way when I walked up. Yeah, he's pissed.

"I take it you heard about what went down in New Orleans?" It was worth a shot, anyway.

He flicked the ash off his coffin nail and took a long drag, exhaling as he spoke. "What you do as druid justiciar is your business. If you chose to help that bastard DeCoudreaux hold his territory, I'm sure you have a good reason for it."

"So—?"

The old man flicked his ash again, unnecessarily. "So, why am I madder than a skillet full of rattlesnakes?" He looked off into the distance before fixing me with a stare. "Why'd you bring her back?"

I glanced around nervously. "I don't think this is the best place to discuss this."

Finnegas made a few gestures with his fingers, not even setting his beer can or cigarette down to cast the spell. Instantly, the world went silent. "She can't hear a thing we're saying. Now, explain yourself, because I'm about two steps away from putting a boot up your ass, just on principle."

"It wasn't my idea, believe me. Jesse and the Dagda worked out that deal behind my back." I sucked air through my teeth and scowled. "Anyway, aren't you going to ask me why I didn't tell you?"

"I know damned well why you didn't tell me!" he shouted, as the ground shook beneath us. It wasn't a good idea to piss off Finnegas the Seer. I decided to remain calm, because escalating the argument would only make things worse.

I closed my eyes and exhaled heavily. "After—after she died, you went off the deep end, just as badly as I did. Honestly, I was just trying to save you from having to lose her twice."

"Come again?"

"Seriously, Finn? Have you spoken with her? The magic has driven her batshit crazy. You don't know how many times I've had to talk her down from killing someone she thought was a threat to me. Or how many times I've stopped her from zapping customers for stepping on bugs or trampling wildflowers in the yard. She's crazy, and she has way too much power. Eventually, I'm going to have to banish her, for everyone's safety."

Finnegas pushed his artfully crumpled straw cowboy hat back on his head, scratching his hairline with a chuckle. "She only wields that power because you haven't claimed the damned oak tree, and the grove within it. Didn't I tell you that you needed to claim it, back when you planted the damned thing?"

"Yes, but I've been busy—"

"Busy avoiding her, eh?"

"So what if I have?" I threw my hands up in the air. "For years, all I thought about day and night was changing what happened back in that cave. And all this time, I've wished we never went after the Caoránach—hell, I wished we'd never become hunters!"

"And I'd have spared you from that if I could, but—"

"Damn it, let me finish!" Without meaning to, I'd raised my voice. I took a few deep breaths before continuing in a quieter, somewhat calmer tone. "All I wanted was a chance to go back and make things right. And when Jesse showed up inside the grove, I thought my wishes had been answered. But I was wrong. She's a menace, and she's been making my life hell since the grove resurrected her in that dryad's body. So yeah, I've been avoiding her."

"And the druid grove." Finnegas leaned forward, elbows on his knees and shoulders slumped. "Do you want to save her?" he asked plaintively.

"Of course. But I don't think she *can* be saved."

Finn sighed. "There is a way. You just have to claim the grove. Claiming the grove will bring her under your control, and it could possibly allow you to rectify the entire situation."

"Fucking hell, Finn, it's not like the damned thing came with an instruction manual." The old man cleared his throat and glared at me. "Okay, so I guess I should have come to you already. Sue me for wanting to spare you more pain."

"Colin, I've walked this Earth for two millennia. I can deal with a little heartache."

"Pfft. Could've fooled me."

He squinted, staring at me with one eye. "Do you want to know how to claim the druid grove or not?"

"If it'll help Jesse? Of course."

He took a long drink of his beer. "Then I'll tell you how —but you're not going to like it."

13

Finnegas was hot on my tail as I stormed out the front gate and into the parking lot. I wasn't even looking at him, intent on reaching my rental and getting the hell out of there.

"Colin, just hear me out—"

I gave Finn "the hand." "Nope! Uh-uh, no fucking way. And, incidentally, that's about the most barbaric, misogynistic, outdated, ass-backwards thing I've ever heard."

"Oh, for goodness sakes—it's no different in principle than tantric magic. And it's not like the druid grove knows the difference anyway. Whatever intelligence the grove possesses simply sees it as a natural act, one that's morally-neutral and necessary to complete the ritual."

"I already told you, my life is complicated enough as it is!"

I got in my car and slammed the door. Unfortunately, I'd left the window open. My wet, muddy clothes were in a plastic bag in the back, and I hadn't wanted them stinking up the car. Finnegas had his hands on the car door, and he was leaning down to look at me. I started the engine.

"Colin, listen to me—"

"For the last time, Finn—no!" I put the car in gear and waited for the old man to back up with his hands on his hips.

"You damned silly fool. Fine, go! But don't blame me when it all goes to shit."

I hit the gas, fishtailing out of the parking lot. Sure, it was juvenile, but somehow satisfying as well. I drummed my fingers on the steering wheel as I fumed about what Finnegas had asked me to do.

I am not sleeping with Jesse.

When Finnegas had mentioned that the ritual for claiming the grove required that I have sexual relations with the "spirit" of the grove—in this case, dryad Jesse—I'd wigged out. Not only did the entire premise repulse me, but I also had no intentions of leading Jesse on in that way. Not to mention the fact that I'd essentially be subjugating her in the process.

The whole thing just sounded way too much like rape to me, even if Jesse was a willing volunteer. What I didn't understand was, why had Jesse been so eager to have sex with me in the first place? Didn't she know she'd be giving up her personal agency and free will by doing so?

Because she doesn't know. Obviously, the Dagda, true to fae and Tuatha form, never mentioned that part.

I wasn't about to broach the topic with her, either. It was better she didn't know. I'd find another way to separate her spirit from that of the druid oak, and then I could deal with "claiming" the grove. The idea of sleeping with what was essentially a golem definitely freaked me out. The whole thing reminded me a bit too much of those lifelike sex dolls, whose facial features still hadn't bridged the uncanny valley—and probably never would.

My very own Cherry 2000. Ugh, gross.

Although I was still pretty pissed off and disgusted, I pushed the whole tawdry mess to the back of my mind. I had bigger problems, namely preventing the apocalypse from happening. Plus, I still needed a shower. A quick sniff of my shirt made me recoil. I smelled like swamp ass.

I stopped at a convenience store and took a sink bath, stripping out of my clothes and grabbing fresh ones from my Bag. I set my phone on the soap dish and checked the time. *Almost dark.* I hit a number on speed dial and turned the speaker on while I dried off with paper towels.

"Druid."

"Sophia, I need some info."

A brief moment of silence ensued. "I am not so sure I should be speaking with you, *chudovishche,* after the mess you made in New Orleans."

"All done under Remy's orders, I assure you."

"So I've heard." I heard fingernails tapping in the background. "Luther is not pleased. He knew some of the *vampyr* you killed."

Shit. "If I'd known, I would have spared them." *Maybe.* "Anyway, that's for me and Luther to hash out. Are you going to help me, or not?"

"Da, I will help you. Ask."

"I need a list of vampire safe houses in the city, locations that may have been recently constructed, or that changed ownership in the last few months."

Sophia Doroshenko chuckled humorlessly. "You do not ask for much."

"Let's not play games. I know that Luther owns the companies that cover all those contracts in the city, because he's the only one who can assure discretion for those clients. And, I know his real estate company handles property transactions for the local vampire community. So, it's not like you don't have access to that info."

"You seem to know quite a lot about Luther's dealings. More than he has told you, da?"

"I'm the justiciar, Sophia. It's my job to know what goes on in this demesne."

It was a half-truth. The fact was, when I'd taken on the role of justiciar, Finnegas had told me everything he knew about each faction, so I'd know how to hurt them if I had to. "Insurance" is what he called it. The old man hadn't lived two-thousand years by not being in the know, that was certain.

More finger tapping in the background. "I will look into this and call you back shortly."

The phone went dead. I finished drying off and got dressed, smelling myself again as I did. *Gah, still a little ripe. Time to let magic do what soap and water can't.* I cast the same cantrip I'd used to cover Fallyn's scent on myself. Another sniff test proved the spell to be a success.

My phone dinged with a text from Sophia.

-List attached. Don't make me regret this.-

I looked in the mirror, checking to make sure I didn't

look like a bum before I headed out. "Hope you're ready, Germain. Because I'm coming for you."

———

THE MOST RECENT real estate transaction on the list was a little country house on some acreage, just outside of town on 290 West. The title and deed information said it had been purchased by Apropos Holdings, LLC. *Germane—Apropos—clever.* I mashed the pedal to the floor to make time as I headed out of town. My watch said 8:17 when I reached the area, late enough for the sun to have dropped below the western horizon.

If he's there, he'll be up. Going to have to do this the hard way.

I drove past the place and parked where the street dead-ended about a block down. The neighbor's houses looked quiet, which was both good and bad. I hoped I could get this done without getting the authorities involved, but it was doubtful. Saint Germain was old and powerful, and he'd put up one hell of a fight.

No time to bullshit around. Better go in with guns blazing.

I jumped the neighbor's fence, staying low and hidden in the trees while I followed their fence line all the way to the back corner. Then, I took several minutes to press scrap silver into the tips of several dozen hollow points. *Jury-rigged silver rounds, just like grandma used to make back in the ol' Hellpocalypse.*

It wasn't ideal because the ballistics would be shit, but they'd do at close range. Once that task was done, I loaded four mags and strapped my tactical belt on, adding my holstered Glocks and silver-plated Bowie knife as well.

Not quite a short sword, but it'll do.

Preparations complete, I stealth-shifted to ensure I could at least match Germain in strength and resilience, if not speed. As usual, I checked for traps, wards, and alarm spells, negating them so they wouldn't trip as I jumped the fence onto his property. Once I was inside, I altered the alarm spell, adding a ward that would specifically prevent anyone from coming in or out without getting zapped by a massive fire and lightning spell.

Okay, Germain, let's see what you got. If you're what I think you are, you'll see the trap—if not, it's barbecue time. Either way, I win.

There were clear cut paths all around the fence perimeter, but I decided to slink through the cedar and oak trees as I made my way toward the house. The paths were likely created to facilitate security sweeps, so I kept an eye out for roaming patrols as I crossed the property. The place was eerily silent, and the woods were so still I could hear my own heartbeat. As I neared the house, everything around me went quiet—birds stopped chirping, cicadas and crickets went silent, heck, even the tiny bit of wind died down to nothing.

It didn't feel right, and I was obviously walking into an ambush or trap. I reached out with my druid senses, and through a screech owl's eyes I saw Germain waiting in the shadows of the home's back porch.

He knows I'm here. Damn.

But as good old Rorschach once said, "I'm not locked in

here with you, you're locked in here with me." I stepped out of the trees and marched in the open toward the house, dropping all pretense of remaining hidden. "Come on out, Germain. You obviously know I'm here, so let's get this over with. I'm long overdue for a shower and a good night's sleep, and the sooner I finish you off, the better."

The centuries-old vampire stepped out of shadow and off the back porch of the home. He was dressed much as he had been when I'd seen him last, in a suit vest, slacks, and dress shoes. Just as before, his sleeves were rolled up to his elbows, but this time he held a walking cane that he twirled in his fingers like a baton. The old vampire stopped just off the porch and across the yard, and I noticed he had a weird leather bandolier strapped across his chest in the moonlight. Instead of carrying bullets or knives, the thing held small glass vials.

Okay, that's just weird.

"Do you always carry your perfume collection around with you? Or did I catch you in the middle of working your side hustle? Trying to earn that pink Cadillac, maybe?"

Germain stopped twirling his cane, resting the tip on the ground between his feet so he could stack his hands on the handle. He set his feet wide, squaring his shoulders as he stared at me through stormy eyes beneath a furrowed brow.

"While you may think this is amusing, I fail to find the humor in the situation. You killed good vampires the other night—many were the offspring of friends I've long held in high regard. And for what? So you can square a debt with that scoundrel Remy?" He scowled. "What a waste."

"It's true that I owed Remy a debt, but the fact is I can't allow a feral vampire to live. After seeing what you did to that man, your existence is something I simply cannot abide."

Germain scoffed. "Seriously? You're upset over *that* human? Monsieur McCool, if you knew anything about the New Orleans coven, you'd be cheering my actions instead of condemning them."

"I know what I saw. And you know you took a risk coming to Austin. As the justiciar for this demesne, I have both the power and authority to take you down—and that's exactly what I intend to do."

"Luther might say otherwise."

"I don't answer to Luther!" I growled, perhaps a bit louder than I intended. I took a moment to calm my voice before speaking. "Now, is there anything you want to say before I separate your head from your shoulders?"

The vampire sighed, a human affectation if ever there was one. *What a drama queen.*

"Are you certain I can't dissuade you from this course of action?" he asked.

"Not on your second life," I said with certainty.

"Then, I suppose I have no choice but to defend myself. *En garde!*"

***

GERMAIN DREW A LONG, needle-thin blade from his cane. He brandished it about like Zorro before assuming fencing's sixth hand position with the cane sword.

"I'm sorry—did you just say 'en garde'?" I asked.

Germain relaxed his posture, standing a bit taller as he answered. "I did. A gentleman always puts his opponent on notice before he attacks."

"R-i-i-ight," I said mockingly. Germain lowered into his stance again, rolling out his shoulders in a manner reminiscent of Bruce Lee. I wanted him good and pissed, not relaxed, so I pointed at his chest. "If you don't mind me asking, what's the deal with the bottles?"

He smiled, and not in a friendly way. "If you decide to use your magic to gain advantage, then you'll find out. Draw a weapon, or fight me empty-handed if you must, because I grow tired of this nattering."

"Nattering," I muttered. "Geez, it's not like you had to make this personal."

Germain sighed. "Are you quite done?"

"Hang on." I reached into my Bag and made a show of rummaging around. "I know have a sword in here somewhere. There it is—nope, that's not it. Maybe this? Nope, *that's* certainly not for public consumption. Ah, there it is."

I pulled out a broadsword and swept it around me in a figure-eight, left-handed. It wasn't silver, and I had no intention of fighting Germain with it. The sword was merely a distraction.

Wait for it—

The vampire relaxed his stance again and rolled his eyes. "Now, are you ready—?"

As soon as he took his eyes off me, I drew one of my Glocks with my right hand, snapping off three rounds just as quickly as possible. The pistol wasn't fully-automatic, but the three-round burst sounded almost like one shot. The first round hit a surprised Saint Germain in the shoulder, then he leaned away before the gun could cycle the second and third shots.

Shit! I was aiming for his head. Should've used the sunlight spell instead.

I kept shooting at him, but damn it if he wasn't zipping around like Speedy Gonzales on a carnival firing range. Realizing I wasn't going to get another shot, I stuck the sword in ground, tip first, in order to release my sunlight spell. Just as I extended my hand toward the vamp, he snatched a vial from his bandolier and smashed it against the ground.

Instantly, a nearly impenetrable cloud of shadowy smoke surrounded Germain. My eyes strained to pick him out in the darkness, but the smoke obscured the vamp almost completely.

No sense wasting my spell. Time for plan B.

I switched my pistol to my left hand and drew my silver-plated Bowie knife in my right. After preparing another spell, I leapt across the clearing and into the smoke. I knew Germain would be waiting for me within that cloud, obscured from view and waiting to rip my throat out, but that was my plan.

It took but the blink of an eye to close that gap, but I was much, much faster in this stealth-shifted form. In midleap, already committed to my course, I sprayed the area where I intended to land with another three-round burst from my pistol. I didn't expect to hit Germain. I merely wanted him distracted while I sprang my trap.

Holstering the pistol while still in the air, I released my second spell. A gust of wind blew up all around, partially blowing Germain's magic smoke cloud out of the way. It didn't work completely, as the stuff seemed to cling to the ground and everything else with a mind of its own. However, it did diminish his cover enough to reveal where the vampire remained hidden.

That's when I cut loose with the sunlight spell. The old vamp covered his face with his arms, leaving the exposed skin on his hands and forearms to take the brunt of it. Instantly, the light caused his skin to bubble and crisp, burning away the top layers to char and blacken the flesh underneath. The old vampire howled in rage and pain as he zipped around the corner of the house, well before I could land and plunge the knife in his heart.

Here comes the finale, in three—two—one.

Somewhere on the other side of the house, lightning struck and a fireball flared into the sky. I holstered my pistol and calmly walked around the house, humming the chorus to The Misfits' "Last Caress" as I rounded the corner. And what did I see but Germain, fried to a crisp and draped across the front gate of the property. He was missing a few fingers from his left hand, his right foot was nearly blown off, and the entire front half of his body was one charred, blackened mess.

I strolled up to him, enjoying the moment as I flipped the huge Bowie between my fingers. Every few seconds, Germain's body would twitch, the residual electricity from the lightning spell attempting to move muscles that were now unable to respond. Most of the flesh on one side of his face had been burned away, reminding me of Aaron Eckhardt's Two-Face in *The Dark Knight*. The vamp's jaw worked as if he were trying to speak, but only a raspy groan escaped his lips.

Strangely, the only stitch of clothing left fully intact was that weird bandolier. And even more strange, every last bottle remained intact as well. I yanked it over his head, tossing it to the side. The thing was obviously spelled. There was no sense in letting him pull any tricks out of his sleeves.

"Mmm-mmm! Nothing like the smell of crispy vampire in the morning." I leaned over his badly burned form, casually batting away a carbon-covered hand as he tried to grab me. "You don't look so good, Germain. But guess what? I know you're going to heal, even without feeding. You old ones are resilient like that. So, I'm just going to sit here casting fire spells at you, burning you over and over again, until you tell me what I need to know."

He stared at me with his remaining intact eye. "A-a-ssk," he croaked.

"Who's your contact at the Cold Iron Circle? And what are they planning to do with the Eye?"

He blinked, once, twice. His chest heaved, and he began to cry. At least, I thought he was crying, at first—then I realized he was laughing.

"You—you thought I was the one?" More laughter, rasping and wheezing. "All this time?"

I grabbed him by the neck, squeezing and shaking him until his crisp skin split beneath my fingers. The vampire still silently shook with laughter. Apparently, the fact that I'd cut off his air didn't affect his mirth the least little bit.

"This isn't funny, Germain, and it's not a game. Believe me, I'll make your remaining time on this Earth a living hell. I've had plenty of practice. Tell me, who else is colluding with the Circle? Names, now!"

He stopped laughing to stare at me, weighing me somehow. The intensity of his gaze was more than a little intimidating, even in his current state and with only one working eye. In that moment, I may as well have been standing in front of Osiris, having my heart measured against the weight of a feather.

"The vampire you want is the one you're working for," he croaked. "Remy DeCoudreaux has been in league with the Circle for some time now, scheming in order to bring the humans under his heel. And I'm trying to stop him."

Fuck.

14

He _could be lying._ In Germain's current state and position, I realized he might say anything to avoid death at my hands. But my instincts told me otherwise. The way he'd reacted to my accusations, his expressions, the certainty in his voice—it all told me I'd been pursuing the wrong person the whole time.

Better make damned sure, though.

I pulled him off the fence, then reset the containment spell. Next, I shackled Germain hand and foot in silver cuffs, dragging him up his front steps where I tossed him on an outdoor bench. As I did, I noticed the vamp's body was healing faster than I might have imagined. Already the muscles on his face were beginning to regenerate, even without the benefit of a feeding. By my estimate, he'd be entirely healed within the course of the next half-hour.

The process will leave him weak, but he could still be dangerous. Best figure this out before he fully heals.

I leaned against his front porch railing, arms crossed

but within easy reach of my knife and pistol. "Alright, I'm listening. Prove it."

The vamp coughed and spat out a clot of black blood and charred flesh. "I was sent by the European coven leaders to investigate DeCoudreaux's dealings with the Circle. Since their inception, The Cold Iron Circle has been at odds with vampires, lycans, and fae alike—more so than their European counterparts. This has *never* changed, not in the many centuries of their existence."

"Yeah, they're not too keen on humans who work with supernaturals either. I was on their shit list for quite some time. They nearly did me in a couple of times, at least until I managed to turn the tables on them."

Germain nodded. "Someone sympathetic to the supernatural races with your powers would certainly be perceived as a threat by the Circle. In days past, they have gone after our human allies—that's almost to be expected. But never before have they allied themselves with *our* kind. Or any of the supernatural species, for that matter."

"How far-reaching is this alliance? Surely there'd be dissent among their ranks if it became known that the Circle was working with their sworn enemies."

"Correct. To our knowledge, only one or perhaps two of their leaders are involved. The Council as a whole wouldn't stand for it, such is their hatred of us."

I scratched the stubble on my chin. "If what you're saying is true, then something caused one or more of the Council members to go rogue."

"Exactly. And now, that person is colluding with Remy DeCoudreaux, but to what end we don't really know. I came back to New Orleans under the pretense of competing with him politically for his seat as coven leader. In actuality, I've been trying to discover who his Circle contact is and what they've been planning."

"Ah—that's why you came to Austin."

He gave the barest smile. "My spies within Remy's coven were unable to determine the identity of his ally. I thought I could find information here that would reveal who that person is and what they want from DeCoudreaux."

I tsked and raised an eyebrow. "Still doesn't explain the guy I found at your mansion."

Germain chuffed. "One of Remy's familiars—and a particularly nasty one, at that. I'd been questioning him for info on his master's dealings with the Circle."

"What was his name?"

"James Broussard, but he went by Jim."

I held a finger up. "Give me a second."

It took only a moment to respond to Sophia Doroshenko's text. Within seconds, I had a reply verifying that, yes, Jim Broussard was one of Remy's favorite Renfields.

Germain rattled his cuffs to get my attention. "Who-ever that is, don't tell them I'm here. I suspect there are spies in Luther's coven working for DeCoudreaux."

"Well, that's convenient."

The old vamp coughed up more black gunk. "Ask Luther about me, if you don't believe me. He doesn't know why I'm here, but he'll at least vouch for my character. I can assure you, Monsieur McCool, I am nothing like Remy DeCoudreaux."

I really should've checked his bonafides with Luther, but I wasn't ready to face the local coven leader yet. He was a trusted friend and always would be, but I had personal issues to work out before that particular reunion could happen.

"I'll take your word for it," I said as I unlocked and removed the silver cuffs from Germain's wrists and ankles. His wounds were healing, but it was clear his body was scavenging itself to make those repairs. "You got any blood around here?"

He tilted his head toward the house. "A few bags, in a cooler in the kitchen. The utilities haven't been turned on here yet, I'm afraid."

"No funny stuff while I'm gone," I warned.

Germain gave me a wry smile. "I assure you, I am in no condition for antics."

I retrieved two I.V. bags of blood from a plastic cooler on the kitchen counter and brought them to Germain. He clipped the tubing off neatly with his teeth before proceeding to suck each bag down like a kid sucking the juice from an ice pop. I looked away as he fed. After my time in the Hellpocalypse, the whole vampire feeding thing still gave me the creeps.

"I see you've had traumatic experiences with vampires. My apologies if this makes you uncomfortable." He paused to assess me anew. "Strange, that someone with such a hatred of my kind should be so close to the local coven leader."

I turned to look at him, swallowing bile as he licked a fleck of blood from the corner of his mouth. "It's a more recent thing, actually."

"Does Luther know?"

I shook my head. "No, and I'd prefer to keep it that way."

"As you wish."

Germain sucked down the last of his bloody meal. Already his body had regenerated, blackened flesh flaking away to reveal new pink skin underneath.

"Sorry about your clothes," I said, not meaning it. I was still finding it hard to have empathy for a leech.

"Mere things that can easily be replaced. I'm much more concerned with discovering what your intended plan of action might be."

I squeezed the porch railing harder than I intended, causing it to creak. "First, I mean to find Remy DeCoudreaux. Then, I'm gonna beat him within an inch of his life and make him tell me who he's working with at the Circle."

"I may be able to help you with that. By now, Remy will know you tracked me back to Austin. We *could* use that to our advantage—"

Germain let the implication of his words hang in the air. I considered what he was suggesting, wondering yet again if I should trust him. Without checking with Luther, I really had no sure way of knowing whether he was on the level.

Well, there's one way to find out.

"Alright, Saint Germain—let's see if you're telling me the truth."

THE NEXT DAY, I was back in New Orleans at the vamp bar, waiting for one of Silvère's flunkies to let Remy know I was here. The coven leader's major domo—or bodyguard, or whatever the hell he was—had refused to let me in, at least not until he got the okay from his boss. Currently, he was standing in the doorway giving me the stink eye while he waited for word from his maker.

"Haven't you guys heard of cell phones? Texts? Emails? It'd be a lot faster than sending someone, you know."

Silence.

I scowled. "Have it your way. I'm going to grab a beer—and I'm putting it on your tab."

Silvère simply stood and stared at me, hands clasped loosely in front of him, shoulders back, a look of smoldering intensity on full display. Obviously, he wasn't a member of my fan club. I didn't care, really—not many vamps would be after I was done with this sad, sorry mess.

I sauntered to the bar to order a pint of Abita, glowering at anyone who so much as looked at me sideways. Every hard stare I received made me question the wisdom of what I was about to do. We'd decided the best course of action was to convince the New Orleans coven leader I'd killed Germain. "Immolation by sunlight spell" was my cover story. That way, Remy wouldn't expect to receive any physical evidence of the act.

Just in case, we'd faked a video of me killing the coven leader's rival. Germain himself had provided the illusory effects for that—and rather convincingly, in fact. His vampire power was alchemy, a weird talent if ever there was one, but one that turned out to be useful in this instance.

I'd triggered the sunlight spell at the exact moment Germain had released an alchemical smoke screen. On video, it looked like he'd been immolated, while in reality the smoke had protected him from most of the effects of my magic. Before the smoke could clear, the old vamp zipped out of frame, leaving a smoking pile of human bone and ashes in his place. I had *not* asked Germain where he'd gotten them.

Personally, I thought the video was convincing enough to fool DeCoudreaux. Hopefully, said "evidence" of Germain's demise and my carefully-concocted story would be enough to get me on the inside with the coven.

Too bad it required me to go alone into the lion's den.

Don't think about what could go wrong. Focus on getting it right.

Once I'd gained Remy's trust, I planned to snoop around and discover the identity of his accomplice. Failing that, I'd abduct and torture him until he revealed that person's identity, and that of every other vamp who was involved in the scheme. Then, I'd ruthlessly hunt them down, one by one, until not a single member of their cabal was left standing.

Was brutality the only option? No, not by a long shot.

However, it *was* the most efficient option. But was it necessary?

Fuck. Yes.

Hell on Earth was coming, and I was the only thing standing in its way. I'd do anything—and sacrifice anything—to prevent that chain of events from coming to pass. I'd risk my reputation, my friendships, and even my life. I would not let them win, not while I still drew breath.

Speaking of my reputation—even if I survive this, that'll be fucked for sure.

It was a foregone conclusion that I'd be despised by vampire society after all was said and done. Wanton slaying of vampire-kind would do that for a hunter. The one good thing I had going for me now was that I had an ally—*if* Germain could be trusted. Perhaps with he and I working toward the same goals, his involvement would at least partially excuse the actions I was about to take.

I leaned against the wall near the bar, sipping my beer and scanning the crowd in case someone decided to try me. As far as I was concerned, every vamp here was a potential enemy. I got a few more hard stares, but the patrons left me alone.

A pretty, careworn barmaid walked up to me with a tray full of empties propped against her waist. "Remy'll see you now."

I nodded, downed my beer, and set the empty bottle on her tray. "Keep the change."

She sneered, cursing at me as I headed to the back. Not wanting to take any chances, I stealth-shifted along the way. Upon reaching my destination, I discovered that the door had been left open, but Silvère was gone. I glanced down the hall and casually checked my flanks, wondering whether I should enter or bolt. Then, Mr. Silent stepped out of a doorway twenty feet from me, beckoning me to approach. I didn't like being beckoned, so I stared at him for a few seconds, then headed in.

Silvère stood at parade rest just outside a nondescript metal doorway. I gave the mute a look that made his lip twitch, then turned and looked into the room.

It was a small office filled with grey metal furniture, a few file cabinets, stacked boxes, and not much else. Piles of receipts littered the desk, and cases of beer and liquor sat in the corners or against the walls—some open, some sealed. The way I'd come in was my only exit.

Remy sat behind the desk, hands clasped behind his head with his legs kicked up. "Tell me you have some good news, druid."

I glanced over my shoulder at Silvère, just to fix his position in my mind. "Depends on what you'd call good," I said as my eyes flicked back to the coven leader. "Germain's dead, if that's the answer you're looking for."

Remy's eyebrows knitted together as he steepled his fingers. "Oh? That's interesting. And tell me, how did this come to pass?"

"I tracked him to Austin, then I killed him. I have it on video if you want to see."

"Video—I'm sure that would be very entertaining, but I'm not the type to enjoy dramatizations and acting."

My left eyebrow shot up. "Dramatizations? Are you accusing me—"

Remy held up a hand. "That's exactly what I'm accusing you of, druid. I had you followed, you see. And just a few hours ago at sundown, my people spotted Germain alive and well at the farmhouse where you left him."

———

Busted.

"Does this mean I don't get my incentive bonus?" I asked, readying a spell in my left hand.

Two things happened next. First, I sensed movement behind me in the hall. And second, I saw Remy's hand slip under the desk. There was a "click," then a sheet of thick, tinted glass slammed down between us, effectively walling him off from my side of the office. He stood behind the desk, straightening the cuffs on the expensive silk shirt he wore.

I glanced at the doorway, where at least three vamps stood in fire-retardant jumpsuits and motorcycle helmets with dark, UV-protective visors. They wore matching Nomex gloves and held electric stun batons in their hands. Based on the additional footsteps I heard, at least a half-dozen more were lining up out of view in the hallway.

I heard Remy chuckle through the speakers overhead. "I am sorry it had to happen like this, cher, but I was suspicious of you from the moment you showed up unannounced in my city. And though I did get my hopes up after the mayhem you caused at Germain's mansion, ultimately you failed the test."

I sniffed and rubbed my nose, mostly to cover the few words I was mumbling as I prepared another spell. I tilted my head toward the hallway. "And them? I suppose they're simply here to escort me from the building?"

The coven leader smiled and shook his head. "I'm afraid my business partner has requested that I deliver you to him as soon as possible, and preferably alive. He didn't say *how* alive, though—which provides me with a bit of leeway, thankfully."

So, his accomplice is male. That'll narrow things down a bit.

"You should know, Remy—once I'm out of here, I'm coming after you."

A hidden door swung open behind the vampire. "If you can manage to escape, you are welcome to try. Goodbye, Colin McCool."

Secret switches, hidden doors, drop-down bullet-proof glass —all this guy lacks is a monocle and a cat in his lap.

The coven leader stepped through the doorway and was gone, the door swinging closed behind him. He was out of my reach, for the moment. Even if I busted through the glass, I suspected the walls beyond would be reinforced concrete behind the plaster and wood facade. I could fight, but I was trapped and outnumbered. If I managed to fight my way through these clowns, I'd still be surrounded by dozens of potential hostiles.

That left me with but one other option—escape. I pulled an object from my Bag, transferring magical energy into it from the second spell I'd prepared as I dropped it to the ground. Then, I leapt straight up, covering my head with my hands and hoping my gamble would pay off.

Plaster, wood lath, and floor planking shattered as I burst through the ceiling and landed in a crouch just to the side of the jagged hole I'd made. I glanced below, waiting until Remy's shock troops had begun to file in before I leaned away from the opening. I triggered the spell and my makeshift frag grenade exploded, peppering the vamps with shrapnel.

The device was nothing more than an M-80 firecracker with silver beads glued to its outer shell, but it became a deadly weapon with a small magical boost of power. While the vamps were protected from fire by their Nomex suits, the material would do nothing to stop speeding projectiles. Several of the silver pellets pinged off the glass, some shot up through the hole, and the rest hit targets below at random.

I didn't wait to see how my pursuers fared, instead opting to get the hell out of Dodge just as fast as my Fomorian-powered legs could carry me. Heading left as I exited the room, I ran toward what I thought was the front of the building. I spied a window at the end of the hallway, boarded up but thankfully not bricked over. By the time I sprinted toward it, my remaining pursuers were already hot on my heels.

Hitting the window at speed in this form was a bit like crashing through balsa wood and sugar glass. While my human skin sustained a few superficial cuts, my Fomorian flesh beneath proved more than a match for the glass and lumber. I shot through the opening and out into the night with the intention of landing in a dead run so I could get a head start on my pursuers.

But rather than finding a stretch of solid tarmac outside to land on, instead there was a magic portal, roughly ten feet across and hovering just above the surface of the street. Already airborne, I had no means of altering my trajectory, so I readied another spell as I plummeted through the portal into the inky blackness beyond.

15

Portals were heavy-duty magic, which meant I wasn't dealing with a bush league practitioner here. Chances were good they'd be waiting on the other side, ready to ambush me with a spell designed to knock me out or otherwise incapacitate me.

Well, this is fucked.

My only chance would be simultaneous retaliation with enough juice to overcome their wards and knock them out. If I was really lucky, I'd recover before they did, in which case I'd dispose of them while they were still incapacitated. I prepped one hell of a lightning spell in one hand and drew my pistol in the other. My plan was to fry them and plant one between their eyes—that was, if they weren't protected by a projectile barrier.

As I plunged through the portal, cold air hit me like a wall of ice. To my shock and horror, there was *nothing* on the other side. Nothing but empty space, that is, because I found myself plummeting out of the sky in the dead of night, from what I estimated to be a distance of many thousands of feet above the Earth. I immediately began tumbling head over heels in dizzying, random rotations, and the stars and moon traded places with the dark earth below with every revolution.

As I approached terminal velocity, I flailed frantically in an attempt to stabilize my descent. Having never gone skydiving, it took several seconds to determine the optimal position for my limbs, one that would flatten me out and stabilize my fall. Once I stopped spinning, I instantly took stock of my situation. While the ground below was nothing more than a dark-gray blob marked here and there by patches and pinpricks of light, it appeared to be rushing up fast. It didn't take much critical thinking to intuit that whoever had sent me through that portal knew *exactly* what they were doing.

And whoever it is, they must know a hell of a lot about me.

I'd fallen from some fairly precipitous heights, back when I was still blaming myself for Jesse's death. During that dark time, I'd tried to kill myself in dozens of different ways, and one of them was by jumping from the tallest buildings I could find. Unfortunately, my Hyde-side had taken over in every instance, saving me from flattening myself like a pancake via gravity and inertia. I didn't remember any of what happened on those occasions, only that I'd wake up somewhere far away with my clothes in shreds, lamenting the fact that the part of me I hated most wouldn't let me die.

Having jumped off both the Frost Bank building and the Fairmont, I knew I could survive falls of five hundred to six hundred feet while in my full Fomorian form. And while that was only about a third of the distance it took to hit terminal velocity in free fall, when I'd hit I was doing about one hundred miles per hour. I knew, because I did the math after I went back to look at each of the impact craters I'd made.

Skydivers in controlled free fall reached speeds of about one-hundred-twenty miles per hour, which meant that if I could shift before I hit the earth below, I'd probably survive. I'd be out of commission while my body healed from the impact, but I'd live. This realization caused me to again reflect that the portal caster knew things about me that only Finnegas, Jesse, and my clued-in lycanthrope therapist could have known.

But I could suss that out later. Right now, I needed to focus on surviving the fall. Knowing that a full shift was my only option, I pulled my Craneskin Bag off and shoved my phone and jacket inside, then I let it flutter away in the wind. The strap would tear as I shifted, so chances were good I'd lose it as I fell anyway. Besides, the thing was semi-sentient, and it had an odd way of showing up again whenever I lost it or had it taken from me. If I was lucky, it'd appear after I'd been locked up by my soon-to-be captors.

Gravity waits for no man. Time to get this show on the road.

I was already shifting to my full Fomorian form as I did the calculations in my head.

Let's see, fifty-six meters a second times twenty seconds

equals about eleven hundred meters—times three-point-two-eight equals about thirty-seven-hundred feet.

Fuck.

Here's to hoping they dropped me from above five-thousand feet.

As I felt the change begin, I did my best to keep my eyes open and on the ground below. I'd lose stability due to the shift every so often, and I'd tumble through the air until I could recover enough to stabilize myself again. Each time it happened, the ground would be that much closer.

Shit, but it's coming up at me fast.

It's weird, the things that go through your head when you think you might die. I wondered who would get Crowley's car back to him. I wondered whether Maureen would be able to keep the junkyard going after my stipend stopped coming in, and whether Bells would miss me when I was gone. I thought about Jesse, and worried that her condition would continue to worsen, and I even momentarily considered whether Finnegas would try to claim the druid grove.

Gross.

It'd never happen, of course. Jesse was like a daughter to him, and he'd find the idea of coupling with her even more repulsive than I did. He might try to petition the Dagda to reverse what had been done, but I doubted the old man could muster enough magic to dimension-hop his way to Underhill. That meant he'd be left with only two options, and neither of them good.

He could let her live and hope she wouldn't become a menace to both mundanes and the World Beneath. *Fat chance of that.* Or, he could join forces with Maeve to destroy Jess, before she became a minor deity in her own right.

Maeve would do it, no doubt about it. She'd happily annihilate anything that threatened her demesne. I knew this, because she'd used me to do just that—more than once, in fact. Maeve was manipulative and merciless that way.

A lot went through my head in the twenty seconds or so that it took me to shift. Once the process was complete, all that was left was the waiting, and that didn't take long at all. Seconds before impact, I realized that I was falling toward Buescher State Park, near where that strange zombie outbreak had occurred.

Damn, I should have thought to check the area near the research labs—

The ground rushed up to meet me in a cruel, bloody, jarring embrace before I could complete that thought. Then, I thought no more.

WHEN I CAME TO, I was bound hand and foot in chains and shackles, hanging in midair three feet off the ground. The room was dark, but I could make out concrete walls that appeared to be new as well as a plethora of magic glyphs and runes. These had been marked in elaborate patterns, weaving an intricate web of anti-magic and talent-dampening wards designed to prevent the casting of spells—and the use of innate magical talents.

Like shifting, for example. Fucking hell, but I am starting to hate this person.

Weaving a levitation spell into an anti-magic field must've been crazy-hard to do, another indication that my captor was a magic-user of no small talent. Interestingly, I noticed an oval area on the wall ahead of me as my eyes adjusted to the light. It was roughly seven feet by three, completely devoid of symbols.

The purpose of that bare spot on the wall was apparent, as my cell lacked both doors and windows. I realized the only source of light came from the weak glow of the wards on the walls, which increased when I struggled to shift or use magic and faded almost to nothing between attempts.

As I hung there assessing my situation, I realized that I really needed to piss.

"Hey! Anyone out there? My eyeballs are floating—can you bring me a bucket or something?"

No answer. My hands were shackled, but I could move them as freely as my chains allowed. The cuffs around my wrists were connected to those around my ankles, so I couldn't scratch my nose—but I could at least reach my junk.

I shrugged and unzipped my now shredded jeans. Then, I whipped it out and pissed all over the cell's floor.

"Oh, man—what a relief," I said, to myself as much as to my captors.

I was certain they were listening and monitoring me, if only to see if I could figure out a way to counter their spells. I couldn't, of course, because it took magic to counter magic—and right now, I was completely cut off from every arcane skill I possessed.

"Wonder what I'm supposed to do when I have to take a shit?" I muttered.

At that, the empty oval on the wall in front of me sparked to life around the edges, pale silver magic dancing in an outline around the rapidly-forming portal. Then, the wall disappeared, opening like a window onto a decrepit office space. A hooded figure stood there, illuminated by the flickering fluorescent lights above. I couldn't make out their identity, because my captor's face was obscured in shadow deep within that hood.

"The thing awakes," a raspy man's voice said. "If only to soil its bed."

The man was tall and skeletal, and hunched slightly like an aged person. Dark, voluminous robes covered him head to foot, made from some sort of rough material that reminded me of Obi-Wan's robes in Episode IV. The sleeves were long enough to hide his hands as they draped at his sides, and the length of the hem was such that it nearly touched the floor. I could make out the toes of a pair of sensible tan work boots beneath the robe, but nothing more.

"Not exactly like you're putting me up at the Sheraton," I quipped. "I mean, there's no mini-fridge to raid, no chocolate left on my pillow, no ice water by my bed—what kind of half-assed operation are you running here, anyway?"

The man stood silent for a moment before answering. "Playing the fool, as ever," he croaked in that same strained voice. "What a waste of space you are—the epitome of human detritus. It never ceases to amaze, how the gods love gifting power to those who have no idea what to do with it."

He coughed, making a wheezing, racking sound. As he raised his hand to cover his mouth with a handkerchief, I noticed he wore black doeskin gloves. My attention was drawn to his right hand, as it appeared to be twisted and deformed—claw-like, even. Such was the deformity that it was readily apparent, even though his hands were fully concealed.

"I take it you're the person on the Council who's working with the vamps."

"I am using them, yes, just as I'm using the vast resources of the Circle."

Well, that's interesting. He doesn't identify as one of them. "But to what end, if you don't mind me asking? I mean, I'll be dead soon anyway, right?"

The man laughed, causing another fit of coughing and wheezing. "Kill you? Hardly. I intend to let you rot here, slowly, while I watch. I can access this viewing portal from anywhere, you see. It works both ways, so you can witness the destruction I'm about to unleash, and I can enjoy your misery as you remain locked in your prison, helpless to intervene."

"No torture? No electric shock, hot wax on the nipples, or plucking out my pubes one by one?"

"Crude, as always," he remarked with disdain. "No— although I'd enjoy torturing you, of that you can be certain. However, I can't run the risk of triggering your ri—your change."

Little Freudian slip there. Damn, but he does know a lot about me.

"Ooo-kay," I said with a frown. "Seems like you've really gone out of your way to make this happen. Why all the hate?"

My mysterious captor harrumphed. "In due time, boy. In due time. Now, I'm off to kill someone you love. I'll leave you to guess who it is."

The portal winked out, and again I was left alone in the near dark, wondering if he'd make good on his threat.

SOMETIME LATER, I heard scratching noises. The sounds continued for a while, only to be replaced by a faint knocking on the walls of my cell. Although my hearing wasn't quite as sharp in my fully human form, I still retained all the benefits of being a born human champion. That meant that while I couldn't hear as well as, say, a 'thrope, my ears were still pretty damned sharp.

As I strained to detect who or what was making the noise, I could barely make out a man's voice, mumbling and cursing in English and French.

"*Fait chier!* No, that's not it. *Bordel de merde*, but this bastard knew what he was doing."

"Germain? Germain, is that you?" I shouted.

"Colin? Thank goodness. The tracking spell brought me to the middle of nowhere, then the signal disappeared.

If it wasn't for accidentally stumbling across that ugly bag of yours, I'd never have known you were here."

Accidentally—if he only knew. "And just where is 'here'?" I asked.

"A moment, please. I must concentrate if I'm to get you out."

I waited for what seemed like an interminable period of time, all while listening to Saint Germain's cursing and mumbling as he puzzled a way to get me out of my prison. Finally, after who knows how long, he said something in French that I assumed meant "eureka!" Then, there was a boom that shook the walls followed by a sizzling noise that gradually grew louder—and closer.

"Close your eyes. I'm using acid to break through the walls."

"Acid? What the fuck? Germain—"

"Just a moment!" he replied in a polite voice, ever the gentleman.

Thankfully, alchemical acid did not start dripping from the ceiling overhead. Instead, the barren oval on the wall in front of me began to melt away, starting in the middle and working out toward the edges. As soon as the stuff had done its work, Germain's head appeared upside down outside the hole in the wall.

"*Est-ce que tu me fais confiance maintenant,* druid?" he asked.

"If you're asking if I trust you now, the answer is yes. Now, if you don't mind, could you please help me down from here?"

Germain wrinkled his nose and sniffed. "Do you smell that?"

"Sorry, the wards on the walls are blocking my enhanced senses. I can't cast or shift. What is it you smell?"

"Besides your urine? Blood. Those spells were painted in blood. They've been there a while, apparently, because the smell is very faint, but quite unmistakable."

"Which tells us that whoever did this has been planning it for a long time."

"Indeed." Germain rubbed his chin, which was weird since he was still hanging upside down. "I wonder…"

He stuck his index finger through the opening, slowly and gingerly. As soon as his flesh crossed the invisible barrier made by the opening, it turned to ash. The vampire snagged his hand back, minus the tip of his finger.

"*Bon sang!*" he declared. "It seems these spells negate all forms of magic, even that which sustains the second life. I'll have to get you out some other way. A moment, please."

Germain disappeared, and I yelled after him. "You keep saying that, yet I'm still cuffed and dangling in midair!"

The vampire returned shortly with a long length of loblolly pine. "I had to borrow this from a tree. I hope that doesn't insult your druid sensibilities," he said as he extended the branch to me from outside the cube.

"I've never been much of a tree-hugger. So long as you get me out, we're good."

I grabbed the end of the tree limb with both hands. Germain began pulling me out, angling the limb so he could pull it up and out of the hole he'd dug to reach me. As soon as my head and arms were out, gravity took over and I dropped, my legs and rear end flopping over the edge of the hole. The vamp grabbed me by the arms and pulled me the rest of the way out, then he snapped my shackles off me like they were made of cheap plastic.

After we'd both climbed on top of the concrete cell—a cube roughly ten feet square that had been buried two feet below ground—I brushed the dirt off and stretched.

"Ah, that's better. I was staring to worry about what I was going to do when I had to take a crap."

Germain eyed me with distaste as he tossed me my Craneskin Bag. "How rude. Now, we should be going. Dawn is coming, and I had to kill a half-dozen Circle operatives on my way here. The woods are crawling with them, and I assume when their dead are discovered, more will be on their way."

"We can't go back to your place, because that hideout has been blown. And if we go back to the junkyard, they're just going to attack during the daytime when I'm on my own. Sorry, but I can't put my people in jeopardy for your sake." I paused and held my hands up. "No offense."

"None taken. Let me reach out to Luther. He'll certainly provide us with refuge until we can plan our next steps."

"Scratch that. I don't want to get Luther involved. Not yet, anyway."

Germain looked at me askance. "I see."

"It's not like that." *Why am I explaining myself to a vamp?*

"Anyway, I have someplace we can go. Did you bring a car?"

The old vampire crossed his arms. "Do you think I turned into a bat and flew here?"

"Right. Give me the keys—I'll drive. Just in case the sun comes up before we get there."

16

We arrived at Crowley's farmhouse just before sunrise. Germain indicated that while he didn't necessarily need to rest during the day, doing so allowed him to operate at peak effectiveness. I assured the old vamp that my friend would be able to accommodate his particular needs.

As we drove down the long driveway that led to the farmhouse and silo, Germain let out a low whistle. To all appearances, the grain silo was still toppled on its side, and the barn looked like it was nothing but ashes and memories.

"*Sacredieu*, what happened here?"

"I sort of got into a fight with Crowley's pet giant."

Germain's eyebrow shot up as he looked at me. "And you're still friends?"

"It's a long story. Although the place looks trashed, in reality Crowley fixed it up good as new. He maintains an illusion to hide it all, says it keeps the Circle from poking around."

"The Circle? Why would they be interested in him?"

"He used to work for them. I think they might want him back. Not many of their wizards can hold a candle to Crowley, after all."

"You have interesting friends, druid."

"Tell me about it," I said as I parked the car and got out.

A "door" through the illusion was waiting for us, just as it had been the last time I visited. I motioned for Germain to follow and walked through.

"Impressive," the vamp said from behind me. "I haven't seen anyone cast an illusion this substantive and convincing since—well, ever."

I looked over my shoulder. "He was trained in Underhill, if that tells you anything."

"Changeling?"

I nodded. "It's a bit of a sore spot, so avoid bringing it up if you can."

"*Mon dieu*, druid. 'Interesting' might have been an understatement."

I chuffed as I stopped short at the entry. Turning my attention back to the tower, I cupped my hands to yell at the upper-story windows.

"Yo, Crowley! Got a vampire here—are your wards going to fry him when we walk in?"

A disembodied voice spoke at a conversational level right next to me. "Already taken care of, Colin. Please, come in and make yourselves comfortable. I'll be down shortly."

"He must be in his lab." A small explosion echoed from an open window three stories above us. "Yep. C'mon, I'll find you a place to sack out."

Crowley's voice replied again, this time from the entry. "There's a trap door under the rug in the sitting room. It leads to the cellar, where I grow certain varieties of rare mushrooms. The place is a bit damp, but you'll find a cot and some blankets in the corner. Mr. Germain can sleep there undisturbed until nightfall."

Germain's brow furrowed, and I shrugged. "I didn't tell him, honest. But if I had to guess, he's been scrying on me. Crowley has a thing for my girlfriend."

"Ex-girlfriend," Crowley's voice replied from somewhere nearby.

"Yeah, yeah. Rub it in, why don't you," I muttered. Germain chuckled at my reaction. I was exhausted and irritated, so I called him to task over it. "A bit childish for someone of your vintage, isn't it? Finding humor in another person's discomfort, I mean."

He bowed his head in apology, although the smile on his face lingered. "It's just that you've seemed so unflappable to this point. It is amusing to me that this friend of yours can get under your skin."

"I'm glad someone finds it funny, 'cause I sure don't. I'd trust Crowley with my mother's life, but hell if the guy doesn't get on my nerves. Anyway, let's get you settled in. I still have a few phone calls to make."

"Sunrise is upon us anyway, so I will take my leave until the evening hours."

"See ya in a few, Germain. Oh, and thanks for bailing

my ass out. Not many would've risked it for someone who just tried to kill them."

Saint Germain cocked his head. "I've been around a long time, Monsieur McCool. I know when someone is worth saving."

I didn't know what to say to that, so I said nothing as the old vamp headed down to the cellar. Once he pulled the door closed behind him, I pulled out my phone and hit one of my speed-dial numbers. The call went to voicemail, so I ended the call and dialed again. I repeated that cycle three times until someone picked up on the other end.

"You must have balls the size of bowling balls, to be calling me right now," Bells said.

"You'd know," I quipped, regretting it immediately. "Wait, don't hang up! I'm sorry for that—for everything, really."

Bells sighed. "If you're trying to make up with me, it's not going to work."

"I'm..." I felt low as hell for doing it, but I figured I may as well spit it out. "I need your help."

Long pause. "Of course you do."

"It's majorly important, Bells. Like, world-ending important."

"It always is with you, Colin. And while you're out saving the world, the people you care about suffer. What's sad is you're too blind to see it."

I could've said a lot in response to that. I could've said she was a jealous lover, that it wasn't my fault the Dagda's druid oak had reincarnated my ex, and that I didn't deserve the way she'd treated me over Jesse. I could've said that I'd never cheated on her, and never would. I might have said that my loyalty was complete and unquestioning, and when I committed, I meant it—so it was unfair of her to question my fidelity.

I also might have said that I'd never asked to be Colin McCool, pawn and puppet in the machinations of fae, gods, and immortals. I could've protested that I'd never asked to have a vampire dwarf try to kill me, or be the sole remaining direct descendent of Fionn MacCumhaill, or to have been chosen by the world's greatest—and only surviving—"good" druid to become a scion of justice in the fight against evil.

But I didn't say any of that. All I said was, "I know."

Because sometimes it's more important to be sorry than to be right.

Belladonna's voice was whisper-quiet on the other end of the line. "Tell me what you need. If it's in my power, I'll do it."

SHE SET up the meeting with the Circle's High Council for three o'clock that afternoon. I requested that time on purpose, because I didn't want Germain tagging along and suspected he'd fight me about it. It was a dangerous gambit, confronting the Cold Iron Circle's High Council on their home turf, and Germain would likely insist on being my backup.

Unfortunately, I couldn't risk it. His participation would likely set the other Council members off, such was their hatred for the supernatural races. The Council was made up of xenophobes and bigots, and people with deep prejudices despised being helped by the people they hated. They saw me as a supernatural threat akin to the fae, vampires, and 'thropes, so it'd be hard enough for them to accept a warning from yours truly. Add in the presence of an elder vampire, and I'd be lucky to avoid an all-out fight.

I showed up at their glass high-rise building downtown at a quarter to three, because I didn't want to piss them off for once and being late might do exactly that. When I walked into the front lobby, I was immediately escorted to a high-security room by three hunter-mage teams in full battle-rattle. They relieved me of my Craneskin Bag and every weapon I carried—even the cold-iron hunting knife I kept sheathed at the small of my back.

"C'mon, fellas—the knife? Really?" I feigned a sudden realization. "Oh, I get it. One of your Council members must be hiding some fae blood in the old family tree. Can't have cold iron around them if that's the case, right? Don't worry—it'll be our little secret," I said with a wink.

One of the hunters didn't find that funny at all, and he butt-stroked me in the back to prove it. "Shut up and start walking. Elevator is straight ahead."

I'd already stealth-shifted, so it didn't even hurt. But I didn't want them to know that. The Circle wasn't aware that I'd just spent six months in the Hellpocalypse learning to be a stone-cold Fomorian killer. They had no idea I could shift while maintaining my human appearance, so those fuckers thought they were safe.

How wrong they were.

I marched to the elevator with two goons in front, two behind, and one on each side. The mages had spells at the ready, standard battle magic stuff, while the hunters had M-4 rifles held at port arms, set to "pew-pew-pew" on the fire selectors. Obviously, they were not fucking around.

After we piled in, the lead flunkie swiped a keycard on the control panel. The doors closed with a whoosh, and I felt the distinct sensation of a magical ward locking itself shut. Within seconds, the elevator car zoomed all the way to the top floor and kept on going. There were buttons on the panel for fifty floors plus the penthouse, but the readout had already hit fifty-nine with no signs of stopping.

I clapped my hands like a child. "Hooray! We're going to Olympus! I just *love* those books. Do you think Aphrodite will be there?" I waggled my eyebrows suggestively. "Hubba-hubba—am I right, fellas?"

Their only response to that remark was another butt stroke to the back.

"Shut the fuck up," the lead hunter growled.

The door dinged at the ninety-ninth floor, and we exited into a rather mundane-looking reception and waiting area. The floors were cheap carpet and laminate, the walls were painted in drab, neutral colors, and industrial office chairs were lined up against the walls to either side. Roughly twenty feet ahead, a pretty receptionist sat behind a rather large metal and glass desk—

the kind you might get at your local office warehouse store.

"Wow, you guys went all out on this place," I remarked, kneeling to rap on the floor. "I bet the bean counters were pissed that you went with *real* Pergo—although I'd have gone with the Pewter Oak instead of the Cocoa Aspen. Would've brought out the flecks of slate blue in the indoor-outdoor carpet."

The guards ignored me, likely deciding that I wasn't worth the effort. They each took up posts around the area, eyes and weapons trained on yours truly. I sniffed and approached the receptionist, who didn't bother to take her eyes off her computer screen.

I leaned forward and took a peek. She was surfing some celeb gossip site online. "The Duchess of Cambridge is preggers again? That little minx!"

She frowned at the intrusion, angling her monitor away from me. "Have a seat, please. The Council will call for you when they're ready."

"I don't suppose there's a bathroom around here, is there? I went a little hog wild on Taco Tuesday at Rosa's, and man, that *queso flameado* is coming back to haunt me." I leaned over the desk and whispered conspiratorially. "I might have even had an accident in my pants."

The receptionist continued to ignore me. "Have a seat, please. The Council will call for you shortly."

"Fine." I flopped down in a nearby chair and grabbed a copy of *Popular Magichanics* from a stack of periodicals on a side table. And I waited—and waited—and waited.

Thirty minutes later, I started tearing out pages of the

magazine to make paper airplanes, which I launched in the air two and three at a time. Using a little druid magic, I kept them in the air with artificial updrafts while weaving in some hidden spell work each time I renewed the wind pattern. After I had about a half-dozen of them going, I began staging dogfights between them, adding my own sound effects and narration, Snoopy and the Red Baron style, just to annoy the guards.

"Here's the World War One flying ace high over France in his Sopwith Camel, searching for the dastardly Red Baron! I must bring him down! Rat-tat-tat-tat-tat-tat-tat— oh no, I've been hit!" I made an explosion sound effect, followed by my best imitation of a diving bi-plane's engine whine. "Gah, more krauts just appeared over the horizon. I'm out of ammo, looks like it's banzai time—"

On cue, the planes flew at each of the guards all at once, triggering a minor cantrip that caused their tails to smolder and release tiny trails of smoke behind them. Two of the hunters merely batted the planes out of the air, while one of the mages burned a plane to ashes with an immolation spell. The other three dodged the planes as best they could, but I kept them flying around in circles, nose-diving the guards before swooping away.

Once the guards were suitably distracted, I marched past the secretary and straight into the High Council's meeting room.

SEVERAL VOICES WERE ARGUING as I approached the door.

"—not even sure if he's human anymore," a high, nasally female voice said.

A deep male voice responded. "He's a menace to humanity, that's what he is. Why we haven't eliminated him already is a mystery to me."

Another female voice chimed in—this one old and raspy, but strong and steady as well. "We tried that already, or don't you remember? Gunnarson was supposed to be my successor on the Council, yet the druid apprentice sifted him like wheat. Pfah! And here we are discussing a parley with a known supernatural who has killed dozens of our people, not to mention a high-level operative. If you would have listened to me ten years ago—"

The door was open, so I marched right in and pulled up a chair as all eyes turned toward me.

"Hey, folks, don't mind me." I sat down and propped my feet up on their huge, cheap-ass conference table, and laced my fingers behind my head. "Please, continue planning my assassination. I can wait until you're finished."

Nasal-Voice stood up and banged her hand on the table. "Why—this is highly irregular. Guards!"

The guards were way ahead of her, already storming into the room by the time she'd finished her first sentence. The lot of them surrounded me, at which point they began lifting me out of my chair by my arms and legs.

"Fuck, but he's heavy!" one of them muttered under his breath.

The old lady made the smallest motion with one hand, and the guards froze. "Leave him be. If he wanted to cause any real trouble, he'd have done it already. I may not like him, and I might even want him dead. But I'm also curious to hear what he has to say."

Like the rest of the Council, she was draped in hooded robes that concealed her identity, but not her age. Her hands were wrinkled and covered in liver spots, and her skin was paper-thin. Yet I noticed that neither her hands nor her voice shook when she spoke.

A male Council member voiced his protest. "Madam Chairwoman, do you really think it's wise to allow this cretin to barge in here like this? At the very least, he should be punished for his insolence."

The Chairwoman waited a few moments to respond. Even though I couldn't see her eyes, I knew that she was staring right at me, because I *felt* the weight of her gaze. You could have heard a pin drop in that room as the seconds ticked by. Finally, she spoke.

"Perhaps. But we should hear what he has to say."

"Sure you don't want to finish planning my death?" I asked, doe-eyed.

The Chairwoman was not amused. "That can wait. Please, speak your piece."

The guards dropped me back into my chair. I made a show of straightening my clothes and fixing my hair, if only to make them wait. Then, I stood and leaned forward, placing my hands on the conference table. I'd heard it was a "power move" that business people sometimes used in negotiations—at least, that's what Dr. Phil once said.

"Ahem. As I was saying..." I looked around at the guards. "Why don't you morons take a break and let the adults have the room?"

Their leader looked at the Chairwoman. She nodded and they filed out, but not without shooting me a few nasty looks on the way.

I popped the cuffs on my coat. "As I was saying—you have a traitor on your council."

17

The room erupted in a chorus of grumbling and protests, only to be silenced when the old Battleaxe —as I was beginning to think of her—raised her hand. "And just what leads you to believe we have a traitor in our midst?"

I didn't want to outright accuse one of them of stealing Balor's Eye from me, so I went with the facts as I knew them.

"Long story short? I recently went undercover inside the New Orleans coven. And why would I do that, pray tell? I did it to check out an anonymous tip that someone on your Council is working with the vamps."

"Preposterous!" Deep Voice shouted.

"Let him speak," the Battleaxe said.

"Now, here's where it gets tricky. My cover got blown, and Remy didn't take kindly to my tricking him. So, he sics a hit squad on me—not to kill me, mind you, but to capture me for his 'business partner.' I escaped by jumping out a second-story window, right into a portal that opened about ten thousand feet above Bastrop."

"Lies!" someone said.

I turned toward the voice, but couldn't tell who'd said it. All the Council members looked the same, and they were spelled up to cover any identifying scents as well. It had been a female voice, so I decided to focus on a slight figure who had curves in most of the right places.

"Tell me something, cupcake—how many mages do you know who could cast a portal ten-feet wide that opened up three miles above a very specific geographic location? Because I can tell you for a fact, whoever cast it knew what the hell they were doing—and they were waiting for me when I hit bottom."

"No one could survive a fall from that height," Deep Voice protested.

"He could," Battleaxe said as she turned toward me. "If he had time to shift. If your story is true, and you really did survive a fall from that height, that means you're getting better at controlling your ability to change forms."

I shrugged. "It takes over when I'm in danger. I'm sure you know that, because you have a whole dossier on me, just like you have on everyone you see as a threat to your"—I spread my hands wide, gesturing at the Council and the building around us—"whatever it is you have here."

Battleaxe's voice took on a serious tone. "You *are* a threat, Mr. McCool. Surely you realize that? Or have you forgotten about how Ms. Callahan died?"

She was referring to Jesse, of course. "Low blow much?

No, I haven't forgotten. But, you should know that my —*condition*—has become much more stable of late." I crossed my arms and pulled my shoulders back. "These days, the only thing I'm a threat to is anything that threatens me and mine. Gunnarson found that out the hard way, as did your man, Keane."

"And Lieutenant McCracken," Battleaxe replied.

"McCracken was a *good* man. You know as well as I do that Keane killed him to frame me, so he'd have an excuse to hunt me down. Of course, you had to disown your pet attack dog after he got off the leash. Wouldn't do for the Council to be seen *openly* breaking the deal you made with the other factions by trying to off the Justiciar. Never mind sacrificing one of their own in order to take out an enemy."

Battleaxe remained silent for several moments. "Continue your story, Mr. McCool."

Thus far, my plan had been to get the High Council together in one place so I could pick the mystery man out. Now that I was here, I realized that had been wishful thinking. At least three of the council members had remained silent through the entire proceedings, and about half of them sat with their hands hidden in their robes.

Even if I asked them to show me their hands, it wouldn't matter. It would only require a simple illusion spell to conceal any disfigurement. Claw hand or no, I couldn't rely on appearances to reveal the traitor's identity. Instead, I was going to have to force my enemy's hand if I wanted to expose the turncoat in their ranks—no pun intended.

I cleared my throat before continuing my story.

"Anyway, when I woke up after falling out of the sky, I was in some kind of cell. And let me tell you, this was no ordinary prison. For starters, the only way in or out was a portal. Plus, the whole thing was warded nine ways to Sunday with negation spells—the kind that cancel spell craft *and* shifter magic. Left me helpless as a newborn babe."

Nasal Voice laughed. "I'd say we need to find this mage and hire them."

I gave Nasal Voice a hard stare. "No need. The person who captured me is in this room." More shouts and protests ensued until Battleaxe settled them down. "Ask yourself, who else knows that much about my powers and weaknesses? Who else could have known how to capture me, and also have the power and motive to do it?"

"Could've been any number of entities," Deep Voice said. "From what I understand, you've pissed off the Fae, the Tuatha De Denann, and several minor gods and demigods from various pantheons. Not to mention all the creatures you hunted back when you freelanced with your girlfriend." He held a hand up as he'd made a faux pas. "My apologies—your *late* girlfriend."

I tsked. "You jackasses just don't get it, do you? Someone on this Council has been manipulating Circle resources and staff to take me down. Think about it—did any of you order Gunnarson to go after me? Or Keane? Even better, who promoted McCracken and appointed him to be my liaison?"

The room grew silent.

"What, no takers? Of course not—because none of you

knows who gave those orders. Or rather, one of you knows, but he's not talking." I looked at each of the Council members who'd chosen to remain silent.

"How do you know this person is a 'he'?" Battleaxe asked.

"Just a hunch. When he came to taunt me, my captor appeared to be male. But then again, that could've been an illusion. Hell, for all I know, Madam Chairwoman, it could have been you."

"It might have been at that, druid," she said with a certain degree of smugness in her voice. "But it wasn't. And I'm not about to tear this Council apart by starting a manhunt for some supposed traitor, based on the hearsay and wild speculations presented by a supernatural aberration such as yourself."

I squeezed the bridge of my nose. "Look, I know you all hate me—some more than others. But I'm telling you, something bad is coming—like catastrophically, world-ending bad—and the traitor on your Council is behind it."

Deep Voice chuckled, condescension in his voice. "Now he wants us to believe he can see the future."

My eyes hardened as I swept my gaze over each Council member in turn. "Believe me, or don't—but it *is* coming. And here's the truth: 'Not one stone here will be left on another; every one will be thrown down.'"

"Is that a threat?" Nasal Voice asked.

"A warning," I said. "Ignore it at your own peril."

Battleaxe pushed herself away from the table and stood. "We're done here, Mr. McCool. Security will show you out."

I sighed and hung my head. "No, Madam Chairwoman. I'm afraid we've only just begun."

UNBEKNOWNST TO THE COUNCIL, I had the mother of all magical barrier wards henna tattooed on me under my clothes. It was a trick I'd learned from Finnegas, and Crowley had been more than happy to do the honors. I believe his exact words were, "Of course—anything to irritate my former employers. And please, do give them my regards when you destroy their offices."

I slapped a hand to my chest and spoke the trigger word, activating the wards. Immediately, a thin barrier of dark, wispy shadow magic enveloped me from head to toe. As a magician, Crowley was easily a match for any of the Council members here. His work would ensure that their spells slipped and skittered off me for the precious twenty seconds or so that it would take me to shift.

The only problem was, shifting would warp the weaves, runes, and glyphs the shadow wizard had painted on my body. So, the further my transformation progressed, the less effective the magic would be in deflecting the Council's spells.

In short, this was going to hurt.

The Council members attacked as soon as I triggered the wards. *Well, that didn't take long.* They threw fireballs, cast lightning spells, and shot cones of frost and shards of ice at me all at once. While the impact pushed me back several feet, none of their spells were able to penetrate the magical shield. At least, not at first.

While the Council launched their initial onslaught, I was already starting to change. As I did, my skin stretched and morphed to accommodate my larger bone structure and swollen musculature. With every inch that my bones lengthened, with every increase in the circumference of my limbs, torso, and head, Crowley's spell weakened. Thus, the Council's attacks began to penetrate the shadow shield, bit by bit.

I was certainly a lot more resistant to damage in my Fomorian form. But until I achieved a complete transformation, I remained somewhat vulnerable to their attacks. Lucky for me, the Council failed to coordinate their attacks, and some of their spells veritably cancelled out the effects of others. Elemental magic was the "rock, paper, scissors" of the spell casting disciplines; thus, the fire spells negated the cold spells on contact and vice versa.

Still, other attacks hit their mark, and those grew more and more effective as the seconds ticked by. Electricity began to singe and burn my skin like a thousand tiny bee stings, and as the effects grew stronger, my muscles began to twitch and spasm. One of the wizards even got the bright idea to use an acid spell. As Crowley's shields began to fizzle out, drops of burning liquid leaked through gaps in the shadow magic, melting away pieces of my skin faster than I could heal.

I covered my eyes and face as best I could, bracing under the sustained attacks of the Council as the seconds ticked by.

The air around me smelled of ozone and acrid chemicals, and I was forced to hold my breath and shut my eyes for fear of splash and inhalation damage. I growled my rage and frustration as I completed the last stage of my change, the point when my skin thickened and hardened, sheathing me in a veritable layer of armor akin to kevlar or rhinoceros hide.

Yet their spells still did their work. As the last vestiges of my friend's magic died out, I suffered under the full force of the wizards' fury. Even though I'd managed to complete the change, I lay in a heap on the charred, singed, melted, and frost-rimed floor, seemingly cowering beneath the combined might of the Council.

Finally, I heard Battleaxe's voice rise above the din of elemental magic.

"Enough! You'll bring the building down if you continue in this manner. He's done for by now. Let security come in so they can bind him, and we'll dispose of him once we've placed dampening cuffs on him."

The sheer volume and ferocity of the Council's magical assault had kept any of their hunter-mage teams from entering the room, but now they filed in to surround me. I continued to lay on the floor, appearing to be nothing more than a shivering, smoldering heap. Once the teams had encircled me, a smile curled the corners of my crooked, deformed mouth.

Without looking up, I spoke aloud with menace in my voice.

"My turn."

I WAS SOMEWHAT magic-resistant in this form, especially against necromantic magic. For some reason, carrying the Eye around in my head for over a year had made it nearly impossible to use necromancy against me. Why, I had no idea—but it had saved my bacon back when the Dark Druid had tried to body snatch me.

Unfortunately, I wasn't nearly as resistant to other types of magic, but I was still a lot tougher than most. So, when the Council's flunkies cut loose on me with their spells, I didn't feel a thing. Sure, their bosses had enough juice to hurt me, but these guys weren't in the same league —not even close.

Most small-caliber rounds were also no match for my hide, which gave me another advantage. Fortunately for me, the hunter teams were packing black rifles chambered in 5.56. While the U.S. military's favorite caliber was fine for chewing up softer supernatural flesh, the tiny .223 caliber projectiles simply couldn't penetrate my thick, Fomorian skin.

I was tempted to tear off a section of the conference table and start swinging, but the truth was I hadn't come here to kill anyone. And while these morons *were* trying to kill me, or at least do me great bodily harm, they were just flunkies doing their jobs. I know, I know—so were the Nazis at Auschwitz. Still, an eye for an eye means every-body goes blind, so I decided to exercise some restraint.

I punched the floor with my huge, hammer-like right hand, sending out a shockwave that made the hunters and mages stumble. While they were recovering their balance, I grabbed their guns and twisted the barrels into pretzels.

Moving at near vampire speed, I gave each of the hunters and mages a "love tap" across the jaw or at the base of the skull. Not hard enough to kill, but plenty rough enough to take them out of commission.

This all happened in the span of a few seconds, and I snagged a body and tossed it at the nearest Council member as I finished. I was banking on the fact that they wouldn't fry or otherwise harm their favorite thugs to save their own asses. All I needed was a moment's distraction to finish enacting my plan, after all.

As the unconscious Circle operative flew toward his intended target, I followed right behind, hoping that the mage would only see one of his own people coming at him and not my huge ten-foot-tall ass. As I expected, the wizard reacted with a spell that froze the operative in mid-air. I dove under the suspended figure, closing the distance between me and his boss.

Rather than attacking the mage, I simply snatched away his robes. With my Fomorian strength, the whole garment tore off like one of those trick outfits on television. To my surprise, the individual I'd disrobed was none other than one of Austin's city council members, Darius Simmons. Simmons was a known slime ball who'd been accused of using government and campaign funds to fuel his lavish lifestyle. Yet he somehow managed to emerge from every scandal looking and smelling squeaky clean.

"Why am I not surprised?" I rumbled. "I wonder, who else among Austin's elite will I find beneath those hoods today?"

With that, the room broke out in sheer pandemonium.

Some Council members cast temporary invisibility spells on themselves as they fled from the room. Others opened portals through which they leapt to make their escape. Still others decided to renew their magical attacks against me, causing poor Darius to dive over the remains of the conference table so he didn't get fried.

Undeterred, I made a beeline for the next closest Council member.

Meanwhile, Battleaxe stood there looking at me, arms crossed and shoulders set as chaos erupted all around. I was too busy shielding my face from a fiery magical missile to catch exactly what she did next, but I did see her clutch her right fist. Instantly, an invisible force field slammed down around me, protecting me from the spells her fellow Council members had cast but also cutting me off from those who remained.

When I reached out to probe the barrier I detected something unique in it, a distinctive quality that sang to me like the song of my people. It was the Eye's magical signature, I was certain of it. I'd lived with that thing inside my head for over a year, and I could recognize its magic anywhere. She had it on her, and the Eye was helping her by boosting her containment spell.

Gotcha.

"Why, Madam Chairwoman," I said. "I do believe you're a liar, and a thief."

Rather than try to push the barrier back, I instead examined the weaves in the magical spectrum to find a weakness in the spell. Once I knew where to strike, I speared my hands into the barrier, forcing my fingers through as I attempted to rip it apart by strength and will alone. I strained my every muscle, exerting myself fully to tear a hole in the invisible cage so I could reach the one who'd cast it.

As soon as I'd made a large enough tear in the barrier, I hocked phlegm from the back of my throat and launched a loogie that hit her square in the chest.

I couldn't see her reaction, but I knew I'd pissed her off by the way her body stiffened. I redoubled my efforts to reach her, but before I could escape, she gestured as if shooing a fly away. Even as I was ripping her spell asunder, an unseen force wrapped itself around me like a giant hand. Then, it lifted me off the floor and tossed me through a nearby window.

18

I crash-landed on a nearby rooftop, suffering a few minor injuries but nothing that would be enough to bench me. After breaking into the roof access stairwell, I stealth-shifted and sprinted back to the Circle's HQ, looking like a typical Austin bum in my ripped, charred, and shredded clothing. I wasn't headed back to nab the Chairwoman, because she'd be long gone by now. I simply wanted to retrieve my things.

I burst through the front doors and sprinted to the holding cell adjacent to the now empty lobby, unlocking the door with a cantrip without slowing down. Once I'd verified the room was as empty as the lobby, I stuck my head out the door to see if the coast was clear. Security hadn't made it back down from their secret hideout above the seventy-umpteenth floor, but the indicator lights above the elevator doors said they were headed my way. After using another cantrip to fritz the elevators, I gathered my possessions and stuffed them inside my Bag before hauling ass down the street.

Once clear of the building and any potential pursuers, I turned completely human and headed into a gas station to change. While I was cleaning up, I set my phone on the sink and hit a number I had on speed-dial.

"Crowley, do you have it?"

"Yes, the signature is very distinct. After you reverted to your human form, the locator spell picked up a second, weaker Fomorian DNA signature immediately. It hasn't traveled far, however—only a few blocks. What do you want me to do?"

"Text me the address and have Germain call me as soon as he wakes."

"Do you want me to come along? I could be of use if you're going up against a member of the High Council."

I considered it, but didn't want him to expose his whereabouts to The Cold Iron Circle on my account. "No, but thanks. We'll handle it from here."

"Very well, then. I'll give Germain the message."

The wizard ended the call without so much as a fare thee well, which was typical of him. While he normally had impeccable manners, Crowley rarely wasted time on social niceties when dealing with me.

Ah, frenemies. Can't live with them, and can't shoot them when they hit on your girl—er, ex-girlfriend.

It was four o'clock, which meant I had some time to kill. My stomach was grumbling—shifting always made me hungry—so I decided to call a ride share and grab a meal before Germain woke from his nap. I was halfway through a huge barbecue beef rib and half a dozen sides at Terry Black's when my phone rang.

Unknown caller. This should be interesting.

"Speak."

The voice was disguised electronically. "I have vital information on your enemies. Meet me at Waterloo Park in thirty minutes, near the entrance to the flood control tunnel."

"Wait—"

The line went dead. *Shit.*

Waterloo Park was about a mile-and-a-half down the road. I could hoof it, but the Circle jerks were on the lookout for me and I didn't want to risk being spotted. I called another ride share and had them drop me off at the southeast corner of the park. When no one was looking, I cast a "look away, go away" spell, then jumped over the side of the spillway, down to the creek bed and the tunnel entrance.

The place was still under construction, part of a flood control and revitalization initiative that had cost the city nearly $200 million. Waller Creek Tunnel was a huge, man-made aqueduct built to prevent flash-flooding in the downtown watershed. Roughly a mile long and thirty feet in diameter, it was designed to divert rainwater and run-off directly into Ladybird Lake.

Why my anonymous caller wanted to meet me here was a mystery to me, but it smelled like a trap. Cursing my curious nature, I pulled a long sword from my Bag and headed for the tunnel entrance.

As I neared the tunnel, I saw a dark figure slip past the

heavy iron grates that were designed to prevent debris and humans from entering. At first, I thought the person had gone incorporeal, which meant either they were a ghost or one hell of a powerful mage. But as I approached the barrier, I saw that the bars had been bent back to create a narrow gap for entry.

Well, that's not good.

Whoever had done that had to be incredibly strong—easily as strong as I was in my stealth-shifted form. I decided to choose discretion over valor, shifting forms under my skin as a precautionary measure. When I reached the gap in the grate, I caught sight of that same dark figure fleeing down the tunnel.

Fuck.

After a moment's hesitation, I squeezed through the gap in the grate and followed the figure at a distance, exercising caution as I searched high and low for any potential ambush. A hundred feet in, the light began to fade into darkness, so I lit a magic orb and set it aloft. While I had decent night vision in my current form, the orb would greatly reduce any advantage that a nocturnal creature with superior visual abilities might have.

I edged my way around a bend, sunlight spell at the ready in case Remy and his thugs were setting me up. Further down the tunnel from somewhere deep within the gloom, a familiar voice shouted a greeting.

"McCool-san, it is good to see you again."

H*IDEIE!*

"You motherfucker!" I yelled as I leapt at the figure in the darkness. My orb tagged along for the ride, and the light it cast illuminated the tengu's face as his strange features registered first amusement, then surprise.

Didn't expect me to be this fast, did you, punk?

As I closed the gap at lightning speed—or, rather, Fomorian speed, which didn't sound as cool but was just as impressive—my blade sliced through the air with a whistle, straight at the tengu's collarbone. Most people think the neck is the proper target for a diagonal downward cut, but it's not. What you want to target is the clavicle and subclavian artery, because it's a two-for-one. Break the collarbone and you hamper the use of that arm considerably. Cut the subclavian artery, and your opponent is going to bleed out PDQ.

Hideie's weird avian eyes widened then narrowed, all in the short span of time it took to make my initial attack. Milliseconds before my blade landed, the mountain goblin beat his wings, which had the dual effect of blowing mud, sand, and water in my face as well as taking him out of range of my attack. I was already stepping through on the reverse cut, left foot shooting forward as I sliced left to right at an upward angle intended to cleave Hideie from his groin to his ribs.

The yōkai was already on the move, again using his wings to propel him away from my attacks. I sprinted after him with a dizzying combination of cuts, forcing him to fly backward down the tunnel and away from me. Finally, he gained enough distance to snap his wings out fully, and with a single powerful stroke they carried him to the roof of the tunnel some thirty feet above me.

I stood there in the shallow waters of Waller Creek, legs spread wide and sword held at the ready in a high two-handed guard. My chest was heaving, but not from the exertion. I simply wanted a piece of this guy, and badly.

"Come down here and face me, coward—sword to sword!" I bellowed, the deep, growling bass of the beast within layered under my own voice.

It sounded creepy as hell, and that was sort of the point. My Hyde-side's voice triggered a primal reaction in most people, so I often used it to intimidate. Shit like that had been freaking people out since the Gerasene demoniac, after all.

But, Hideie was no person—he was a demon himself, of a sort. And he was not impressed by my outburst. In fact, the mountain goblin smiled, in that weird way that only his strangely-pliable beaked mouth could. Truth be told, seeing him smile was almost as creepy as my double-voice trick.

Almost.

"McCool-san, you are full of surprises!" Hideie exclaimed with a gleam in his fucked-up bird eyes. "Days ago, you were hardly a match for my skill and speed in your human form. Yet here you stand, forcing me to use my other talents to avoid your wrath. Not only do you manage to surprise—you present a mystery as well. How delightful."

"Draw that meat cleaver and come back down here, and I'll unwrap this mystery for you up close."

His beak twitched slightly, and those big black pupils in his eyes widened a tad. Then, the birdman made a crisp bow, deeper than the last time we'd met.

"It would be my honor to accept your challenge, McCool-san. First blood, or to the death?"

The corners of my mouth curled into a wicked grin. "If you think I'm letting you walk out of here after you tricked me into giving up the Eye, you ought to share what you're smoking."

"Hah! To the point as always, if lacking in eloquence. So be it." He drew his sword from midair, as if pulling it from an invisible sheath. "Let us begin."

The tengu floated down from the ceiling without any apparent use of his wings. As soon as his feet hit the floor, he settled into *gedan no kamae*, a low guard stance. It was a defensive posture, which told me he was taking this duel seriously.

I cracked my neck. "Alright, fucker. Let's dance."

I ran at him, sword held high. Hideie responded by raising his sword into an offensive guard, *hassō no kamae*, as he sprinted to meet me.

Holy shit—this is just like Rurouni Kenshin.

We clashed blades as we passed each other, but I deflected and snuck in a cut just a tad faster than the tengu. I felt my blade catch on something, but I was already spinning on heel with a backhanded cut, so I didn't have time to see if my blade was wet. Damned good thing, too. That ugly fucker was already dropping a straight vertical downward cut at my back.

I managed to perform a decent roof block as I stepped

off the X, then it was on. Human eyes couldn't have followed what happened next, but I caught the action just fine in my stealth-shifted form. In the span of ten seconds, we traded dozens of blows. Cut, parry, counter, deflect, riposte—our exchange almost became a rhythm as we sliced and stabbed at each other from every angle imaginable.

At the end of that exchange, we ended up in a bind, locking blades in equal *forte* so neither of us had an advantage over the other in leverage. I leaned in, not showing my full strength but matching his, sinew for sinew. Hideie's weird bird eyes narrowed again, those black and citrine globes closing to slits as he considered the situation. My instincts told me he was about to pull some hinky shit, so I readied a spell.

That's when the fucker whipped a wing around to smack me right in the eye.

THE IMPACT WASN'T HARD ENOUGH to injure or stun me, but that hadn't been the point. Hideie had been trying to distract me, and getting hit in the eye with a giant-sized wing did exactly that. The tengu used the opening to break away from our bind, and by the time I realized what had happened, I felt cold steel at my neck.

"Drop the sword, please."

"That was poorly done," I protested, doing as he asked and letting my longsword clang to the concrete beneath our feet. "After our last encounter, I at least expected a fair fight."

Hideie's feathered eyebrow arched at me. "And you were not cheating? Come now, McCool-san—you can't expect me to believe that you aren't using magic to enhance your physical attributes. Certainly, for a human you are at the peak of your potential. However, you could never match my strength, speed, and reflexes without some sort of supernatural assistance."

Obviously, Hideie thought I'd enhanced my physical capabilities with some sort of spell. I wasn't about to disabuse him of that notion, so I decided to let him think he was onto something.

"Do I need to point out you have every advantage over me in my human form? Oh, wait—of course I don't, because you just did. And after having my ass served to me on a platter the last time we fought, did you really expect me to take you on *without* using magic?"

"A fair point," he replied. "Now, if you don't mind, I'd like to conclude this business. The damp in here is playing havoc with my feathers."

"Better hope my other half doesn't decide to come out before you slice my head off."

The tengu craned his neck and let out a cackling, crow-like laugh. "Oh, McCool-san. You are a very funny young man. If I had wanted you dead, I'd have killed you when we first met. No, I think I will not kill you, today. Shall we call a truce?"

"A truce? Then why did you lure me down here and ambush me?"

"If you'll recall, it was you who attacked me. Right after I had greeted you, in fact. I am not the aggressor here."

I had to admit he was right, but hell if I would admit it out loud. "Alright, a truce it is."

He drew his blade away from my neck with a flourish, as if flinging blood from the blade. Then, he sheathed the weapon and deposited it back into the weird pocket dimension from whence it came. I pointed at my sword, which was partially submerged in a shallow stream of water.

"Do you mind? I'd rather dry it off now than have to polish the rust off later." The birdman nodded, so I picked the blade up and wiped it dry on my jeans. Then, I sheathed it and stuffed it into my Bag. "So—if you didn't bring me down here to kill me, can you tell why I'm standing in the world's biggest storm drain having a convo with the yōkai who stole my magic rock?"

Hideie clasped his hands behind his back, reminding me of Chow Yun-fat in *Crouching Tiger, Hidden Dragon*. "As to why we're inside a storm drain, well—you are the one who is currently being hunted by the Circle, yes?"

I shrugged. "I suppose."

"As I understand it, you were tossed from the eighty-fifth floor of their headquarters building this afternoon. After starting a fight with the entire High Council, that is."

"Yup."

"Which tells me you know the stakes, and what is at risk if my former employer is able to carry out his plans."

I scratched my head. "You'll need to elaborate on that one, Hideie."

The tengu frowned. "Hmm. Suffice it to say that Welsh gods are not the only ones who can walk the Twisted Paths."

"You're surprisingly well-informed regarding my companions, Hideie."

"We tengu usually are."

I sat on a nearby ledge and let out a sigh. "How much do you know? Wait, I have a better question—if you can see the future, then why did you help them steal the Eye in the first place?"

"What do I know? I know those fools are about to trigger an apocalypse—one they think they can control, but they will not. As for your second question, I'm a demon. Any sufficiently powerful mage can summon me, bind me, and place me under a geas."

"Just curious, how many mages are capable of doing that?"

"Not many—a handful. And few would be foolhardy enough to do so, considering the consequences that would follow."

I gave a sympathetic nod. "So, why haven't you taken this fool out yet?"

"Because, McCool-san—he's found a way to control the Eye."

Well, fuck.

19

"So, explain this to me again. Especially the parts that involve time travel and seeing into the future."

I was sitting on a concrete escarpment roughly six feet above the tunnel floor, with my legs dangling over the edge. Hideie was perched next to me—apparently wings make it difficult to sit like a normal biped. He'd been explaining events that occurred after he was summoned and placed under a geas by the mystery wizard-slash-stalker on the Circle's High Council.

"As I said, I was told to retrieve the Eye by any means necessary. That left me some leeway as to how I gained possession of the artifact. Understand, while we tengu can be forced into servitude by a sufficiently powerful magic-user, such service still requires a contract between summoner and subject. Thus, we use our natural cunning to negotiate the terms of our service down to the most minute detail. The idea is to wear the summoner out so they will eventually agree to less stringent demands than they had originally intended."

"Makes sense to me."

Hideie shook out his wings. I was starting to figure out his bird-like mannerisms, and I'd learned to interpret that particular gesture as a sign of displeasure.

"It is distasteful for my kind to dissemble, because there is no honor in it. However, we do as we must to ensure our powers are not used to disturb the natural balance and order of things. And in this case, I suspected such an outcome would be difficult—if not impossible —to avoid."

I blew my cheeks out in a long exhale. "So, you decided to walk the Twisted Paths to see what might happen if you succeeded."

"Indeed, and what I saw chilled me to the bone. I know the Welsh trickster showed you a possible future, the most likely one. I saw that world myself, and it wasn't just your beloved state of Texas that suffered. The repercussions were felt worldwide." He paused to lick the edge of his lipless mouth. "McCool-san, did you know there are no references to vampires in Japanese folklore?"

"I wasn't aware. Why is that?"

"Because they reminded the god Izanagi too much of his undead wife. After he trapped Izanami in the under-world, he saw to it that every last vampire in Japan was destroyed. To this day, they are seen as an abomination, and we have not tolerated their kind in my homeland since they were banished ages ago." The tengu drew a long, shuddering breath. "Yet, in the future I saw, my beloved country had become infested by the creatures and their offspring."

"Revenants, ghouls, and zombies."

Hideie hung his head slightly and gave a weak nod. "Hordes of them. Like locusts, they destroyed everything in their wake and left the nation in ruins. The only humans left alive were gathered into concentration camps, cattle to feed the vampires who had invaded after the outbreak of undead. The sight haunts me still."

"I know the feeling."

"So, you see, I could not allow that future to come to pass. For that reason, I traveled other branches of the Twisted Paths until I found one where disaster had been avoided."

"Let me guess—it was the one where I traveled to the future and lived out an entire season of *The Walking Dead*."

"Yes, or at least that future where you survived your encounters with the wizard who is now in possession of Balor's Eye."

"Ahem—if you don't mind me asking, how many time-lines did you travel where I didn't die?"

Hideie looked away. "Eh, only one."

"And you said 'encounters,' as in plural. How many times do I face him?"

"Three, and as you know, one battle has already passed. However, in most timelines, it is the third encounter in which you lose your life." He paused, as if he wanted to say more. "I would provide details, but I fear it would cause you to act in a way that would ensure your defeat. Humans were not meant to know their futures."

"Yeah, you minor deities keep saying that, yet you play with time travel like it's a Slinky."

"Not at all. Unlike that crazy Welsh magician, I rarely risk it. In fact, I would not be surprised if his meddling caused this entire mess."

I buried my face in my hands and chuckled humorlessly. "I can definitely see that happening." I rubbed my face and blinked a few times, then looked the tengu in his weird raven eye. "Okay, so now I'm all caught up. What's the play?"

Hideie sighed, which sounded weird coming from his beak-like mouth. "Unfortunately, I cannot assist you directly in your attempts to get the Eye back. That was one of the stipulations in our contract. And believe me, it was a struggle to find a loophole that would allow me to provide any information on my former employer."

"Can you at least tell me his name?"

"I cannot. He was quite clear about that during our negotiations."

I grabbed two fistfuls of hair and growled. "Gah! So, what *can* you tell me?"

"A few things, which may or may not be useful. For one, you will bear witness to a great tragedy before your final battle with this person, so I implore you—do not lose hope."

"And when have I not witnessed great tragedies? My life has been one long tragic comedy since I learned about The World Beneath."

Hideie blinked. "I am sorry you feel that way, McCool-san. May I give you a bit of advice?"

"Sure, why not?"

"If you don't want to be a pebble on a *goban*, then you need to become the person placing the stones on the board."

I chuffed at that remark. "I've been thinking that very same thing myself lately. Any other advice or info?"

"Second, speak with the trickster again before your final confrontation with the enemy. And third, you should muster your forces before facing your third and final battle."

"So, stay positive, go see the arguably-insane trickster god, and bring back-up. Something tells me this whole thing is about to go sideways off a steep cliff."

Hideie blinked again, and his wings went still. "I am sorry I cannot be of more assistance. When this is over, please seek me out again so that I might offer retribution for any troubles I caused you while in service to your enemy."

I clapped a hand on the birdman's shoulder, causing him to stiffen. "You know what, Hideie? For a demon-slash-goblin who stole my magic rock and made me think my mom was dead, you're not half bad."

BY THE TIME I was done conversing with the tengu, night had fallen. Due to the geas placed on him, Hideie refused to verify the location of our mystery wizard. Despite his reticence, his eyes twinkled when I mentioned the address Crowley had given me, and he said something to the effect of, "*When threatened, a swallow will always fly back to its nest.*" I took that as confirmation enough.

Germain and I had decided to surveil the place to make certain the wizard would be there. He seemed to think that Remy would show his face as well. I badly wanted a piece of the guy, but if it came down to choosing between the Eye and revenge, I could square things with the New Orleans coven leader another day.

Crowley had indicated our target was currently located in one of the penthouse suites at the 360 Condo building. So, we set up shop at the ugly jigsaw-looking tower that was under construction across the way. It was several stories taller than the high-rises adjacent to it, allowing us a direct view of the penthouse suites in the other building. And while we didn't see Mr. Mysterious, we did spot Remy DeCoudreaux himself hanging out on the rooftop balcony, soaking in a hot tub while he snacked on a couple of human hotties.

Bullseye.

I tapped Germain on the shoulder. "Time to go. If we hurry, we can catch them with their pants down—maybe literally, the way Remy is going."

The old vamp held up a hand, motioning for me to wait. He was still casing the place with a pair of binos. "Ah-ha, I knew it. See for yourself."

I grabbed the binoculars and checked the windows, doors, and balconies again. It didn't take long to locate a couple of familiar faces.

"Gaius and Cornelius? I thought they were working for you."

"Apparently not. Perhaps our recent alliance has something to do with it. You did behead their beloved Lucius, after all."

"Meh, he deserved it. But should we be worried?"

Germain absently stroked a bottle on his bandolier. "Gaius is no concern at all. But Cornelius—well, he does present a problem. He is an old and skilled combatant. And since you killed his son, he will be out for blood— quite literally, I believe."

"Yeah, I've seen him fight. He had magical assistance at the time, but he nearly beat Luther. Even for a cheat, that's no easy challenge." The vampire chuckled at the understatement. "How do you want to play this?"

"It's your city, monsieur. You tell me how we should handle the situation."

"Honestly, I'd like to shift and hop right the fuck in their laps, guns blazing and dick swinging. I figure I'll start off by throwing Remy right off the fucking balcony, followed by Gaius and Cornelius. Then, I'll squeeze that freaky wizard until his head pops off like a champagne cork. Unless you have a better plan."

"Might I remind you that I cannot fly? And that Cornelius and his son can?"

"Ah, hell. I forgot about that." I considered the problem for a moment. "I could throw you."

"How—unseemly. Perhaps if I just entered through the front door? I'm certain I can get past Remy's 'goons,' as you called them, and cause enough of a distraction so you can make a surprise entrance. I for one would very much like to see you toss Remy off the roof. He does not fly, either."

"What *is* his talent, anyway?"

Germain's lips curled into the barest hint of a frown, as if someone had farted in his vicinity and he was pretending he didn't notice. "Pheromones. He charms women and gets them to do his bidding. I'll leave the rest to your imagination."

"Now I *really* want to kill him."

"Indeed. And while I cannot fly, I do move rather quickly. Give me two minutes, then you may initiate your attack."

"Will d—"

The vamp had already vanished in a blur before I could answer him. *Much as leeches give me the creeps, I gotta admit, that's pretty cool.*

THE MAP APP on my phone said it was about four hundred and fifty feet from the edge of this building to the penthouse. Fully-shifted, my top speed on foot was about fifty —and that was if I had enough space to get up to that speed. That meant I'd need to be airborne for six seconds to make it across the gap.

I'm going to need some elevation to stick this jump.

I headed up to the highest level and backed up to the other side of the building. Then, I set the clock on my phone to count down from a minute-thirty and started shucking clothes so I could make the shift. After the change was complete, I placed a few goodies at the top of my Bag and waited.

Five seconds before my timer went off, I saw Remy's head snap toward the front door of the condo.

Showtime. Ready or not, motherfuckers, here I come.

The top level had just been added, so it was mostly an empty shell. That allowed me to get a running start—and let me tell you, a Fomorian at a full sprint is no joke. I launched myself over the side of the building at top speed, leaping as high as I could to add some arc to my trajectory. Legs and arms flailing to maintain flight stability, I soared through the air like the Hulk with the wind whistling in my ears.

Speaking of wind, when I was about halfway across the chasm between the two buildings, I realized I'd failed to account for two things—air resistance and wind shear. Not only was I going to miss my mark; I was going to hit the building about four stories below the penthouse level.

Well, shit.

On instinct, I curled into a ball and covered my face to protect my eyes. Two seconds later, I landed on someone's balcony and smashed through a sliding glass door at roughly forty miles an hour. The glass they use on high-rises is laminated safety glass, so it doesn't shatter into a thousand little pieces the way they show in the movies. Instead, it spiderwebs as it gives, but that kind of glass is designed to stay in the frame when it breaks.

So, my ten-foot-tall, eight-hundred-pound ass took out the entire door frame on my way into the building.

I rolled as I hit the floor of the apartment, shedding the glass and door frame as I popped up on my hands and knees. The ceiling was too low to stand upright, so I remained in a crouch as I got my bearings. A couple stood in the apartment's kitchen just off the living room, utterly still with their mouths agape.

"Um, sorry about the mess. I'd help you clean up, but I have somewhere to be."

The couple continued staring.

"Ma'am, can you tell me your unit number? That way I can send an insurance adjuster over to assess the damage."

The lady blinked a few times before stuttering a reply. "U-unit f-four-zero-one-six."

"Great, my insurance agent will be in touch. Enjoy your evening!"

I made a mental note to have one of Maeve's fixers mind wipe the couple in Unit 4016. By the time I hit the balcony, I could tell it was already a shit-show up on the penthouse level. The first indication was that my sensitive ears caught the familiar sounds of violence and mayhem coming from above. And second, a body plummeted past me flailing and screaming bloody murder. They were moving way too fast to get an ID, so I glanced over the side to see if it was someone I knew.

Ew. Nope, not anyone important. Time to get my ass moving.

I started speed-climbing from balcony to balcony, scrambling up the side of the building like a crack-addicted spider monkey going after the last rock in the bag. I hit the top floor and vaulted myself over the edge, but I was on the other side of the building from the mystery wizard's penthouse suite. With no time to waste, I climbed up and jumped the walls that separated the balconies until I reached my destination.

Holy hell—what a fucking scene this is.

There were body parts everywhere, and from the smell I deduced they were almost all vamps. One of the girls Remy had been feeding on floated face down in the hot tub, her blood gradually turning the water a pale shade of pink. The other girl cowered behind a large potted plant—apparently, she hadn't yet been tapped by any of the vamps present for a quick heal or boost of energy.

The glass doors leading from the balcony inside had been shattered and torn from the frame. A bedroom lay beyond that entry, where more charred and dismembered corpses adorned the floor and furniture nearby. From somewhere inside the penthouse apartment, I heard Remy, Cornelius, and Germain yelling curses at each other in various languages, a conversation that was punctuated by the sounds of furniture breaking and the occasional small explosion.

I grabbed the girl hiding behind the planter, lifting her gently and setting her on the other side of the wall, in the neighbor's patio balcony.

"Get the fuck out of here—and stop hanging around vampires."

She nodded nervously while avoiding my gaze, clutching her bikini top to her chest as she padded off into the neighboring condo.

Guess nobody locks their doors up here—why would they? Rich people, go figure. I shook my head and turned my attention to the fight going on inside. *Time to make my entrance.*

I barreled through the entry to the bedroom at a crouching run, shattering the doorframe as I continued straight through to the living room. The scene there was a mess. There was broken glass everywhere, along with burned and charred furniture and body parts. The thick, dark blood of vamps painted the walls and ceilings, and the sofa was half-melted by what looked like an acid of some sort and half on fire.

The wizard stood on the balcony above, surveying the carnage. He'd reverted back to the male version of himself that I'd seen through the portal of my prison cube, so I assumed that was his true form. I still couldn't make out a face, but I did notice that weird clawed hand of his poking out from his sleeve.

On the lower level of the condo, mayhem reigned supreme. Gaius lay in a broken and unconscious heap, sprawled across the kitchen counter with a toupee clutched in his hand. *Guess the hair hasn't grown back yet—shame.* The other three vamps darted to and fro, human-shaped blurs that chased each other around the space. Every so often, one blur would throw a glass vial at another, missing for the most part, but still doing a tremendous amount of damage.

Each time those vials struck the floor, or the walls, or a piece of furniture, they exploded and released their contents into the environment, some of it splashing on Germain's intended targets. Fire, acid, frost—it appeared he knew a thing or two about using elemental magic via alchemical means, at least enough to hold his opponents at bay. But, he couldn't keep it up forever.

I gathered in the scene in the span of a few seconds, then jumped into the fray, grabbing a passing blur by the neck with my huge Fomorian hands. As my prey squirmed in an attempt to escape my vice-like grip, I took a moment to determine the unfortunate bastard's identity. On confirming that I'd nabbed Remy Decoudreaux, I tossed him through a nearby window, hard enough to separate the pane from the frame.

"Surprise, motherfuckers!" I shouted to no one in particular. "Look who's back!"

20

As Remy went sailing out into the Austin night, the tableau before me froze for a brief moment. Cornelius glared at me from across the room, then glanced at the now empty window frame. Proffering me one final scowl, he leapt after the NOLA coven leader.

That left me, Germain, and the wizard—and Gaius too, but he didn't count.

Now that the playing field had been leveled, I wasted no time going after my prey. Knowing that it took a little time to rev up the Eye, I also knew my ability to withstand its blasts would be useful, yet limited. My Fomorian body was uniquely capable of channeling the Eye's energies, giving me at least some resistance to the destructive capabilities of that magic.

But that didn't mean I was immune to it. Not by a long shot.

As soon as I moved, the wizard released a spell at Germain with that withered, deformed hand. I sensed rather than saw the magical energy he released—a powerful stasis spell that froze my companion in place, taking him out of play.

Whoever this guy is, I can't match his magic on my best day.

The hairs on my arms stood on end, indicating that the wizard was spinning up another hellaciously strong spell. My eyes zeroed in on him as I leapt toward the balustrade above. Once again, I noticed that silver nimbus of light, the same one that had shone on the runes in the prison cube.

Where else have I seen that before?

I'd reached the balcony railing when the wizard released his spell, another invisible magic barrier designed to prevent me from getting to him. A quick look in the magical spectrum showed me that the protective spell he'd cast was spherical, designed to keep me at bay while he figured out what he was going to do next. Such spells were stationary by nature, so he had nowhere to run.

Gotcha, you prick.

I plunged my hands into the barrier, tearing a small opening in the weaves as I wriggled my fingers inside. Once I'd gained purchase, I began pulling the edges of the hole apart using my Fomorian strength and knowledge of warding magic.

All the while, I kept my eyes on the wizard behind the invisible shield just a few feet away from me. "You're done for—and I will have my Eye back."

"The Eye doesn't want you," he rasped. "I've agreed to its terms, and now the artifact and I are fully integrated, symbiotes working synchronously to achieve converging goals."

I grunted with the strain as I tore the hole wider. "And what—goals—would those be?"

"The first you already know," he sneered. "To free the Earth from the influence and presence of the Tuatha Dé Danann. That has always been the Eye's intent and purpose, and if you'd only cooperated with the artifact in achieving it, you'd still be in possession of its power."

I'd ripped a decent-sized hole already, but it wasn't enough to allow me to squeeze through the barrier. Eager to get at my enemy, I tore at it with even greater intent.

"You know—it'll be free—once the fae—are gone, right?"

I could hear a sneer in his voice as he responded. "Yes, but by then I'll have achieved my own goals. Thus, it will not matter."

"Not—if I stop—you two—first," I growled.

By this point, I'd almost made the rip wide enough to squeeze through. I stepped on the lower edge with one foot, pulling in three directions to make the opening wide enough to get at the wizard. At the same time, my enemy pulled the glove from his twisted right hand.

He shouted with triumph in his voice. "I think not, McCool. Behold!"

"Behold? Seriously?" I had to laugh at how ludicrous the whole thing was. My laughter didn't last long.

The wizard held that deformed appendage up, palm extended toward me. The thing was a withered, dead version of my claw-like left hand in my current form. And dead in the center of the palm, Balor's Eye was embedded into the dried, decayed flesh, a red-hot lump of molten mineral with a pupil that darted to and fro, looking for something to incinerate.

Fucking hell. The crazy bastard grafted a mummified Fomorian hand onto his arm. That's how he's managing to control it.

Seeing Balor's Eye embedded in that hand triggered a slew of ideas and emotions in me. Chief among those thoughts was the realization that I'd needlessly blinded myself each time I'd used the Eye.

Wait a minute—this whole time, I could have had that thing embedded in my hand instead of behind my eyes? Are you fucking kidding me?

I expected the wizard to unleash the Eye's formidable, deadly energies on me. But instead, he turned his head toward another high-rise to the northwest—a forty-story, glass and steel residential building. Nodding once, he raised his withered hand, palm extended, to point the Eye at the other building.

"No, don't—!"

My protest fell on deaf ears. As the wizard cut loose with the Eye's full power, a beam of pure molten energy instantly vaporized another of the penthouse condo's windows. Once that obstacle had been removed, the beam shot forth, connecting with the other high-rise at its leading edge, somewhere around the twenty-fifth floor.

THE RUTHLESS SON of a bitch moved his arm just a hair, but

at this distance it was enough to direct the beam of energy clean through the neighboring structure from one side to the other. Wherever the glowing shaft of light hit, that section of the building went up in a cloud of ash and smoke. When the dust cleared, I saw that the magic heat ray had disintegrated an entire floor of the building, save for a few concrete and steel support columns that miraculously remained intact.

My face twisted in a mask of rage and horror.

"*Mallacht Dé ort*, wizard!" I howled, meaning every word of the old Irish curse.

"There is no god but magic," he rasped in reply. "You of all people should know that by now."

I glanced back at the building, which somehow still remained standing. *Someone needs to evacuate the building —now.*

"When I'm done with you, your god will be pain," I snarled, releasing my hold on the barrier.

In the blink of an eye I was in motion, my huge Fomorian legs pumping like pistons as I sprinted toward the hole the Eye's blast had left in the side of the wizard's apartment. As I neared the edge, I leapt with everything I had at the teetering remains of the other tower, all while its remaining support columns screeched under the sudden stresses placed on them.

I was still airborne when the building began to collapse upon itself. I hadn't been old enough to witness 9/11 firsthand, but I'd seen the footage, and this was a mirror image of each tower's collapse. Heat from the blast must have weakened the steel in the remaining support columns, causing them to fail catastrophically, just as it had in the Twin Towers. First, the top floors fell while remaining relatively intact, crushing the next floor down. This caused a chain reaction as the lower floors each buckled sequentially under the weight of the falling structure above.

Floor after floor gave way, and as they did the upper half of the building gained momentum, dropping faster and faster toward the ground below. Finally, the upper floors hit ground level with an earth-shattering boom. The impact threw dirt, dust, and debris up in a rapidly expanding cloud, obscuring the area around the building for an entire city block and busting out windows in every nearby building.

When I landed on an adjacent five-story apartment complex, the entire area below was completely concealed in the dust cloud caused by the building's collapse. But what my eyes couldn't reveal, my other senses might. I cupped a hand to my ear, hoping and praying I'd pick up something, anything to indicate survivors were in the rubble.

All I heard was the sound of steel creaking and straining, electricity sparking, fires burning, and a forty-story collapsed superstructure settling into its final grave.

I fell to my knees and buried my deformed face in my hands.

"My God, what have I done?" I whispered.

Then, the screams started. Not from the structure, but from the surrounding area. People who had been asleep in their beds awoke to a horrific tragedy. The concussive force of the collapse had sent debris, including glass fragments, steel, and concrete, flying in all directions, injuring passersbys. Others were picked up by the pressure wave caused by the displacement of air as the building fell, tossed like rag dolls against cars and other buildings.

Multiple motor vehicle accidents had been caused by the debris cloud. As the cloud continued to spread, I heard the sounds of cars screeching to a halt only to be struck by those vehicles coming up behind. Every few seconds, the squeal of tires and brakes would be followed by the sickening crunch of glass and steel, echoing through the streets below.

I froze. Never in my life had I witnessed such destruction—at least, not all at once. Certainly, I'd seen the aftermath of nuclear war and an undead outbreak during my time in the Hellpocalypse, but this was happening in real time. And it was horrific.

My nostrils filled with the smells of burning plastic, wood, and bodies, as well as fresh blood and human waste. My ears now heard the sounds of dozens of people, all calling out for help at once. Grown men and women were shouting the names of their loved ones or screaming in abject terror. Children were crying for their parents. I might have even heard someone's final death rattle.

I wanted to help, but I had no idea where to even begin.

From the dust cloud below, Germain whizzed up next to me in a blur of motion and supernatural grace. "*Sacré Dieu... 'cest un cauchemar,*" he exclaimed in horror.

His voice snapped me out of my stupor. *I can engage in*

self-hate later. Right now, people need our help. I stood and faced Saint Germain, swallowing a lump in my throat before I spoke.

"Dozens of bystanders were injured when the building fell, and there may still be survivors in the debris. Call Luther and tell him to bring the coven to help with the rescue efforts. Then, I want you to use that blood-detecting nose of yours to look for anyone who still might be alive."

The old vamp nodded. "It will be done," he said before speeding off.

I shifted to look as human as possible while still retaining much of my Fomorian strength, speed, and durability. Then, I slipped on a pair of jeans and a t-shirt, forgoing shoes to save time and so I'd look like just another survivor. Listening intently for the location of the closest victims, I locked their positions into my memory, then took a moment to send out a text to everyone who mattered.

Huge tragedy at Fifth and West. Please come help.

With a sigh, I tucked my phone into my Bag and leapt down to street level to begin searching for survivors.

THE RESCUE EFFORT lasted through the night and into the following day. Luther and the oldest members of his coven showed up first, darting in and out of the scene while they could still use the settling dust cloud to disguise their movements. They saved quite a few people. Could've been more if Luther had brought the entire coven. But with all the blood around, well—the young ones might have gone crazy and started feeding on the survivors.

Yeah, imagine that.

Bells and several independent hunter crews showed up after that, along with the entire Austin Pack. Samson organized his people into teams, and Belladonna did the same with the hunters who arrived. Bells was a natural leader, and she did a hell of a job keeping the human hunters on task as the day wore on.

Despite the tragedy all around, I couldn't help but feel my heart swell with pride a bit at watching the girl work. But I kept it to myself. Too much to do, and all that.

Maeve portaled in on a local rooftop with every healer she could muster, plus a mind mage to make sure none of the survivors talked. Vamps, 'thropes, and hunters shuttled the injured into makeshift field hospitals manned by Maeve's people, and the Faery Queen kept prying eyes away with her magic.

Finn and Maureen eventually turned up as well, pitching in at a couple of medical stations without saying a word. They just went to work, healing the wounded and saving lives where they could. Throughout the night, I caught them casting concerned glances my way when they thought I wasn't looking. Not in the mood for conversation, I let them think I didn't notice.

Meanwhile, Chief Ookla, Guts, and most of the Shank-tooth troll clan arrived via the sewers, along with a shaman to keep their odor-negating spells working—that way, they wouldn't harm any potential survivors with their smell. The lot of them worked below ground level to search for anyone who might still be alive and buried in the rubble. At first, they were enthusiastic about their task, but after a while, it was like watching a search and rescue dog working a dead scene—heartbreaking.

The trolls found body after body, all deceased, as they picked through the rubble well into the next day. By the time the human crews from above began to penetrate the dark below, the disappointment and sadness around the clan was more palpable than the powerful odors they usually emitted. Everyone knew they were retreating from more than just the deadly threat of encroaching daylight when they headed back to their homes.

And me? I kept working the area—righting flipped cars, going through apartment buildings, and searching every side street and back alley for any living survivor. I'd started with the rubble, but my senses soon told me that no one had survived the building's collapse. Not. One. Soul. Worse, the debris was a charnel house, with body parts everywhere. I decided to leave the recovery of the dead to the authorities.

Finally, sometime during the afternoon of the next day, I was about to head back in when I felt a hand clamp on my shoulder. There stood Finnegas, his white, pearl-buttoned cowboy shirt and jeans stained with blood. He had dark circles under his eyes and a look that said it'd been a long time since he'd seen such tragedy.

"It's done, son. Time to pack it in."

I looked out the front windows of the restaurant. Maeve had set up one of the aid stations here the night before, and I'd been delivering the wounded here since then. I'd lost count of how many people I'd pulled from wrecked cars and debris.

"There may still be survivors. Just one more search, then I'll call it quits."

Finn's eyes brimmed with sympathetic tears as he responded. "Colin, you're exhausted. It's been hours since you had to shift back to your fully human form, and your mortal body can't keep this up forever. There are plenty of human rescue workers on the scene now, and we've done all we can. It's time to let the mundanes pick up the pieces."

I rubbed my face with my hands and looked out the window again. "Maybe you're right."

Practically falling into a nearby chair, I took a deep breath as I released the tension I'd been holding. Immediately, exhaustion set in. A quick survey of my person told me I had cuts and scrapes everywhere. I was also bruised and battered from climbing into overturned cars and through debris, and energy-wise I was running on fumes. Nearby, a television tuned to local news coverage announced the body count at 702 and climbing.

I leaned on the table and hung my head. "This is my fault, Finn. If I hadn't given up the Eye to save my mom, none of this would've happened. Those people might still be—"

Smack!

The sound of Finn's hand slapping me across my face echoed inside the restaurant.

"Stop!" he shouted at me, shaking me by my shoulders. "You stop that shit right damned now!"

"But—"

"But nothing!" Finnegas said as he wagged a finger in my face. "As long as I've known you, every time something bad happens around you, you blame yourself. 'Poor me, everything I touch turns to shit. Poor me, my life is a tragedy, and I'm the cause of it all.' It's fucking pathetic, the way you beat yourself up for shit you had no control over and that wasn't your fucking fault in the first place. It's time you stopped."

I glared at him. "So, you're saying it wasn't my fault that Jesse died?"

Finn's face turned red, and he blew out his cheeks in frustration. "No, it was mine! I'm the damned fool who sent you in there, knowing darned good and well that the *ríastrad* was going to surface sooner or later. Did I know that bitch the Caoránach was going to be at her full strength? No, and that was someone else's doing. But hell if I wasn't the one who sent you in there to die, and that's what caused the change to come over you." He poked me in the chest to emphasize every next word. "It. Was. Not. Your. Fault."

"So, what?" I whispered. "I'm just supposed to absolve myself from the consequences of my own actions?"

Finnegas hooked his thumbs in his jeans and closed his eyes with a slow sigh. Then, he took a seat across the table from me. "No, you're not. But you do have to stop taking responsibility for every single fecking tragic thing that happens. You're not God—hell, you're not even *a* god, even though you've somehow managed to kill a few. So, stop acting like you hold the fate of the world in your hands. Even though you'll likely live a very long life, you're only mortal. You cannot know or control the future."

I looked down at the table, poking a molar with my tongue as I nodded. "And what if I did? What if I knew something terrible was going to happen, and I was the only one who could stop it?"

"Ah, there it is—the savior complex rears its ugly head." He tsked and frowned at me, crossing his arms over his chest. "Son, when are you ever going to learn that you can try to save the world, but you don't have to do it all on your own?"

I chose not to answer that question. Finnegas stood and gently clapped a hand on my shoulder.

"Go home, Colin. And when you figure out where that bastard of a wizard went, you call for help. Family goes deeper than blood, you know—and we'll always have your back."

21

After getting home around five o'clock, I showered and collapsed into bed. Not long after I fell asleep, I heard Jesse's voice echoing from just outside my room.

"Colin? Psst! I'm lonely, come talk to me!"

I tried covering my ears with my pillow, but hell if she wasn't standing right outside and magically projecting her voice through the walls. *Damn it—her ability to range away from the oak must be increasing.*

Jumping out of bed, I stormed out of the warehouse barefoot and in my underwear, but she was nowhere to be found. So, I marched my ass right over to the druid oak, where Jesse was hanging off a tree branch from her knees.

"There you are! You'd been gone so long, I was worried sick—"

I'd already started stealth-shifting on the way over from the warehouse—a sure sign that deep down in my gut, I really did not trust dryad Jesse. I snarled, and a bit of my Hyde-side slipped into my voice as I answered her.

"Jesse, I have had one hell of a shitty week. I'm injured, I'm tired, and I just want to sleep and forget about everything that's happened."

"Ooh, someone's a little grouchy-poo. Did I wake you, sugar bear?" She disappeared, popping up behind me with her arms around my waist. "I bet I know how to make you feel better," she purred.

I felt Jesse's hands slide down the front of my Jockey shorts, and that's when I lost it.

Quick as a wink, I grabbed her wrists and yanked her around in front of me. Using all the restraint I could muster, I pushed the dryad firmly but gently against the tree trunk with her wrists pinned across her chest. Despite my obvious anger, she was still acting like it was all a game, looking up at me with doe eyes and a smart-assed grin.

Time to set this basket case straight.

I didn't like getting physical with a creature who looked so much like my ex, but enough was enough—and being sexually assaulted by this doppelgänger was the final straw. She was an abomination, one that needed to be put down.

But not today.

I was tired, and cranky, and not thinking straight, and the last thing I had wanted was a confrontation. I decided that a warning would suffice for now. My voice was low and dangerous as I spoke, because by this time, I was about halfway to completing the change.

"You need to *back the fuck off*. I don't have the patience to play your games today, Jesse—or whatever you are." I saw something flicker in her eyes when I said that last bit.

"Hmm—you don't like it when I insinuate that you're not who you say you are, do you? Well, you're nothing like the Jesse I once knew, the woman I loved. She was kind, and strong, and considerate—and she didn't pester and push herself on me constantly, like a needy fucking whore!"

"You're hurting me," she whispered.

"Hurting you? You're a monster, and from what I've seen, practically invulnerable! If anything, I'm being *gentle* right now."

"Still," she hissed, "*I don't like it.*"

Jesse wrenched an arm free and punched me square in the face. The force of the blow snapped my head back and sent me head over heels in a reverse somersault across the yard. I landed in a three-point stance, roaring in anger as I finished shifting into my full-on Hyde-side mode.

"That fucking does it!"

I leapt at the dryad who looked like my ex-girlfriend, closing the space between us faster than any mortal could manage. In response, she merely blinked out of existence, much the same way Click had when I'd tried to teach him a similar lesson. Being close to my full height now, my head almost reached the lower branches of the druid oak. Unfortunately, that placed me within punching range of my crazy ex.

"Surprise!" she said as she popped out of the leafy canopy above to strike me directly on top of my head.

The force of the blow was sufficient to stagger me, but I recovered in time to leap up in an attempt to pull her out of the tree. Again, she vanished from sight, only to pop her head out of the foliage on the opposite side of the tree, several yards away.

"Wow, you look really mad," she exclaimed with glee in her voice. "I bet it makes you super-angry that you can't rip me limb from limb like you did in that cave in Kingsland."

"Stop messing with my head!" I roared as I leapt up into the branches of the tree.

Once aloft, I swung from limb to limb, chasing the dryad as she blinked in and out of sight, always just beyond my reach. This went on for a few minutes, and with each passing second my anger increased dramatically. I was angry enough when I was human, but changing into my Fomorian form intensified those emotions. That was my weakness in this form—my rage.

By the time several minutes had passed, I was fuming while Jesse laughed her head off. If I'd been human, I would have realized the ludicrousness of the situation, and I might have even apologized and laughed it up with her. But in this form, I was incapable of calming down once my ire had been raised.

I swung down from a tree branch to the ground below, steaming mad while Jesse clung to the oak's trunk several feet away, sticking her tongue out at me. I was about to leap after her again when I experienced a rare moment of clarity.

The tree—that's her source of power. That's how I can hurt her.

I launched myself at her, knowing she'd simply disappear again. And that's what I was counting on. I turned that leap into the hardest Superman punch I'd ever thrown, making myself into a virtual ballistic missile. When my fist impacted the side of the druid oak, it crushed the outer layers and shattered the cambium and sapwood beneath. Bark and splinters flew everywhere, and on the other side of the tree, Jesse let out a yelp of pain and surprise.

So, I struck the tree again. And again, and again, each time eliciting a cry of pain from the dryad. Before I knew it, I'd pulverized a good portion of the trunk, and soon I was nearly to the heartwood of the tree. I reared back for another blow, but just as I was about to unleash it Jesse snapped into existence in front of me, shielding the tree with her body.

"Please, Colin, stop—you're killing us," she panted.

<hr />

SHE WAS BRUISED AND DISHEVELED, with dark brown contusions all over her body and face. Thick green sap ran in rivulets from her nose, ears, and mouth, and her skin color had paled considerably from her normal shade of vibrant green.

I flashed back to what had happened in that cavern in Kingsland, when we'd gone after the Caoránach and the ríastrad first came over me. Once the warp spasm had taken hold I'd gone straight for the dragon, that ancient mother of demons and monsters, diving down her gullet and tearing her apart from the inside out. But that hadn't been enough, because by that point my Hyde-side was in complete control.

Then, Jesse was there, trying to talk me down. In my mind, I could still see my Hyde-side pummeling and ripping her to pieces. All I could do was watch.

Oh, my poor Jesse.

I clenched my fists, gritted my teeth, and howled at the sky.

Jesse—not my Jesse, but this green imitation of her—cowered in a heap at the base of the oak.

"Thank you," she whispered.

I shook my head and shifted back into my human form. I was still fuming, but at least now I had full control of my faculties.

"Why'd you come back, Jesse? Why risk insanity and losing your identity for good? Why not just move on, leave this world behind and accept your eternal reward?"

"I came back for you, Colin," she whispered. "You need me, even if you don't realize it."

"I need this? A crazy ex-girlfriend with god-like powers to stalk and harass me, and make my life hell? You moved into my backyard, sabotaged my relationship with my girlfriend, and got me into a fight with—"

It felt like my brain skipped a beat. What I'd been about to say hung just on the edge of my memory, only to slip away like quicksilver.

"I'm not that bad," she protested through pouty lips, breaking me out of my reverie. Her wounds were already healing, but the tree wasn't for some reason. "And I'm not a monster," she whispered, looking down at the ground.

"You're not a—?" I stopped myself from saying it again, because this day had been cruel enough as it was. "You know what? I *never* asked you to come back. That was your decision, and if you'll recall, you never once consulted me about it. You just decided to make a deal with the Dagda to have him resurrect you, and in exchange for what? So he'd have a means of controlling me through you?"

"That's not what he wants," she said, so softly it was barely audible.

"You know what? I don't care what he gets out of the deal. All I know is that you've made my life hell and turned it upside down ever since you came back from the dead in this body."

"I really don't understand why you're so upset. You forget that I watched you mourn my death for months on end. I watched you try to kill yourself, time and time again. And I heard you cry my name deep in the night, as you hugged one of my old sweatshirts and rocked yourself to sleep. So, why would I not try something—anything—to come back to you?"

I covered my eyes and squeezed my temples, because what she said was true. "Yes, Jesse, I mourned you. And I hated myself for the way you died. But I also moved on. I got over your death, started a new life, a new relationship—"

"Do you love her?" She was looking up at me, and those deep green doe eyes brimmed with tears.

"I—what does that have to do with anything?"

"That's what I thought," she replied matter-of-factly. "Because you never really did get over me. Admit it, Colin —you still love me."

"No, you're wrong. I still love Jesse, but *you're not her*. And you never will be."

I spun on heel and stormed off, the sounds of Jesse's lookalike sobbing behind me. It took everything I had to resist turning right back around to comfort her.

Don't do it—don't give in.

After a moment's deliberation, I kept on walking. When I exited the yard, Maureen was waiting on the front steps of the warehouse. "Lovers' spat, I take it?"

"Maureen, I'm not in the mood. I just watched seven hundred people die and spent eighteen hours pulling survivors from the wreckage. All I want is to curl up in bed and sleep for a week."

Maureen cocked her head, arching an eyebrow at me as she spoke. "As I'm aware—I was there, ya' know. But that's hardly the end o' yer problems. Fecking hell, lad! You've got the dryad who looks like yer ex to deal with, that wizard is still out there running around with the Eye doing who knows what with it, and yer walking around with a haunted look in yer eyes, like ya' just did a tour o' duty on the front lines in the Middle East."

"So?"

"So, I thought ya' might want ta' talk about it."

"Nope," I said as I stomped up the steps past her.

"Ya' know, that tree won't heal on its own. Ya' have ta' claim it and order it ta' heal itself."

I stopped at the entrance to the warehouse with my hand on the door knob. "Did Finnegas send you? Because he and I already had this discussion."

"I came o' my own free will, out o' concern for a certain

dolt of a druid apprentice who has a tendency to muck things up. The oak was slowly dying on its own before. Now that you've damaged it, the process will accelerate. It may be only a matter of days."

"At which time what? The tree will die, along with Jesse?"

She pursed her lips. "Yes. Forever diminishing yer power and puttin' an end to the reign of druidkind, forever."

I scratched at my hairline, yawning. "Honestly, Maureen, right now I could give a fuck."

"An' fecked ye'll be if that tree dies. It's more important than you know."

I gave a halfhearted wave and slammed the warehouse door behind me, then headed off to bed and the blessed forgetfulness of sleep. But sleep didn't come for a long, long while. As I lay there tossing and turning, all I could think about was seven hundred lives, lost because I'd chosen my family over the greater good.

I woke up some time later with bright light shining all around me. Sitting up on the edge of my bed, I yawned and balled my fists to rub the sleep from my eyes.

Sheesh, what time is it?

Cracking open my eyes to look for my phone, I saw it wasn't there. In fact, *nothing* was there. Not my phone, not my milk crate bedside table, not my cinder block and scrap wood bookshelves, not my espresso machine—not even my room. My bed was there, of course, but by all appearances the bed and I had been transported to some weird alternate dimension.

The place looked like a setting from a Harry Potter flick, the Magic Mountain ride at Disney, and Whoville had kinky sex while tripping balls on shrooms, and this was the resulting offspring. There were weird floating pathways and conveyor belts going everywhere, like a big ball of spaghetti that made zero sense to my tired eyes. Each followed winding, circuitous paths between floating islands in space, upon which sat ornate warehouse shelves that were easily two or three stories high.

The paths and conveyor belts were lit, but by no visible light source I could determine. Beyond those spaces it was pitch dark—hell, darker even, if that was possible. If I could describe the complete absence of light, it would not suffice to explain how black it was beyond those lit areas. Yet the pathways, conveyors, islands, and the shelves thereon might as well have been sitting in the middle of a field on a bright, sunny day.

Speaking of which, those shelves were stacked with all manner of odds and ends, including: swords, shields, and armor from various historical periods; other armaments of every type and kind; horns, drums, gongs, chimes, and other strange musical and noise-making devices; gems, jewelry, clothes, and various types of footwear; food and drink; firearms, ammunition, small kegs of gunpowder, crates of explosives, and various other munitions that seemed to range over several centuries and time periods in origin; and other miscellaneous items that were too numerous to identify by name.

Even more strange, here and there feather dusters, hand brooms, and polishing cloths floated from item to item of their own accord, cleaning and straightening the inventory, and generally keeping everything neat and tidy.

What do the Japanese call those? Tsukumogami?

It was a scene straight out of the *Sorcerer's Apprentice*—that is, if Walt Disney had been smoking crack instead of his usual Lucky Strikes.

I rubbed my eyes again. *Nope, still there.*

"Okay, this is one fucked up dream. I'm going back to sleep."

I closed my eyes and laid back down, pulling the covers over my head. Just as I was drifting off to sleep again, I sensed someone or something watching me. Moving ever so gingerly, I pulled the covers back to see who was there.

"Gah!" I cried, scrambling back toward my headboard and pulling the covers with me. "What the fuck, Click?"

The youthful-looking god-slash-magician was floating in the air above my bed, laid out prone as if he were lying face down on the floor with his chin propped on his intertwined fingers. Yet, he wasn't contemplating a flower or a line of ants on the ground. Instead, he was staring directly at *me*.

The Welsh trickster slowly drifted downward, shifting his position in midair to sit on the foot of my bed. "Ah, the lad awakes! Ye've been asleep for"—he checked his wrist, although he wore no timepiece—"oh, thirty-two Earth hours and seventeen minutes, ta' be precise. Not as though time matters in a place like this, but I was beginning ta' grow concerned about ye."

I gathered my wits, sitting up with a bit more dignity as I let the covers fall to my lap. "Ahem—and just where did you bring me, anyway?"

"Look familiar?" he asked as his lips curled up in a sly smile.

"Yeah, but I just can't place it."

"It should—we're inside yer Craneskin Bag, after all."

22

"Say what?"

"Yup, we're inside the Bag—or, should I say, inside the pocket dimension that can be accessed via the portal that represents the open end of said Bag." He opened his arms in an expansive gesture and looked around. "So, whaddya think?"

"Well, I've never been in a pocket dimension before, so—"

"What? O' course ye' have, lad. The druid oak's interior is just such a place, in fact. And it would have been my first choice for a training location, since time moves at a snail's pace inside there, fer sure. But, ye damaged it right good in yer tussle with the dryad, and now it's not safe to venture there, what with the Void and all tearing away at its edges. Damned shame, 'tis."

There wasn't much to say to that. "I screwed up—so sue me. Still doesn't explain why we're here."

"Why ta' train ye, lad—or didja' not just hear me say it?"

I leaned back and scratched my head. "Ah, chronomancy."

"And chronourgy—don't ferget that."

"Well, Hideie did say I'd need to speak with you before I faced the wizard for the final time. But honestly, Click, I don't have time to waste right now—I need to be going after the Eye."

Click leaned forward and thumped me with his middle finger, right between my eyes. "Too much sleep has made ye daft, lad. Time doesn't pass inside here, not like it does in yer realm. The whole place is one huge stasis spell, but a unique one in that beings like you"—he thumped me between my eyes again—"and me can function and act, independent of the standard stream of time."

"So, while I'm here, time isn't passing back in the real world?"

The Welsh trickster frowned. "What's 'real,' after all? This is just as real to you as yer room back home, is it not? But that's beside the point. Time is passing back in yer realm, but yer not currently in that time stream. Thus, when ye exit this pocket dimension, ye'll re-enter yer realm's timeline at the exact point ye left it."

I considered what he'd just said for several seconds, then stretched out on the bed and pulled the covers back over my head.

"If that's the case, I'm going back to sleep."

"Yes, well—there's going to be a problem with that."

I peeked out with one eye and glared at him like a pirate. "What 'problem' might that be?"

Click grinned sheepishly. "Well, ya' see, I brought ye here during yer natural sleep cycle. But now that's done with, yer body won't *need* sleep until ye leave here."

"What do you mean by need?"

"Ah—I mean that ye won't be able to sleep until I take ye back to yer own timeline."

I sighed as my chin hit my chest. "At least tell me there's a place to shower and a coffee maker here."

"Um—would it help if I said ye won't need either while yer here?" he offered cheerfully.

"Nope, not at all," I said, throwing off the covers and swinging my legs over the side of the bed. "Still, I refuse to do whatever *training* it is you have planned in my Jockeys. If you want me to do participate in whatever it is you intend for us to do while we're here, you'll need to find me a clean set of duds."

Click smirked. "Ahem—turn around."

I slowly looked behind me. A complete set of the clothes I'd recently purchased came marching down the pathway toward us. It looked as though the invisible man had put my clothes on, and he was headed over to greet us. When my shirt, jeans, socks, and boots arrived, the clothes folded themselves neatly next to me on the bed, and my boots unlaced themselves and turned around, toes pointed away from me.

"Huh. I could get used to this. Now, if you could just rustle me up some breakfast—"

Click winced. "Eh, I'd be careful what ye eat here, lad,

an' how much. Although there's no shortage of void space in which ta' drop a load o' shite, time stasis tends ta' cause constipation. Plus—"

"Plus, what?"

He gave a wary look at the darkness that sat just on the edge of the pathway we were on. "There are *things* out there, in the Void, things better left alone. And human waste has a tendency to attract them."

"Great," I groused, rubbing my face with my hands. "So, I can't sleep, eat, or take a shit while I'm here—is that all?"

"Er—don't step off the paths?"

"Don't tell me—I'll start chanting 'Ph'nglui mglw'nafh Cthulhu R'lyeh wgah'nagl fhtagn' if I venture off?"

Click straightened and drew his eyebrows together. "What? Oh no, that's just a myth, lad. But there would be a very slight chance ye'd be devoured by Yog-Sothoth—that is, if it happened to be passing by."

"Holy fuck, you're giving me a headache."

"I aim ta' please," he said as he leapt off the bed to give me a small bow. "Now, get dressed so we can start yer lessons. I figure it'll take, oh, six of yer timeline's months in order ta teach ye the basics of time manipulation."

"Any chance of arranging a conjugal visit during my stay here?"

The Welsh trickster looked at me with wide eyes, then clutched his belly and laughed out loud. "Oh, I suppose we might if there was a woman in any o' the realms right now who'd be willing ta' lay ye. But then again, ye've mucked it up wit' every single one o' yer female companions, and right handily, I should say." He tapped a finger on his chin. "Then again, the she-wolf might still bed ye, although she was a bit miffed that ye spurned her outright. Hmm—let me think about it, lad. If it comes ta' ye busting a gasket, I can always scrounge up a succubus or wood nymph for ye ta' diddle."

I didn't know what frightened me more—being eaten by Yog-Sothoth or letting a trickster god arrange a date for me.

"Um, Click?"

"Yes lad?"

"Let's never bring this topic of conversation up again, alright?"

"Certainly, lad, certainly. But the option's always there if ye change yer mind."

A TRULY INDETERMINATE amount of time later—nearly a year according to the trickster, but no time at all according the passage of time back home—Click delivered me and my bed back to the junkyard warehouse.

"Well, yer not completely hopeless, lad—but yer close."

"Ah, thanks—I think."

He clapped a hand on my shoulder and smiled like a proud father sending his son off to college. "Don't mention it. Now, I'm off to—well, I s'pose I've no idea. But I'll think o' something. Now remember, third chronourgic finger position requires a fifteen-point-seven-five degree angle at the last joint of yer pinky, else ye'll cause a pin-sized worm-hole that'll slowly suck the planet into the other side o' the universe. Good luck!"

With that, the youthful-looking deity winked out of existence.

I glanced at my phone, which was right on my night-stand where I'd left it. *Just past midnight—plenty of time to catch some sleep before I figure out how to kill what's-his-who's-it.* I started peeling off my clothes, which strangely were not the least bit ripe after having been worn for nearly a year. It occurred to me that it *had* only been a split second since I'd left.

Time travel is weird, I thought as I kicked off my pants. *Ah, freedom.*

I'd taken to going commando inside the Bag, since I didn't need to bathe. But I hadn't slept in the nude—or slept at all, in fact—in almost a year. So, I was looking forward to free-balling it while I went comatose for a day or two.

I was pulling back the covers when Click suddenly blinked into existence in front of me.

"Gah!" I shrieked, snagging a pillow from the bed to conceal my nakedness.

Thankfully, the trickster was oblivious to my state of undress, looking me in the eye as he spoke. "Oh, I almost fergot—remember ta' take Dyrnwyn with ya' when ye face that bloody, er, wizard! Yer goin' ta' need her, fer sure." He glanced down at the pillow. "And put some clothes on, or ye'll like to catch a cold."

"Have you been standing there the whole time?"

"Well, I was tryin' ta' decide what ta' do." The youthful-looking deity scowled. "Oh, fer Arawn's sakes, I weren't standin' here watchin' you. No offense, but yer not my type."

"Um, none taken." I made a shooing motion with one hand, nearly dropping the pillow. "A little privacy, please?"

"Everybody does it, but alright—if ye need ta' be alone ta' yank yer *pidyn*, who am I ta' keep ya' from it?"

"I'm not—"

But, Click was already gone. I hesitantly probed the air where he'd been standing, then made a circuit of the room just in case. Once I was certain the little Welsh god had left, I changed my pillow case, then hopped into bed and started drifting off to sleep.

That is, until Finnegas came bursting into my room.

"What's the meaning of you trying to kill that druid oak?" he blustered.

When Finnegas got mad it was easy to tell, because lightning flashed in his eyes and thunder rolled in the distance. Sometimes, the ground even shook a little. All that was going on and more. My bed was actually shaking from the tremors.

"Oh, holy hell," I muttered, covering my head with my pillow. "You fucking immortals are going to be the death of me."

Finnegas paced back and forth from one end of the room to the other, which wasn't far—maybe three long paces, if that. "Damn it, Colin—how many times do we have to tell you, that druid oak is essential to your future existence?"

"I don't know, I don't care, and I don't plan to care until I get some sleep."

The old man ignored me, because he was on a tear. "And Maureen tells me you did it trying to kill Jesse. *Jesse!* For years, I've had to put up with your self-piteous whining over the fact that she died, and I've had to watch you mope around pining for the girl. Now, she's back, and not only do you reject her advances—you try to kill her, too?"

"Well, that might have something to do with the fact that she's batshit crazy and slightly homicidal," I deadpanned.

"Do I need to explain this to you twice? I told you, as soon as you claim the druid grove she'll likely regain her sanity. It's the *power* that's making her crazy, all that Tuatha magic. She's not meant to wield it, but you are. For the life of me, son, I have no idea what's going on in that head of yours these days!"

"Finnegas, have a seat, roll a cigarette, and calm down. I know I screwed up, and I'll find a way to fix it. But right now, I have bigger fish to fry."

"Bigger than the future of the druid order?" he asked, exasperated. Throwing his hands in the air, he grabbed a rickety old kitchen chair from the corner and sat down heavily. I waited, counting in my head.

One one-thousand, two one-thousand, three—

BOOM! A huge thunderclap sounded in the distance.

"And there it is," I remarked. "Nicotine for you, caffeine for me, then we talk."

THE OLD MAN glowered at me, but I ignored him and got dressed. Finn had seen me naked dozens of times, so modesty was no concern around him. During our survival training, Finnegas would send me and Jesse off into the woods for days without a stitch of clothing or a single piece of kit. We went through our very own version of *Naked and Afraid* long before the show ever aired. I once considered suing the production company, but came to realize I'd never have a way to prove my copyright to the concept.

By the time I'd started heating the espresso machine up, he was rolling up a cigarette. "I'll take a cup too," he muttered. "Black."

"No problem."

I served him a double-shot espresso, fully caffeinated, and prepared the same from a half-decaf blend for myself. Then I sat on my bed facing him, sipping my coffee while he settled down. Halfway through his second cancer stick, he broke the silence.

"I know things are hard on you," he offered. "I just wish you'd listen to me, is all."

"I do listen to you, Finn, more than you know. But you don't know everything that's going on with me, not anymore. I'm a grown man now, in case you haven't noticed. So, no matter how much it irks you, I'm going to make my own decisions."

He looked at me with hooded eyes. "I know. I probably don't say it enough, but I'm proud of you. You've grown into a fine young man. In many ways, you're still a pup in my eyes, but then again, Fionn was leading entire armies at your age."

I sipped my coffee, considering what he'd said. "I won't let you down, old man."

He shook his head and blew smoke from his nostrils. "That's not what concerns me. What worries me is that I've let you down to this point by not preparing you for the challenges you're facing. That's why I need you to claim the grove, so we can accelerate your training and give you a fighting chance to survive."

"Survive what? Obviously there's something you're not telling me, so spill."

He chortled at that. "As if I were the only one keeping secrets."

"I have my reasons."

"So do I, but I s'pose it's time you knew. You're going to figure it out anyway, before long." He took a long drag off his coffin nail and blew smoke out his nose again. "Remember when the Fear Doirich showed up, and I disappeared for a while?"

"How could I forget? That's when you left me the Gremlin."

"Yeah, well—I never did tell you what I found out, when I went off looking for answers to those questions I had."

I chortled. "Hell, old man, you never even shared the questions."

"True," he said, taking a sip of coffee. "I went to spy on the gods."

"Huh," was about all I could muster. "You can do that —watch them without being seen?"

"Yup. Although it got pretty hairy there a time or two. Thought the Morrígna were onto me, but it was really just Badb I had to worry about."

"Ah. I never did really understand her—er, them. Different gods, but the same or something? It's weird to me."

Finnegas flicked ash off his cigarette and shook his head. "No, they're different entities, of that you can be sure. Badb the Raven is the trickiest of the three, although you really don't want to mess with any of them. Nemain will take you out directly if she doesn't like you, Macha will curse you—and believe me, her curses last. But the Raven —she's another matter entirely. She loves to cause confusion and strife for her enemies, weakening them until she decides to go in for the kill. And you'll never see her coming."

"Sounds nasty," I said. "And like you know her well."

Finnegas mumbled incoherently.

"Uh, what was that?" I asked, although I had a pretty good idea what he'd said.

"I said, I might have slept with her once," he grumbled, looking away from me.

"Glad I'm not the only one with questionable taste in women."

Finn's eyes snapped back to me. "You've only been with two women, both of them good, honest folk. Be kind."

"I was only making a joke about you know who."

"She can't help herself. And if you won't help her..."
Finn let his words trail off.

"You know how I feel about that," I said with an air of
finality. "Now, you were about to divulge deep and guarded
secrets concerning my health and well-being."

The old man went back to glowering, but this time he
didn't mean it. "Smart-ass. As I said, I went to get some
answers. I've been around long enough to recognize the
signs of divine meddling when I see them. Somebody had
been pulling strings from on high, sending you trouble at
every chance possible. And it's only gotten worse with the
passing of time."

"Go figure."

"Yep. So, I spied on the gods and found out a few
things. One, that the Avartagh studied under the Fear
Doirich. Two, that the dwarf was his one and only son.
And thirdly, that the Dark Druid was the one who raised
him from the dead—turned him into one of the *neamh-
mhairbh*. In fact, that was when he first turned to necromancy. Not that he wasn't an evil bastard before."

"Weren't you the druid they consulted before they
brought Fionn in to kill the Avartagh the first time?"

Finnegas nodded. "Yep. And the first time around, we
hid the Avartagh's grave but good. This meant we unwit-
tingly prevented his father from raising him again—
although we didn't make the connection between the two
at the time."

"So, he shows up out of the blue looking for revenge,
and you're wondering how the hell he escaped his grave."

Finn started rolling another cigarette. "I didn't think

much of it, really. Damn dwarf had been buried for nigh on two-thousand years, so he was bound to get out sometime. Wasn't 'til I heard the Dark Druid chatting with Badb that I learned the whole story."

"Wow, no wonder the Fear Doirich has had such a hard-on for Fionn's descendants. Not only did old MacCumhaill free Sadhbh from the Dark Druid's curse, but he also killed his son."

Finnegas licked his cigarette to seal it. "Can't blame him, really."

The old druid lit up for the third time since he'd arrived. *Damn, but he's worried.* "This is all fascinating, but we already knew that the Fear Doirich hates me and wants to see me dead. I trapped him in a decrepit, decaying body, after all."

"Still waiting for the other shoe to drop, eh?"

"Is it that obvious?"

Finn took a deep drag from his roll-your-own, exhaling the thick grey smoke as he replied. "So, here's the kicker—since you and the Eye kicked his ass, the Fear Doirich has been knocking on doors. And he's convinced a good number of the Celtic gods that you're a threat to their future existence."

23

"Meaning?" I asked.

"Meaning there's a price on your head, and every day you grow in power, every time you defeat some new and greater menace, that price increases."

I shrugged. "I've survived this long with them gunning for me. For the life of me, I can't understand why you're so concerned."

He leaned forward with his elbows on his knees and flicked ash on the floor. "Son, they've been throwing their third string at you to this point. But soon, I fully expect them to start sending demigods and minor deities after you. You might be a badass by the standards of the supernatural races, I'll give you that. But when it comes to surviving the full and undivided wrath of the gods—quite honestly, you are not yet up to the task."

"So that's why the Dagda gifted me with the acorn."

Finnegas clapped his hands, silently. "Finally, the dumdum gets it. Yes, the druid grove was supposed to provide you with a safe haven from the gods who have it in for you, and to provide you time to grow into your powers. Also, the damned thing isn't limited to just one location or plane of existence. It's a sort of nexus, capable of traveling anywhere the master of the grove so chooses. Meaning, you could stay clear of the gods indefinitely if you had complete control of the damned thing."

"But now?"

"Now, it's dying—a preview of things to come, if you don't get off your high horse and couple with that dryad." I began to speak, but he held up his hands in protest. "I know you don't like it, but that's just the way it's going to have to be if you want to survive what's coming."

"It's not right, Finnegas. She's not even completely Jesse. The magic twisted her, turned her into something else. The thought of having any romantic feelings toward that thing—it repulses me."

The old man rolled his eyes. "Oh, you youngsters with your modern sensibilities. When I was your age, we didn't mate for 'love' or because we had 'feelings'—we did it for the strength of the tribe, to survive." He flicked ash at me. "There are more important things at stake than your fecking feelings, son."

I decided to change the topic. "You really think this is the Fear Doirich again?"

"Does a bear shit in the woods? You bet your ass it's him. Think about it. You locked him in an aged body, you wounded him with the Eye, and after carrying the damned thing inside your head for over a year, you're pretty much immune to necromancy, his favorite weapon. Did you think he wasn't going to try to weaken you to even the odds?"

"Shit, I should've have seen it already. Every time that wizard used magic, his spells took on a silver glow."

"It's him alright. That's druid battle magic, or I'm Donald Trump."

I tsked. "Orange hair wouldn't suit you."

"Yeah, but being an asshole does. Supermodel wife wouldn't hurt, either."

"Sheesh, but the porn stars? C'mon, a man has to have his standards."

The old druid cracked a lecherous smile. "Hey, strippers and porn stars need love, too."

"You're incorrigible, old man."

"Look who's talking." He stood, dropping his cigarette to the floor and crushing it with his boot heel. "Say, a certain Maori warrior came 'round looking for you earlier while you were still asleep. He said he'd be at his old place, and to come find him when you were ready."

That news perked me right up. "Hemi's back?"

"Uh-huh. Had a hot looking little number with him, too—I'd have pegged her for an Irish lass, if I didn't know any better."

I couldn't help but crack a wide grin, despite all the horrible, crazy, weird stuff that had happened to me of late. "Seriously, that's the best news I've heard in years."

"What do you mean, years? It's only been, what, seven months or so since he fell off that mountain in Underhill."

"Never mind. Thanks for conveying the message."

"Yeah, yeah—I'm a walking answering machine."

"Holy shit, you know nobody has those anymore, right?"

"Yes, damn it. I'm old, not senile. Live to be my age, and you'll get your decades crossed too." His smile faltered and his eyes hardened. "The Dark Druid is no joke, Colin. He stands separate from the gods, as I do, and with the Eye he's more dangerous than ever."

"He killed all those people, Finnegas. He could have turned the Eye on me, but instead he murdered hundreds, just out of spite. And more people will—"

I caught myself before I said something I shouldn't. "Someone needs to stop him, and I guess it falls to me to do it."

Finnegas clucked his tongue. "Not alone, you won't. I told you before, and I'm telling you now—you have family that goes deeper than blood, and they have your back. You *will* call on them, just like you did when you organized the rescue efforts last night."

Last night—right.

"Yes, Finn. I'll bring the cavalry with me when I figure out where the bastard went. Speaking of, did anyone see where that fucker and his vampire buddies went?"

"Hmm—Saint Germain relayed the story of what happened to us, since you were too busy living out your savior complex to communicate. You know he's highly-placed in the European covens, right? Anyway, Germain said that after you took off, Cornelius came flying back with Remy, who was in bad shape but alive. Cornelius scooped up his son and the wizard—the Fear Doirich, probably—and flew them the hell out there. Stasis spell held Germain 'til they were long gone."

"No telling where they're hiding now. I'll check with Luther, see if he knows anything."

The old man stroked his beard. "Check with Hemi as well. That new girlfriend of his is much more than she appears. Something tells me he didn't bring her along for eye candy."

"Alright. Any other major insights, Yoda?"

"Yoda was a journeyman, compared to me," Finn said as he popped a pair of imaginary suspenders. "If Luke would've had me to teach him, he wouldn't have lost that hand."

I WAS ABOUT to knock on the door to Hemi's old apartment when the door swung open, only to be filled by seven-plus feet of Maori warrior. He wore a hoodie that kept his face concealed in shadow, much like my mysterious nemesis. Only on Hemi, it just made him look like a K-Road thug—especially with the tall boy of malt liquor he had in his hand. The way he carried himself told me he'd changed a lot since the last time I'd seen him.

Hemi nodded at me and held up the can. "Hey bro, care for a cold one?"

I arched an eyebrow. "Seriously? We haven't seen each other in forever, and you greet me by offering me a beer? Dude, the last time I saw you, you died in my arms. I carried your freaking body all the way to New Zealand—"

"He means Aotearoa," Hemi said to someone in the background.

A female voice answered from behind him, sweet as honey and with a Kiwi accent as thick as Hemi's. "I know what he means, Hemi. I've been topside before, aye?"

"Sorry," he replied, chastened. "I forget you didn't spend your whole life in the Underworld."

Okay, so, this is getting weird fast. I cleared my throat. "As I was saying—"

"I think he wants a hug," the female voice said.

"Oi, I'm not hugging *him*, that's for sure," Hemi replied over his shoulder. He looked back at me. "No offense. We're best mates and all, but I'm not keen on the bromance, yeah?"

"Then greet him with a hongi," the female voice interjected.

By this time, I was trying to look around my friend to see who was speaking, but his considerable bulk blocked the entire doorway.

"Ah, yeah—that I can do. C'mere, bro."

Before I knew it, the big guy grabbed me with one hand on my shoulder and another behind my head. He leaned in, and for a moment I thought he was going to kiss me. Instead, he pulled me forward until our faces were touching, forehead to forehead and nose to nose.

"Well, this isn't awkward at all," I muttered.

"Considered to be an honor," Hemi replied, staring into my eyes. "Formal greeting, warriors do it all the time." He released me, clapping me on the shoulders. "C'mon in and meet Maki."

My friend turned and headed inside, motioning for me to follow.

"Right," I said, straightening my jacket and looking anywhere but at my resurrected friend. "I think I'll have that beer, by the way."

His back was turned to me, so he waved over his shoulder as he headed to a small refrigerator. "Comin' right up. Colin, say hi to my girl, Maki."

As soon as the big guy stepped out of the way, my eyes were drawn to a tall, lithe redhead with pale skin and the brightest blue eyes I'd ever seen. Her chin was tattooed in the traditional Maori manner, in intricate swirls and patterns that accentuated her striking beauty. Except for her full lips, her face bore the fine, elfin features of the fae, but her hands were callused and her arms lean, like a laborer's or perhaps those of a craftsman.

I didn't have to look at her in the magical spectrum to know she was a witch.

Stepping forward, I held out my hand. "Pleased to meet you, Maki. I'm Colin."

The woman smiled warmly as she took my hand in a dry, firm grip. "I know who you are. Heard heaps about you."

"All good, I hope?"

Hemi chuckled as he handed me a tall boy. "As if. Have a seat." He plopped down on a couch that sat in the middle of the one-room efficiency, and Maki sat next to him.

The place wasn't large inside, since it was a converted garage that sat behind a house just off Manchaca. Hemi had rented for as long as I'd known him, and while it'd been perfect for a single guy, it was a bit cramped for company. I sat cater-corner in a dilapidated easy chair. Hemi pulled back his hood, revealing a face both familiar and radically different.

"Dude, you got your facial tattoos!" I leaned forward and toasted him with my can, and the big guy clinked his against mine. "When did that happen?"

Hemi smiled broadly. "Well, Maki's... um, granddad.... is a tattoo artist. That's how we met, actually."

She elbowed him. "There's more to the story. Tell him."

He did, and for the next twenty minutes I listened, enrapt as the two took turns explaining all that had happened to Hemi during his journey to the Underworld. I barely said a word, sipping my beer and nodding until they finished their tale.

Maki beamed at the big guy, hugging his huge arm as she wrapped up the story. "And so, we came here."

Hemi's expression soured. "Needed to get as far away from Ruaumoko as possible. He's still pissed off."

"Wow," I replied. "I think that beats any meet-cute story I've ever heard."

Maki chuckled and looked at her man. "He's a bit metro, this one."

Hemi gave her a knowing nod. "Yeah, but he grows on you."

I finished off the rest of my beer. "Gonna need another one of these if I have to take that sort of abuse."

Maki snapped her fingers, and suddenly I had a fresh, unopened cold one in my hand.

The big guy looked at her with real affection in his

eyes, and mock disapproval in his voice. "Show off." He let that look linger before turning back to me. "I hear you're in deep, as usual. What's up?"

I shrugged with fake nonchalance. "Meh. I'm about to hunt down an evil magician who may or may not be the Dark Druid back for revenge. Once I find him, I plan to kill his evil vampire army and take back Balor's Eye. Oh, and I have to figure out a way to get Belladonna back. She dumped me."

Hemi nodded. "Heard. Sucks. Need a wingman?"

"If you guys aren't doing anything later, sure."

Maki held up her hands, palms out. "Have to sit this one out. Laying low, and all that."

"I kinda snuck her out of the Underworld against a greater god's wishes," Hemi added. "Oi, Colin—you know where to find these jokers?"

"Beats me. We slapped a locator spell on the mage the last time, but he'll be wise to that now. Any ideas?"

Maki rubbed her hands together. "How powerful is the artifact he stole?"

"Very," Hemi and I both said at once.

The Maori witch frowned her disapproval at our obvious stupidity. "Then why don't you look for that instead?"

AFTER MAKI POINTED out what should have been painfully obvious, she volunteered to cast a finding for mystical artifacts of immense power, using a map of Texas spread out over their breakfast table as her focus. I watched closely as she did her thing, and damn it, she was good. As in, ancient fae good—god-like, even.

Who the fuck did you get mixed up with, Hemi?

Dark tendrils of magic swept out over the map as she chanted and wove her fingers in intricate patterns. Like druidic magic, her casting used both vocal and physical elements, but I got the feeling she was sand-bagging and doing all that stuff just for my sake.

As the little black wisps of magic sunk into various points on the map, they coalesced into small, intense points of light, starting with the Austin area and spreading outward. First, I noticed a bright green blob, right around where the junkyard was located. *Druid oak, for sure.* Then, a white point of light, along with several smaller pinpricks of light, roughly in the area where Maeve's manse was located. *Tricky, tricky, Maeve. Someone is hiding a ton of serious firepower under their house.*

Once the magic began to spread out, more dots of light emerged. Another green dot appeared in my hometown, and while I couldn't be sure, I'd almost bet it was right over the Éire Imports warehouse. No telling what Finnegas had hidden there. Other dots popped up at various spots on the map, in shades of blue, green, violet, orange, yellow, and even black once or twice. One of those black dots was in the general vicinity of Crowley's farm. I made note of where those markers were located, for future reference.

Finally, a red dot appeared, bright as the noonday sun. I shielded my eyes until the light faded into a glowing red ember, somewhere southeast of Dallas.

"That's it," I exclaimed. "Has to be."

Maki concurred. "Based on your description, I'd say it is."

Hemi squinted with his face over the map. "Nearest town is Glen Rose. 'Squaw Creek Reservoir' is the spot, though."

I pulled up Squaw Creek Reservoir on my maps app, zooming in so I could see what was there. "Shit. It's a fucking nuclear power plant."

My friend frowned. "Oi, language."

"I can take it, Hemi," Maki said. "I've been around worse."

"Maki, what would they need a nuclear power plant for, you think?" I asked.

"Two possibilities, neither good," she replied. "Sabotage, or for extra power to fuel a major working."

I knuckled my forehead. "If they blew that plant up, it'd be another Chernobyl. But I don't think that's this wizard's game. In order to get the Eye to lend its power, he had to agree to its demands."

"What does it want, anyway?" Hemi asked.

"To wipe the fae from the face of the Earth, including all remaining Tuatha Dé," I said, chewing on my thumbnail. It never hurt to spark a little of Fionn's wisdom when I was sussing out a plan. "I think this wizard is using the vamps to help the Eye achieve its stated goal. 'Quid pro quo, Clarice—quid pro quo.'"

"What's he mumbling about?" Maki whispered to Hemi. He shrugged and made the universal symbol for "crazy" by twirling his finger by his temple.

I looked at them, exasperated. "It's a movie quote, for heaven's sakes. *Silence of the Lambs*? No? Anyway, the wizard said they were symbiotes now, each helping the other achieve their ends."

"And what does the wizard want?" Maki asked.

"Honestly? I think he wants me dead," I replied.

"Wouldn't be the first bugger who did," Hemi said. "You attract haters like flies."

"Gee, thanks. Next time you die, you can get someone else to drag your fat ass back to your mom's house."

Hemi's face fell. "Hey, that hurts. I'm just big-boned, is all."

Maki pinched his cheek. "I think it's cute."

I rolled my eyes. "Ahem. I'll leave you two lovebirds to get all shmoopy together, while I make some phone calls and round up the cavalry."

Hemi and Maki looked at each other quizzically. "'Shmoopy'?"

"It's a quote from a sitcom! Damn it, but do I have some work to do on you two before this is all over," I muttered, storming out the front door of the little apartment.

My sensitive ears caught Maki whispering to Hemi behind me. "You weren't kidding, Waara. He *is* a touchy one."

24

When I said I was calling in the cavalry, I meant it. And when I called, everybody came. While I couldn't tell them just how high the stakes were for this mission, they all wanted a piece of the wizard, as well as the New Orleans coven.

Every faction had lost someone in the high-rise collapse—except for the druids, of course. After all was said and done, the death toll stood at 849 humans, five vamps, two fae, and one local Pack member. Moreover, the Coven had lost several of their closest human allies, people who lived in the tower that had voluntarily fed Coven members.

The price for my failure had been steep. I would *not* fail again.

When we rolled into Glen Rose, the assault *team* was more like an assault *platoon*. Luther had insisted on making a personal appearance, and with him came several of his enforcers—Sophia Doroshenko and, of course, Saint

Germain. Samson had brought along Sledge, Trina, and Fallyn, along with a half-dozen of his best brawlers. Maeve sent her favorite assassin team, Lucindras and Eliandres, along with a healer and a squad of eight fae hunters. Bells came with Crowley as her wingman, both of them apparently repping for the human faction.

As for the druids, Maureen and I were it. She wasn't officially a druid, but she definitely had honorary status. I was glad to have her watching my back, along with Hemi of course, who had declared himself Team Druid by default. I might also have brought along some trolls, because Guts was itching for a fight. But I thought the chance of them getting killed by a stray beam from my sunlight spell was too risky, since a single ray of sunlight could turn a troll to stone. After much grumbling, they'd agreed to sit this one out.

Once we arrived, we set up shop about a half-mile south of the place and downwind, in a metal building near some tennis courts and a baseball diamond that I was pretty sure was owned by the power plant. It was across a lake inlet and through the woods, well-hidden from prying eyes that might be on lookout at the facility. We weren't certain what we'd be facing during the assault, so we decided to reconnoiter the place rather than charge in blind.

Luther was our natural choice for scouting the place out. While Lucindras and Eliandres had wanted to do the honors, once Luther did his Nightcrawler routine they relented and let him do his thing. He disappeared in a cloud of black fog that dissipated almost instantly, returning five minutes later with an unconscious vamp over his shoulder.

"Found a young one on perimeter duty. Figured I could interrogate him and compel him to divulge what he knows about their plans."

The vamp he'd abducted was young, maybe mid-twenties, and male, of average height with olive skin, a military haircut, and a muscular build.

I nodded. "Have at it, then."

Things had been tense between us. Luther had sensed my "sudden" resentment toward vampires, but he couldn't figure out why. He had no idea what had happened to me, so for all he knew I was blaming all vampire-kind for what Remy and his chuckleheads were up to. Plus, I'd killed some of his friends' offspring back at Germain's mansion, so that wasn't helping matters.

"We are going to talk later, you and I," he whispered as he passed me carrying the abductee.

"Mission first. The girl-talk can wait until after I kill a wizard," I replied. He gave me a look that could peel paint, so I raised my hands in supplication. "Just making a joke, Luther. I'm trying to relieve some of this tension, is all."

"Can cut with knife," Sophia Doroshenko said. "Is good you use humor, *chudovishche*. We must have minds on mission, not on feelings."

Luther turned that look on Sophia, and she wisely said no more. Then, he laid the vampire on the floor and knelt beside him, whispering in his ear.

"Wake, and be still."

The vamp's eyes popped open, but the rest of him remained stiff as a board.

"Have you ever been under the thrall of a master vampire, young one?" Luther asked, in the creepiest damn voice I'd ever heard him use. "Ah—from the fear in your eyes, I can see you have. When you were turned, yes? I can smell his scent on you, and from that I know he was one of mine. I turned Gerard in the spring of '76. That's 1876, in case you're wondering. Yes, he's old compared to some in your coven. But I made him, and he made you. That means I can control you, if I so choose. And I do."

The young vamp's eyes darted all over the place, taking in the scenery. He was surrounded by a sea of unfriendly faces—vampire, 'thrope, fae, and human alike. Many of us bristled with weapons, while others bristled with rage. Combine that with Luther's calm, creepy voice and the fact that he was completely under the Austin coven leader's control, and it was a sure bet the kid would've been pissing his pants if he could still urinate.

Luther ran a razor-sharp fingernail down the young vamp's chest, drawing a thin line of dark, almost black blood from his skin. "Now, young one, you're going to tell me everything you know about what your coven leader and the Circle wizard have planned. And, you're going to tell me what kind of resistance we can expect when we enter. I want to know every last detail—numbers, race or species, locations, fortifications, everything. If you lie, I'll know, and it will not go well for you. Blink if you understand."

The kid blinked twice.

Luther nodded. "You may begin."

I almost felt sorry for the kid as he spilled the beans. Almost.

THE YOUNG VAMP was very cooperative. He told us that my mystery nemesis was holed up in the main facility along with most of the New Orleans coven's leadership, including Remy, Cornelius, and Gaius. Just as Maki had speculated, they intended to use the reactors to fuel some sort of dimensional portal through the Veil. That would allow them to bring in a bunch of heavy-hitters from the other side—primary vampire spirits, for the most part.

Primaries were immortal entities that couldn't die. Oh, you could kill their physical body here on Earth, but they'd just come back in a few hundred or few thousand years good as new and ready to go another round. All the gods and some demigods were primaries, as were the progenitors of every supernatural race. Dracula? Primary. The Beast of Gévaudan? Also a primary, as was the Caoranach.

Primaries were bad news, because they were the strongest of the strong, with god-like abilities compared to their offspring. Oh, that's right—primaries could make more of themselves, either by infecting humans as with vampirism and therianthropy, or via standard reproductive methods, which was how the Caoranach shat out litters of demons by the bushel.

I guess that explains why there were so many vamps after the apocalypse went down.

Primaries could turn out their own kind by the score, and the ones they turned tended to be hellions in their own right—secondaries, we called them. From what I'd gathered, Luther was a secondary, as was Samson—a clear indication of the benefits of getting the vyrus from the source.

For that reason alone, we simply could not allow the wizard and Remy to open that gate. No way, no how.

The young vamp went on to explain how they'd hired a cadre of heavily armed therianthrope mercenaries for security, and those fuckers were pulling sentry duty at all points in the inner cordon. Remy figured we'd show eventually, so he'd sent his cannon fodder out on perimeter duty, leaving the pros to do the heavy lifting. That was how the sorry little turd had found himself on the wrong end of Luther's compulsion. And did he ever. The kid talked a mile a minute, giving us sentry locations, patrol timetables, body counts... the works.

"Is there anything else we should know?" Luther asked.

"Corpses," the young vamp eagerly offered. "We brought corpses in by the truckload. Plus, there are dead bodies everywhere. We killed all the staff when we took the place over, all except for a couple of engineers who understand how the reactors function."

Dead bodies—interesting.

"Very good, young one. You've done well." Luther's hand moved quicker than a cobra striking, snapping the kid's neck. He stood and gave me an inscrutable look. "Now that we know what we're up against—what's your plan?"

"Okay, here goes." I looked around the room to make sure I had everyone's attention. "Lucindras, Eliandres, Germain, Luther, and the rest of the vamp crew will be responsible for taking out the flunkies before we attack. I want a timed, concerted effort so they all go down at once. Then, you'll go after the mercenaries, taking out as many as you can without causing a ruckus. I want maximum time to get in before the wizard knows we're hitting them. Bells, Hemi, Crowley, and the 'thropes will follow, along with the rest of the fae.

"At some point, the leaders *will* figure out they're under attack. By then, I plan to be right in the wizard's lap. Which is why sometime during the assault, I'll break off and sneak past the cordon into the reactor control room.

"Listen carefully—those dead bodies are likely meant for necromancy, and I'd bet my left nut the Dark Druid is under that wizard's cowl. That's why I want our vamps to stay out of the reactor control room. I don't need to explain what would happen if a necromancer were to gain control of Luther or Germain. So, leave the control room and everyone in it to me.

"Now, are there any questions?"

Hemi raised his hand. "How are you going to get into the control room without being seen?"

I smiled, faking confidence while my stomach did somersaults. "I have a few tricks up my sleeve, but they'll only work for me. That's why I have to go in alone."

Eliandres scoffed, his pretty fae mouth twisting into a sneer as he spoke. "To face a coven of vampires and a skilled necromancer alone is suicide, justiciar, even for you. You should take back-up with you, or this will all be for nothing."

"Trust me, I have that covered. When I make my presence known, it'll be down to me and the wizard—er, the Fear Doirich, that is. I'm the only one who can withstand the Eye's powers for any length of time, so let me handle it."

I looked around the room, making eye contact with everyone present. "Any more questions? None? Then, kit up. We roll in twenty."

———

THE FAE ASSASSINS and elder vamps rolled over Remy's low-level goons like a steamroller at an Easter egg hunt. They were the Black Plague made manifest, Death itself moving like a fatal mist through the young, inexperienced vamps on the outer perimeter. Within seconds, the enemy's first line of defense had fallen.

And that was the last easy inch we took.

No sooner had we hit the fence line than we started taking rounds, both from small arms and emplaced machine guns. A couple fae and one of Luther's vamps went down under heavy automatic fire.

"Keep your heads down!" Samson yelled. "They're bound to have snipers on overwatch."

The grizzled old wolf was right. One of the fae hunters popped her head up to take a quick look at the hot zone, and she took a round right in the eye. *Er, sorry about that, Maeve.*

The mercs Remy had hired were good, and they knew their stuff. They'd set up motion and heat sensors that crisscrossed every last inch of the security fence, and had kill zones in place with intersecting fire covering every single approach to the main plant. They were also shooting both silver and cold iron rounds and alternating ammunition types in their magazines to cover all their bases.

We took cover behind parked cars and a few buildings that were adjacent to the fence. I whistled to grab everyone's attention. "Crowley, locate those snipers. Germain—when he points them out, I want you to drop a couple of those nasty vials on them, as well as on the machine gun emplacements."

"Fire or acid?" he asked.

"Does it matter? They're 'thropes, so either one will do."

Crowley knelt and meditated behind a parked truck, bullets whizzing overhead. Three black spheres made of shadow appeared in front of him, then they spun out into the night. Moments later, he opened his eyes.

"Three snipers. Water tower, two o'clock. Southwest corner of the main building. Top of the far reactor."

Germain was still fumbling with his vials when Bells yelled, "Got it!"

She leaned out from behind cover, snapped off a shot from her Steyr, and leaned back before I could blink. Then, she did it again, and a third time.

Bells yelled from her position. "Headshots, silver

rounds. They won't be getting back up. Germain can clear the emplacements now."

Damn, and with open sights too. Apparently, serpenthropy has been good to her.

I wasn't about to argue with results like that, so I signaled Germain to finish the job. The old vamp tossed three vials from behind cover without even looking. They landed on the machine gun emplacements in rapid succession, exploding and spreading liquid fire over everything within a ten-foot radius. Six humanoid figures screamed at once, each jumping out of their emplacements and sprinting toward the nearby lake.

Belladonna dropped two with her rifle, while Eliandres and Lucindras took another two with throwing knives to their spines. The elven hunters took out the remaining pair with a few well-placed arrows in eye sockets.

"Crowley, sit-rep!" I yelled. He was still in *seiza* posture, kneeling behind the car with his eyes closed.

"About a dozen more therianthropes of various species are waiting in ambush inside the buildings. You're clear to approach, but expect to meet heavy resistance once you enter the structures."

"Alright, split into teams and move out—and I want explosives or incendiary spells tossed in every door before anyone makes entry!" I yelled.

Samson gave me a mock salute and a wicked grin, and Fallyn slapped my ass as she ran by. I ignored them both, because my mind was on getting inside the main building. Since everyone on the assault team was a supernatural creature of some sort, they crossed the ground between the fence and buildings in seconds.

My team approached the nearest entrance. Germain opened the door and tossed in one of his vials quicker than I could blink. We heard a loud *boom!* as the door flew off the hinges, then screams followed from within. Bells, Maureen, and the fae assassins were stacked up beside the door, and they entered with Belladonna's rifle blazing and the two fae tossing blades like candy at a small-town parade.

Once they cleared the way, I planned to sneak off and take revenge on my enemies. It was all going so very smoothly, except for having our cover blown this early in the game. Bells yelled back with the all-clear, and I was about to enter the building when the dead started to rise.

'Thrope undead, that was.

Sophia Doroshenko was the first to notice the corpses getting up. "Druid, we have problem!" she yelled, catching my attention.

When I turned, she was already locked in combat with an undead werecat. The merc had been burned to a crisp and he had an arrow sticking out of his eye, but it didn't seem to be slowing the damned thing down. The vampire was holding her own with a Cossack saber that she spun, slashed, and stabbed in dizzying combinations. But no matter how many times she cut the undead thrope, it just kept on coming.

Soon, my whole team was engaged with the merc 'thropes we'd just killed. Above the din, Hemi yelled from somewhere close by.

"Hey, bro, we got trouble!"

The big Maori had been laying into the zombie 'thropes with a massive war club that was shaped like an axe or an adze. Of course, he was just as deadly with the damned thing as he was with that whalebone spear he used to carry. He spun it in a quick circle overhead, ending his swing against an undead lizardman's head, separating the thing's skull from its neck and sending it sailing. After admiring his handiwork for a second, he pointed his war club toward the other side of the plant.

I looked and nearly shat my pants. There were dozens of nosferatu running en masse from the opposite side of the compound to the north. We were about to be overrun, and I hadn't even reached the main building.

Shit on a motherfucking stick!

Nos-types were normally easy to deal with, since they were dumber and slower than higher vamps. I'd only ever met one that had given me fits, and it had been thousands of years old. These looked young, but they easily outnumbered us three-to-one. Combined with the undead 'thropes, we were about to be fucked in the ass without lube.

No way was my team going down, not on my watch. I had the power to turn things around. The problem was, I only had one spell that could do it, and I'd been saving it for Remy and the rest of the NOLA coven's leadership.

Damn it. I stealth-shifted on the fly and spun up my sunlight spell. I'd spent plenty of time charging it up, so things were about to get interesting.

"All vamps, take cover now!" I yelled. The vamps had

heard about what I'd done at Germain's mansion, so they knew what was coming and beat feet. "Everyone else, shield your eyes on three."

The remaining team members were now engaged in a running battle, since the vamps had left them to deal with the remaining handful of undead 'thropes. I watched the line of nosferatu coming for us, loping across the ground on all fours like apes—but with hairless, wrinkled gray skin, weird bat-shaped ears, long claws, and mouths full of long, sharp, crooked teeth.

Wait for it—let them get in range.

When they were thirty yards away, I crouched and started my countdown.

25

"One... two... three!" I hollered as I leapt ten feet in the air, fist extended over my head. I opened my hand and said the trigger word, shielding my own eyes with my other arm.

Searing white light infused the entire area, turning night to day. Unholy screams of pain and terror pierced our ears as four dozen nosferatu screeched in defiance and agony. As soon as the light died, I uncovered my eyes and looked around. All that remained of the nosferatu were ashes and smoldering skeletons.

Only necromancers I know who could control that many are the Fear Doirich, and maybe Fuamnach. I called Crowley over, and he sauntered across the courtyard, obviously not wanting to appear too eager to heed my call.

"What's your take, Crowley?"

He knelt next to an ash pile, sifting it with his hands and rubbing a bit between his fingers as he took a sniff. "It's the Dark Druid, I'm certain of it. I'd recognize the stink of his magic anywhere." As he stood, his eyes turned to slits and his voice took on a calm menace. "Colin, you cannot face him alone. Without that sunlight spell, the New Orleans coven will tear you apart. I insist that I accompany you into the control chamber, and that you take Luther with us as well. He and I are more than capable of remaining hidden until you strike."

I shook my head. "I don't know, Crowley—one blast from the Eye, and you and Luther are toast. And if it is the Dark Druid, and he gains control of Luther—"

He smiled, and since Crowley never smiled it was creepy as all hell, like Wednesday Addams when she was up to no good. "You'll just have to deal with the Fear Doirich quickly, then, won't you?"

Of course, Luther had already heard our conversation —vampire ears were nearly as sensitive as a werewolf's. "He's right, Colin. You can't go in alone."

"Fine, but stay back until I make my move. And remember, the Fear Doirich is mine."

I called across the courtyard, where Samson, the fae, and Sophia Doroshenko were cleaning up the remaining undead 'thropes. Samson had shifted to his wolf-human form, and he was savaging the neck of a were-panther with his massive jaws. There was a loud pop as the were-panther's head went rolling. The alpha stood, licking blood from his lips and snout, and I waited until he was finished before I addressed him.

"Alpha, you're—well, alpha, right now. Take care of any stragglers and keep everyone away from the main control room."

I remembered too late that Samson's wolf didn't like taking orders, and I saw his hackles rise at the way I'd addressed him. He locked eyes with me, the man fighting the wolf, resisting the instinct to crush this usurper standing before him. Then, he nodded once and turned away, barking orders at the rest of the team as he organized squads to sweep the facility.

Well, that was close. Note to self, don't boss the alpha wolf around after he shifts.

Releasing a lungful of air I hadn't realized I'd been holding, I started shucking clothes so I could make the full change. Unsurprisingly, that earned me a few catcall whistles from Fallyn. I glanced inside the building where Bells stood watch, her lips pressed into a tight line. Once she realized I was watching her, she gave me a hard look and turned her attention back down the hallway.

Hah, thought I didn't see that, didn't you? Looks like someone isn't as over me as they think.

Once I'd stripped to my skivvies, I spent the next twenty seconds or so transforming into my bigger, badder self. Luther was fascinated by the metamorphosis, while Crowley looked away. Couldn't blame him for it. He had some bad memories associated with my Hyde-side.

"Alright," I said to the wizard and master vampire in my now very deep, rumbling voice. "Let's go fuck some shit up."

With that, I took off at a crouching lope, squeezing through the doorway to approach Bells, Maureen, and the fae assassins in the hall.

"Maureen, make sure no one follows us, alright? I don't

want to risk losing anybody to one of the Eye's heat blasts tonight. Well, except maybe Crowley."

Belladonna's eyes narrowed at me. She slung her rifle over her shoulder, then grabbed Crowley by his leather jacket and hoodie, pulling him close to kiss him on the lips.

"Don't get killed for his sake, hear me?" she said to the shadow wizard as she stared into his eyes. The girl didn't spare me a glance as she spun on her heel and walked out of the building.

Maureen hid her mouth behind her hand and snickered, while the assassin twins looked on, bored. Crowley wore a dopey, shit-eating grin, and Luther's face was a mask of barely restrained mirth. I rolled my eyes and sighed, then took off down the hallway toward the control room.

———

WE RAN through a maze of halls, passing a small museum and a training center that included an exact scale-replica of the plant's control room. Of course, we popped our heads in to take a look. The room was roughly thirty by sixty feet, oblong and octagonal at the ends, and filled with banks of lights, monitors, and switches.

"Well, that's handy," I rumbled. "At least we know what the layout will be when we go in."

"That's if they're even in there," Crowley commented. "To access the reactor rods, he'll need to be inside one of the reactors."

"I guess we'll find out when we get there," Luther said, looking at me quizzically. "How do you intend to get the drop on them, anyway?"

"You'll see," I replied, loping off down the hallway.

Minutes later, we reached a hallway with a sign above it that said, "Security Checkpoint Ahead." I motioned to Crowley, but he was way ahead of me. A small ball of shadow and smoke appeared above his hand, changing shape and coalescing into a tiny salamander-shaped creature. He whispered to his creation and the thing leapt from his hand to the wall. The shadow golem scurried toward the ceiling, then it darted around the corner and out of sight.

Crowley closed his eyes, and moments later he relayed what his mystical servant saw up ahead. "Two vamps, on alert. Older, I think, in modern ballistic armor and armed with firearms and shock batons."

"Remy's enforcers," Luther hissed. "Don't worry, I got this."

The old vamp disappeared in a cloud of dark smoke and mist. He reappeared a moment later, brushing off his dinner jacket and straightening the collars on his dark silk dress shirt. He was the only person I'd ever know who would show up to a fight looking like he was headed to dinner at the The Driskill.

"The way to the control room is clear," he said, examining his nails. "Oh dear, I've ruined my manicure. Well, I suppose sacrifices must be made for the greater good."

"You don't know the half of it," I muttered.

He looked up at me, concern in his eyes. "At some

point, we're going to have a serious talk about whatever has happened to you—and don't you expect to squirm out of it."

"Yes, Mom," I said, earning me a sharp slap on the arm.

"I might be a queen, but don't you ever refer to me as your mother," the vamp said, meaning it. "Now, are you ready to do this?"

"Trust me, they won't see me coming," I replied, rubbing my arm. Even in this form, it hurt when Luther slapped me. "When you hear the shit hit the fan, you guys come running. But, Luther, if you come in there and the Fear Doirich is still on his feet, I want you to turn right back around. And watch yourselves, the both of you. If that fucker pulls his glove off that creepy, fucked-up hand of his, both of you should run."

Without waiting for a reply, I reached into my Bag and pulled out Commander Gunnarson's cloak of invisibility. It was semi-sentient, and the damned thing still fought me like a motherfucker when I tried to use it. However, we'd come to a certain understanding during my time in the Hellpocalypse. It let me use its powers every so often, and I promised I wouldn't feed it down a garbage disposal.

It was a strained relationship, but it worked.

I threw the cloak around me, knowing it was way too small. From past experience, I knew that I looked like Chowder from *Monster House* with the man-sized cloak draped across my massive Fomorian shoulders.

The corner of Crowley's mouth curled up as he took it all in. "That is a very good look for you, druid. You should wear it more often."

Luther covered his eyes and shook his head. "At the very least, they should die of laughter when they see you. Well done."

"Like I said, they won't see me." I willed the cloak to do its thing and winked out of existence before their very eyes.

"Where'd he go?" Luther asked.

"Invisibility cloak," I said after sneaking up behind them. "Pretty cool, huh?"

Crowley rolled his eyes at my antics, but my prank did elicit a small startle response from the Austin coven leader. He spun with murder in his eyes, which darted everywhere as they tried to determine where I was standing.

"Boy, don't you ever sneak up on a black man like that! You are like to be shot or bitten doing that, and not necessarily in that order."

I chuckled. "Remember, when all hell breaks loose, that's your signal."

Then, I took off down the hall, absolutely silent. Since I took it off Gunnarson, I'd spent a lot of time trying to figure out how the cloak worked. I never could suss out how it functioned—all I knew was that I couldn't be seen or heard by anyone while I was wearing it, unless I wanted to. The cloak's only limitation was that it took an immense effort of will to control it and use it; thus, I couldn't wear it but for a few minutes at a time. Any more than that, and I'd start getting a headache that could put down an elephant.

I'd learned that the hard way. Getting a migraine in a post-apocalyptic world flat-out sucks. You can't just run to the corner store for a blister pack of Excedrin and a four-pack of Red Bull. The only solution was either to sleep it off or boil a shitload of willow bark and sip it 'til I was pissing buckets. Thus, I'd have to make this quick.

I crept up to the control room entry foyer and waited for someone to exit. It didn't take long before one of Remy's shock troops came out, pulling a pack of cigarettes from his pocket as he exited the room. Of all the human stuff that a vamp might choose to do, smoking seemed like it'd be the last habit they'd want to retain. Then again, when cancer isn't an issue, I guess you can do whatever the hell you want with your body—who am I to judge?

Moving with all the grace and speed I could muster, I barely squeezed my huge bulk through the door before it closed. Even on all fours, my shoulders scraped against the door frame as I entered. Thankfully, the noise was muted by the cloak—but what I didn't count on was snagging the damned thing on the latch.

There was a loud ripping sound as Gunnarson's cloak tore from around my neck. Inside the control room, a dozen pairs of eyes looked my way in response to the noise, along with one hooded, concealed face. Figuring I was fucked any way I sliced it, I stood to my full height and waved at the room full of vampires.

"Hiya, folks—ya miss me?"

WHEN THE VAMPS sprang into action, they came at me in force. The room was large, maybe the size of a small house, but with all those banks of control panels and worksta-tions it offered me little room to maneuver. Lacking the room to evade their assault, I went at them head on as they zipped across the space to attack me.

The first two came at me high and low, likely in an attempt to take me down to their level. It didn't work. I snagged each of them by their scrawny little heroin-chic necks, crushing them like papier-mâché dolls.

Yet it was a Pyrrhic victory, as the sacrifice those two vamps made created an opening for the rest of their number to surround me. A half-dozen more of the sneaky bastards and bitches zipped in and out, faster than the human eye could see, stabbing and punching and scratching and biting at me like a school of piranhas while Remy, Cornelius, Gaius, and Silvère looked on.

My skin was tough enough to repel small arms fire, but blades and fists moving at vampire speed were another matter—as were vampire claws and teeth. The vyrus hard-ened a vampire's tooth enamel and nail keratin when they changed, and the older they got, the tougher that tissue became. Vamps who were as old as these, in the one-fifty to two hundred range, could chew and scratch their way through concrete and mild steel without chipping a nail. Nail *polish*, of course, was another matter—much to Luther's displeasure.

Within seconds, I was bleeding from dozens of wounds. I could heal rather quickly in this form, but I wasn't invulnerable. The longer this went on, the more likely it would be that they'd hit something vital, and then the tables would truly have turned. Lacking alternatives, I decided to switch to my Plan B.

"Crowley, a little help in here!" I shouted out the door as I held one vamp off the ground by his ankle and another by the scrotum.

I squeezed on both counts, and my efforts were rewarded by a satisfying snap on the one hand and a girlish screech on the other. I swung the vampire with the crushed testicles overhead until said nut sack separated from its owner. That one crashed head-first into the wall with a sickening crunch, still clutching his groin like a school boy who'd just got racked. Meanwhile, the other vamp was doing a hell of an impressive inverted sit-up, gnawing at my arm like a chihuahua attacking a leg of lamb. I tossed her across the room at a bank of lights and switches, buckling it. Neither vamp got back up.

Oops—I hope that control panel wasn't too important.

That still left four of the bastards, plus the peanut gallery across the way. I was honestly getting a little concerned at my odds, but then three of the vamps attacking me got yanked out the door by tendrils of smoke and shadow. The fourth vamp got distracted by that little development, so I punched a hole through his chest. Shaking blood and goo off my hand, I turned my attention toward the rest of the group.

On the other side of the room, the Dark Druid spoke in a conversational tone to Remy DeCourdreaux. "Don't kill the shadow wizard—he may be of some use to me yet. Do as you will with the rest."

Remy grinned like a barracuda sizing up a school of herrings. "Gladly."

The Fear Doirich's only response was to open a portal and step through. I managed to catch a glimpse of what was on the other side, and knew exactly where he'd gone. *The reactors—but which one?*

I had little time to puzzle it out, because Remy was already barking orders at the other remaining members of the New Orleans coven. "Silvère, Cornelius—you take the druid. Gaius and I will deal with the wizard—but remember, Gaius, *he* wants him alive."

"Oh, cut the shit," I grumbled. "I know you're all working for the Fear Doirich."

"How alive?" Gaius asked, ignoring me. "Nevermind. Just leave a piece of the druid for me. I owe him for what he did to Lucius."

He zipped toward the door with Remy not far behind. But just as Gaius reached the exit, a tall, dark figure appeared in a cloud of black smoke in front of him. Luther extended an arm, snatching the much younger vamp off the ground by his neck. He squeezed, cracking the kid's neck, then dropped him to the floor like a dirty snot rag.

Nope, they definitely did not see that coming.

"No!" Cornelius screamed, darting toward Luther.

Remy stepped aside to let Cornelius pass, and soon Luther and his old rival were going after each other like two wet cats in a burlap bag. The outcome of that encounter was a foregone conclusion, so I turned my attention to the New Orleans coven leader and his right-hand enforcer. I had no intentions of bothering with them.

I simply wanted to make certain Remy and Silvère didn't slip away.

"Crowley, you got this?" I asked without taking my eyes off the vamp.

My enigmatic frenemy came floating into view, "hovering" several feet off the ground by use of several thick tendrils of shadow magic that extended from his torso. Smaller wisps of shadow whipped and tore at the air all around him, and his eyes were two jet-black orbs so dark they sucked in light, making the surrounding sockets look bruised and sickly. Black energy danced from his fingertips, and a general sensation of *despair* came off him in waves.

All-in-all, it was a fucking impressive entrance.

The shadow wizard turned his freaky eyes on me. "I wouldn't mind having a few choice words with my stepfather regarding my supposed utility. However, I am content to allow you to handle that worm of a necromancer for me while I deal with his lackeys."

"I'll leave you to it, then," I replied, bounding on all fours out the door and down a hallway with an arrow and "Reactor One" painted on its cinder block wall.

REACTOR ONE WAS void of life, so I backtracked and took the opposite hall to Reactor Two, entering it on the ground level. I had no idea what sort of radiation I'd be exposed to in there, nor did I know whether or not my Formorian body would be able to withstand the effects of radiation poisoning. I had my suspicions it would, simply based on my one-hundred-percent survival rate during past exposures to the Eye's energies.

At least, that's what I hoped.

When I walked into the reactor, the Fear Doirich was standing on a balcony above the fuel rod cooling pool, hood down with his Fomorian hand extended toward the waters below. The Eye was glowing a bright, cherry red. It didn't take a genius to guess that the two of them were building up enough power to zap the fuel rods, vaporize the water in the cooling tank, and cause a meltdown.

"You're not looking so great these days, bub," I said, meaning it.

His face was a grayish color, and streaked with dark, blue-green veins, as if his whole body were gangrenous and sickly. Which, of course, it was. The body I'd locked him in was long past its expiration date, and since he couldn't hop over to another one, it was only a matter of time before the damned thing started to spoil.

"One more step, and I overload the reactor core," he croaked. "It'll be like Fukushima but ten times worse, since the Eye has the power to send the rods into an instantaneous meltdown. The resulting explosion will send up a cloud of fallout that will blanket that little burg to the south and east of here, and thousands there will die. That poisonous cloud will then spread, contaminating thousands of square miles of your beloved state. Ten of thousands will be affected. Babies will be stillborn, cancer rates will increase, and birth defects will skyrocket. It will make what I did in Austin pale in comparison."

"I know," I said calmly. "But no matter what I do, you're going to do it anyway."

"Oh? And what makes you think that?"

I ignored him, instead looking at his hand—the one with the glowing orb embedded in it. "Eye, you sure you don't want to change sides again? Final offer."

Balor's Eye answered me with that big, booming voice it'd used the first time we met.

-YOU KNOW I CANNOT, COLIN MCCOOL. I AM BOUND BY THE GEAS BALOR PLACED ON ME TO SEEK THE TOTAL ERADICATION OR REMOVAL OF THE FAE AND TUATHA DÉ FROM THIS REALM. I WILL NOT REST UNTIL I COMPLETE MY TASK. I MUST BE FREE.-

I stuck a finger in my ear and wiggled it around, meeting eyes with the Dark Druid. "Fucking hell, but that thing is loud. Wasn't like that when it lived inside my head —we actually had normal conversations. How do you stand it?"

"Your nonchalance won't buy you any time, MacCumhaill. You are correct; I do intend to send this reactor into meltdown. Once I trigger the reaction, I'll portal myself a hundred miles away—but you won't have near enough time to escape with your friends. And even in that body, you won't withstand the energies that will be released. Your skin will peel from your muscles, bit by bit—"

I held up a hand. "Let me stop you right there, because I know what comes next. I die in the blast, and the energies that are released will thin the barrier between this plane and the Veil, allowing a bunch of primaries on the other side to punch through. They'll immediately inhabit the bodies of all the plant employees you killed, and probably a bunch of highly-ranked officials and military personnel who will show up during the clean-up efforts. How am I doing so far?"

"B-but—who told you this?" he rasped.

"Hang on, not done yet. So then, those primaries—who are now inhabiting the bodies of many very important people—multiply, turning other well-placed individuals into vampires, at all levels of government, both here and abroad. And that's how the nuclear war starts—the vamps cause it all. Then, they help you and the Eye chase the fae and the last remnant of the Tuatha Dé Danann from the face of the Earth, who will be more than happy to flee a world sickened by radiation and infested by the undead. Because if there's one thing the fae can't stand, it's sickness and death."

The Fear Doirich threw his head back and let out a mad cackle. "I truly must hand it to you, I would never have thought you'd figure all that out."

I gave him a thumbs up. "Admittedly, I had a little help. A bit of old Fionn's wisdom still remains, you know."

"Ah, I see. Well, the question still remains. How will you stop me?"

"Oh, that," I said, nodding. "Like this."

I changed back into my stealth-shifted form and twisted my hands and fingers exactly the way Click had taught me. We'd drilled this spell over and over and over again, thousands of times in the void space of the Bag's interior. By now, I could cast it in my sleep.

The Welsh trickster god had said I was his worst student ever, because I couldn't affect a very large area with that spell at all. But I didn't have to. All I needed was a stasis field large enough to encase a large gemstone—or, perhaps, the hand that held it.

The spell released, latching onto the Fear Doirich's Fomorian hand, surrounding it and the Eye as well. Now, both the hand and the Eye were useless—at least until I released the spell. That wasn't going to happen, not even if the Dark Druid killed me. Moreover, the spell froze whatever was inside it, which meant that he was anchored to that spot.

Or, at least, his hand was. And that was all I needed.

I made a running leap onto the balcony, pulling Dyrnwyn from the Bag and willing it to light. Once Click told me what it was, I realized why it had failed me in the past; I hadn't been using it for a worthy cause. Fortunately, this cause *was* worthy, like saving the entire fucking world worthy, which was probably why the sword lit up with a white-hot flame that nearly seared my eyeballs.

I landed next to the Fear Doirich, severing his arm at the elbow just as he released the mother of all lightning spells at me. I took it square in the chest. The spell blasted me off the balcony, right into the fuel rod cooling pool below. I hit the water with a splash, then blacked out.

26

I awoke next to the fuel rod cooling pool, coughing up water while Click leaned against some equipment nearby.

"Sorry, lad, but mouth to mouth just isn't my thing. I like ye, but not like that."

I completed my coughing fit and looked up at him. "You pulled me out?"

He nodded. "I couldn't let me favorite pupil in—oh, the last five minutes or so—go an' drown in a radioactive pond, now could I? Not after he risked his life ta' save humanity from a future too terrible to imagine." He squinted and wagged a finger at me. "But don't ya' go lettin' that go ta' yer head now."

"I won't," I said calmly. Then, something occurred to me. "Wait a minute—you were here all along?"

He frowned, wavering his hand back and forth. "Sort of. I was watching from a parallel plane of existence, just in case ye failed. No sense in having us both glow in the dark, eh?"

"Why in the fuck didn't you help out earlier?" I asked.

He sighed, clapping his hands on his thighs. "Ya' see, that's just the sort of thing that got me in hot water in the first place. Ya' go an' mess with the timelines, interferin' and what-not, and soon ya' have a primordial goddess of chaos wantin' ta' rip yer head clean off yer shoulders." He waved his hands back and forth. "Nope, not me, not anymore. No way, no how, no siree. I only work through champions these days. And you, lad, are me current pick."

I looked around frantically. "The Eye! Shit, did he get away with it?"

Click smiled and pointed above his head. "'Twas a fine spell, and I daresay even Cú Chulainn in all his madness could'na budge it from where it remains." He held a hand up beside his mouth, whispering to me conspiratorially. "If I were you, I'd stuff that thing in that Bag o' yers and keep it there until ye can pawn it off on someone who knows what ta' do with it."

"Sure, I'll get right on it. But first, I have questions."

Click shut one eye and rolled the other in a sour expression that almost made me chuckle. "Oh, I suppose."

"After falling in that pool, am I going to get cancer or grow a third eye?"

Click pursed his lips and looked up at the ceiling. "Hmm. No, not likely."

"Where's the sword?"

"Safe and sound back in yer Bag, lad. Safe and sound."

Now, the big one. "Did we just prevent the apocalypse?"

The trickster smiled and gave me double-guns with his

fingers, Fonzie-style. "You did, lad, 'twas you. With a little help, o' course." He huffed on his knuckles, polishing them on his motorcycle jacket.

I heaved a sigh of relief. "What about the other timeline, and all those people in it? Will that happen—er, has it happened?"

"And can ye go back ta' save them? Am I right?"

I gulped and nodded.

"Think back ta' yer lessons, lad. The Twisted Paths got their namesake fer a reason. Once ya' walk them, the things ya' see and experience will haunt ya' all yer days. O' course you can go back—once ya' learn to walk those paths yerself. And I'm willing ta' teach ya', if ya' truly believe it's what ye want ta' do."

"I do, Click. I can't just abandon them in that desolate timeline. I couldn't live with myself if I did."

"So be it, then. I'll teach ya' how ta' walk the Paths— but it'll take years, even decades. Lots o' time inside that Bag. Or yer—oh, never mind, ferget I said that."

"Forget what?" I asked.

He pointed over my shoulder. "Yer friends are comin', lad."

I looked over my shoulder, but no one was there. And when I turned around, neither was Click, the magician and trickster god once known as Gwydion.

A youthful voice echoed from the empty air nearby. "I'll be in touch," it said, trailing off into silence.

Footsteps behind me caused me to spin, crouched and ready for violence.

"Whoa there, it's just us," Luther said, walking into the

reactor trailed by Crowley. "I take it you handled the Dark Druid?"

I exhaled heavily, blowing a strand of hair from my eyes. "I managed. What about Remy, Silvère, and Cornelius?"

The two looked at each other. "We managed," Luther said.

Crowley's eyes zeroed in on the balcony overhead. "There's a hand floating in the air up there—a hand with an extremely powerful magical artifact embedded in it."

I narrowed my eyes at him. "Don't even think about it."

"Well, I was going to ask, but since you're so prickly about it," he said, clasping his hands behind his back. "Then again, it *would* make it so much easier to power a few experiments I've been working on."

Luther and I both looked at him and shouted in unison, "No!"

Crowley gave a small shrug and the barest of smiles. "It was only a suggestion."

TWO WEEKS LATER, things had settled down considerably. The city was still reeling from the disaster downtown, but people are resilient, and there's no end to what they can survive or accomplish when they band together. It would be weeks before the area would be deemed "safe," but except for those still grieving, lives were getting back to normal.

The nuclear power plant was another matter. Maeve

portaled in with her fixers at Samson and Luther's request. The mages cleaned the place up as best they could, but they had to stage a minor disaster to cover for all the deaths that night. And with three major "terrorist attacks" in Texas within the span of a week, rumors started to fly that certain people in Washington were taking notice.

People who were clued-in to the World Beneath.

That had even Maeve worried, so she and her people took extra care to do the cover up right. A few mind wipes and a little media manipulation later, and the battle had been forgotten by all but those who were clued in on the supernatural. But, as in Austin, the city of Glen Rose lost a lot of native sons and daughters that night. They'd be hurting for a good long while.

Both cities received several generous, anonymous donations to the families and victims funds for their respective disasters. Maeve, Samson, Luther, and Finnegas had all pitched in their fair share, but the bulk of it came from the Cold Iron Circle. After I threatened to expose how they'd had an impostor on their High Council working with a rogue vampire coven, well—they couldn't pony up the funds fast enough. It wouldn't make up for the lives lost, but it was a start.

As for the Dark Druid, he was still in the wind.

I buried myself in my studies, both practicing what Click had taught me in private and learning the deeper secrets of druidry from Finnegas. We trained everywhere but the junkyard. Finn made excuse after excuse, but I knew the truth; he simply couldn't stomach seeing that wounded, withered, dying oak tree.

As for the status of the New Orleans coven, their leadership had been gutted. "Good riddance" seemed to be the sentiment all around. Germain agreed to stay on for a time, both to serve as temporary coven leader and to prevent some worse entity or faction from filling the power vacuum left by Remy's sudden, unexpected demise. I had a pretty strong feeling that Luther would be running Austin and New Orleans soon, but first he'd have to take over Houston, which was a no man's land.

All things in their own time, I suppose.

I had other issues to contend with, namely the disposal of the Eye. For that reason, I was sitting in Maman Brigitte's parlor. We sipped on pepper-infused rum while engaging in polite conversation, waiting for a certain third party to arrive. Well, the conversation wasn't that polite—this was Maman Brigitte, after all. Madam Bawdiness herself.

She was telling the punchline to a very dirty joke involving a one-legged sailor, a midget stripper—her words, not mine—and a mutant, two-dicked merman. Thankfully, I was rescued from the embarrassment of blushing through another of her jokes when the guest of honor arrived.

Maman Brigitte looked over my shoulder, smiling demurely at the door. "Hello, Lugh. It's been a minute. Have you been well?"

I stood and turned to greet him. "Lugh, good to see you, I—"

He cut me off. "Let's jest get this whole affair over with, shall we?"

I was taken aback by his abruptness, as he'd been so friendly when last I'd seen him in Underhill. He was practically glaring at me now, clenching his jaw and his fists at his sides. *What the hell?*

Maman Brigitte broke the ice. "Might I remind you, there'll be no violence in my home. 'Tis neutral ground, and you'll be respectin' my rules, yes?"

"Um, yeah. Sure."

Lugh nodded, tight-lipped.

"It be settled, then," she said. "Shall we make the exchange?"

I pulled the Fomorian hand, with the Eye still attached, out of my Craneskin Bag. "It's, um, in stasis. I had some help procuring it."

Lugh scowled. "Time magic. Nasty stuff. Ye'd best be tellin' the mage who cast it ta' watch their back. The gods have a way of knockin' off those who fart around with chronomancy."

"Yeah, I'll do that." I handed him the Eye which, although suspended in time, seemed to glare at me from within the stasis field.

That was a weird thing in and of itself. When I set the hand down on a solid object, the stasis field sunk into that object, freezing time for anything that came within its radius of effect. Yet, I was able to handle the stasis field as if it was a physical object, like a bowling ball or a potted plant. Click hadn't explained that part, and I had no idea how it worked, so I handed it off to Lugh with a warning.

"Ah, be careful with it. The stasis field—"

"I know how ta' deal with time magic," he snapped. "It's not my first time around the fidchell board."

"Right." I watched as Lugh placed the hand inside a magic bag of his own. He was almost shaking with anger, and something inside me said I couldn't let this be. "Maman Brigitte, could you give us a minute?" I asked.

The goddess frowned. "I suppose, but don't you boys be tearing my parlor up or I'll skin the both of ya'." She fixed me with a stare. "And you—you'd best call my grand-daughter, just as soon as you get back to Austin."

I mumbled a "yes, ma'am" and Lugh nodded, standing silently as Maman Brigitte left the room. Actually, he was looking at her ass, and frankly I couldn't blame him. The goddess was quite a looker. Once she left the room, I cleared my throat to get his attention.

"Lugh, did I do something to offend you?"

He looked at me like I was nuts. "Didja' what? Offend me? Oh no, not at all. Kick me out o' yer druid grove, steal me spear and sword, and hold 'em ransom. No, ye did nothin' o' the sort."

"I did what?"

He squinted, his mouth a taut line that split his face. "Ye really don't remember, do ye?"

"Um, no."

He exhaled heavily and sat in a nearby chair. "I came ta' warn ye about the dryad, ta' tell ya' no good would come o' it. We fought, ye managed ta' kick my tail by usin' the power o' the oak—else I'd o' had ye, mind—and then ye stole me weapons and used that tree ta' toss me seven leagues."

I blinked and frowned. "I did what? When did this happen?"

"Not long ago, lad." He squinted at me again, then stood and got up in my face. Not angrily, but to stare at my forehead. "Ah, I see what happened now. That crazy lass used my spear ta' erase yer memory."

"Um, how would she do that?"

───────

HE GAVE ME A RUEFUL SMILE. "I believe yer physicians call it a 'frontal lobotomy.'"

Of course, I agreed to get Lugh his weapons back, but I wound up putting it off until I could figure out how to get rid of Jesse. I did everything I could to avoid her, but she wouldn't take the hint. Finally, I resorted to placing a containment ward around the druid oak—an invisible, magic fence that kept her confined to the tree and its environs.

Hah! Try waking me up in the middle of the night now, bitch.

After that, I simply pretended she wasn't there. I'd walk through the yard, ignoring her presence, and she'd just sit against the dying oak, staring at me. Some days, she'd bury her face in her hands and cry.

I wasn't falling for it, but it was hard seeing her like that. Still, I'd chosen a course and was determined to stick to it no matter how much it hurt. I'd wait until the druid oak died, and Jesse with it, and hope her spirit would decide to move on to her final rest. Then, I'd find a way to reach the Dagda—maybe through his daughter, Brigitte—and ask him for another acorn.

It'd work. At least, that's what I kept telling myself.

Once things had settled down, after I'd truly allowed myself to process all that happened, I came to a few realizations. First, I definitely still loved Jesse, just not *that* Jesse. Second, I missed Bells.

Belladonna was another matter. We'd been texting back and forth, talking about simple, everyday stuff. How many monsters did you kill today, what was the bounty, who was your client, things like that. But when the topic of conversation rolled around to the status of "us," she clammed up tighter than a nun's knees.

It was obvious she still had feelings for me, just as I did for her. Even after all that time in the Hellpocalypse and training with Click, I still carried a flame for her. But there was a chasm between us that I didn't know how to cross, and for that reason I had no idea if she'd ever come back to me.

A few weeks later, after coming home from a *disastrous* date with Janice, I was fast asleep in bed. I heard a knock on my door, so I flipped on the light and grabbed Dyrnwyn from my Bag. The light was for the benefit of any mundanes who might not understand how I could see in the near dark, and the sword was just in case the Fear Doirich showed up.

I opened the door, sword hidden behind it as I peeked out. My jaw nearly hit the floor when I saw who was standing there.

"Um, Bells—wow. Is something wrong?"

She smiled and pushed a strand of hair behind her ear, obviously embarrassed to be there. "Hi, Colin. Can I come in?"

I tossed the sword in the corner. "Sure, come on in."

Kicking dirty clothes and the debris of my sorry, lonely life in the corner with the sword, I cleared a pizza box, a game controller, and a stack of Doc Savage novels from my only chair. After dusting off a handful of residual crumbs, I motioned to it.

"Please, have a seat," I said as I reached into my mini-fridge to grab her a bottle of water. "Um, let me get you something to drink."

When I turned around to hand Belladonna the water, she was standing right behind me, so close we ended up nose to chest.

"I don't want water," she said in a breathy voice as she caressed my face. "I just want you."

Half of me wanted to take it slow, talk it out, and ease back into things. But the other half of me, the half below my waist? Yeah, that half said it had been nearly two years in Earth time since I'd gotten laid—and that half wanted to fuck and be fucked like a stud bull in a Viagra factory.

I dropped the bottle and reached for her, and she jumped at me, wrapping her legs around my waist and her arms around my neck. She kissed me hungrily, so I spun around and dropped us both onto the bed. As soon as her back hit the mattress, she used a jiu-jitsu sweep to flip me over so she was on top. I wasn't wearing much, and she was wearing a skirt, so it didn't take long for things to happen.

As soon as I slid inside her, I knew something was wrong.

For starters, she had me pinned down on the bed. And not just with her hands and hips; there was another power, an outside force holding me down. Second, her voice changed. We had both been panting and groaning, what with all the heavy petting and dry humping, but as soon as we began to consummate the act, her voice went from husky and sultry to high and girly.

And third, she didn't move like Bells. Sure, it had been a while, but I'd had a lot of sex with Belladonna—lots. I knew every curve of her body, every and scar and blemish, and I knew how she liked to move her hips when she was on top. Bells like to grind, but whoever was on me was bouncing up and down like a cowboy riding a bronc.

Not that it didn't feel good. It felt amazing, in fact. And with every stroke, every time I plunged into her, a *warmth* spread from that region out to my entire body. I wondered, honest to goodness, if Click hadn't hired a succubus and sent her to my room as a favor—one of his twisted trickster jokes.

Then, we began to glow.

I looked down, because my head was the only part of my body I could move, and where our bodies were conjoined we were glowing. It started as a pale light, almost like a trick of the imagination, then it gradually increased in intensity until it became a bright, golden glow that lit up the whole room.

Soon, her rhythm sped up as the sensations became more intense. Despite my misgivings about the whole bizarre interlude, I was about to climax, and by the sounds that this mystery woman was making, she was too. But when I achieved my release, she didn't moan, or shudder, or cry out in ecstasy.

She *screamed*.

It was a high, lonesome sound, like a banshee's warning cry or a woman howling for her lost child. The scream went on for a long time, and in it I heard echoes of despair and pain and loss. As the woman screamed, she began to transform before my eyes. Belladonna's dusky skin faded away to be replaced by a rough, alien dermis. Her hair changed color as did her eyes, and her features faded into a face that at first was unrecognizable—but gradually, it became oh-so familiar.

Within seconds, all was made clear. This woman on top of me wasn't a human or succubus at all. It was Jesse, *dryad* Jesse. And she was in agony.

At that moment, my door crashed open. "Colin, is everything okay? I got your text, and—"

Belladonna stood there looking at us, her mouth agape and her eyes wet with tears.

I looked over at her, wanting to say something, anything to explain what was going on. But before I could, the light that suffused Jesse and I intensified into a brilliant, vibrant glow, the color of sunshine and growth and life. It continued intensifying, rising to a crescendo until there was a blinding flash, so bright I had to shut my eyes.

When I opened them again, my room, Jesse, and Belladonna had all disappeared. I was lying naked in a patch of withered brown grass, beneath the oak tree inside the druid grove. I sat up and looked around, and to my horror most of the grove was gone, eaten away and replaced with—nothing. Apparently, it had been unraveling bit by bit over the days and weeks since I'd injured the oak.

All around, the Void encroached, threatening to sweep me and the oak away as the tiny island of dirt and grass and roots beneath us slowly crumbled like sand into the black Abyss below. Instinctively I reached for the oak, willing it to send me back to my own plane of existence.

But when I touched the tree, I felt absolutely *nothing.*

My connection to the druid grove had been severed, stranding me in a pocket dimension that was gradually, inevitably giving way to the entropy of the Void.

Well, this is fucked.

I quickly assessed the situation. Then, I did the only thing I could do in that moment, the only thing I knew that would save both me and the grove. Straining to marshal every bit of magical skill I possessed and stretching the boundaries of my abilities to meet the demands of the task, I prepared to cast a stasis field around myself and the tree.

For just an instant, I hesitated. If I did this, I'd be trapped eternally in a place called Nowhere, frozen like a bug suspended in a drop of amber.

But I'd be alive.

I had no choice. With a single thought I released the spell, and in the next instant, everything *stopped.*

This concludes *Druid Vengeance*, but the Junkyard Druid's adventures will continue in Book 8, *Druid's Due*!

Subscribe to my newsletter to get a free ebook, and to be among the first to know when new installments in the Junkyard Druid series release:
https://mdmassey.com